FOGGY
SUNSET

FOGGY SUNSET

Peter McGarvey

Cliffhouse Publishing

Cliffhouse Publishing

Toronto, Ontario, Canada

www.CliffhousePublishing.com

Edited by Amy Mark

Cover Design by Lesley Stodart

Author Photo by Marcus Ames

ISBN: 978-0-9950470-1-3

DEDICATION

For Amy, my long-suffering editor who pushes me to be better.

ACKNOWLEDGMENTS

Thanks to my beta readers Sandee Brown, Don Hutchison, Arleen Mark, Brett Randall, and David Warren.

Special thanks to Rita John and Alfie Iannarelli for generously allowing me to appropriate their names.

FOGGY SUNSET

... it is grief that develops the powers of the mind.

Marcel Proust

ONE

Paradise Falls Mobile Home Park, March 1967

FOG raced off the lake and smothered the highway.

Arnie Voxx slowed his cruiser to a crawl and turned on the Ford's rotating roof light. The flashing turret made no difference. It couldn't penetrate more than a few feet beyond the hood.

Arnie shuddered at the thought of some trucker blindly barreling down Highway 31 toward him. He considered hitting the siren, something he very much wanted to do during the two weeks he'd been on the job. But in this thick fog bank, it wouldn't make a difference. He pulled onto what he presumed was the shoulder to figure out what to do next.

It was going to be impossible to find the trailer park in this soup. Dispatch had mentioned the park had a lighted sign on the highway, but that wasn't going to help. Arnie flicked on the driver's side searchlight and rolled down the window to swivel it around. The brilliant beam became a diffused glow within a couple of feet. Arnie decided his only option was to continue driving slowly and hope he'd see the illuminated sign.

"The manager's in the gatehouse. I've got back up on the way, but for now you're on your own," the dispatcher told him when he got the call forty-five minutes earlier. Someone in the park had reported a loud argument followed by screams. That meant it was likely a domestic. As his instructor at the academy had so forcefully put it, "More cops get killed on domestic calls than any other crime."

Arnie shivered from the cool, damp air drifting through the cruiser's window. He rolled it up and turned off the spotlight. His hands were shaking, but Arnie knew it wasn't from the cold.

PRIVATE First-Class Arnie Voxx wrestled frantically to keep his panic down. If he lost it now, he'd be dead.

He'd lagged behind the rest of his six-man patrol as they moved deeper into the A Sau Valley. They'd been warned about the low cloud cover which could flow down the mountainside and into the valley at the speed of a pyroclastic storm. And that's what had happened. One moment the patrol was there, the next they'd disappeared into a cloudbank. Arnie froze, every sense attuned to the shrouded jungle surrounding him.

He raised a hand and moved it tentatively away from his face. It disappeared a few inches from his nose and a lightning bolt of adrenalin shot through his body. Instantly, he was soaked in sweat. He listened desperately for any sound that would lead him back to his patrol.

Silence.

Arnie gripped his rifle like a talisman and crouched, willing his eyes to penetrate the fog. He neither saw nor heard movement, but he sensed it. Around him, beyond the curtain, the forest was alive with predators armed with either guns or fangs. Arnie held his breath to control the panic that was begging him to break and run. Instead, enclosed in a hostile wilderness, he clutched his M-16 and waited.

SEVENTEEN months after returning from the jungles of Southeast Asia, that fear still permeated Arnie's thoughts day and night. He constantly wrestled with his terror and had started to get the upper hand. But now, lost in this thick fog, the irrational fear flooded his soul again, and Arnie desperately fought to gain control.

Arnie slowly increased pressure on the accelerator and the vehicle crawled forward, swirling fog in its wake.

Relief flooded Arnie when he saw the glow of the sign marking the entrance to Paradise Falls Mobile Home Park. In retrospect, Arnie felt it might have been a mercy if he'd missed the entrance and had continued on through the fog.

When he reached the park's main gate, the manager came out of his shed and crouched down, so he was eye level with Arnie.

"It's quiet now, but they sure were going at it a little while ago."

"What number?"

The manager combed thin fingers through greasy blond hair.

"One sixteen, but I'd better show you the way. You'll never find it in this shit."

Arnie reached over and opened the passenger door. The manager got in and pointed ahead.

The man was right. Arnie doubted he would've been able to find the mobile home even without the fog. It was on a lot set back from the road with no others nearby. With its faded paint and torn canvas awnings, the trailer looked neglected. No lights inside or out only increased his sense of foreboding.

Arnie picked up the radio mike and called in his location.

"How soon is backup expected?" He worked hard at not sounding anxious.

Arnie had a bad feeling, and he'd learned to trust his bad feelings after eighteen months in Viet Nam.

"Tremblay figures he's a few minutes away. He says it's hard to tell in the fog."

"Tell him to look for the sign. I'll send the manager out to meet him." Arnie looked at the manager. "Ten-four. Out."

The manager eyed the dark trailer with apprehension then strode back the way they'd come.

Grabbing the flashlight clipped to the dashboard, Arnie walked swiftly to the wooden porch at the side of the mobile home. The beam wavered as his hand trembled from a mixture of dread and anticipation when he saw the screen door hanging askew.

Arnie debated whether or not to wait for Mike Tremblay, but he sensed something was very wrong. As if in confirmation, he heard a low moan from inside the trailer. Arnie unhooked his holster and removed his pistol while keeping the flashlight trained on the broken screen door. He shivered involuntarily and rapped his flashlight against the doorframe.

"Hello? Sheriff's department. Everybody okay in there?"

A whimper came from inside the trailer, like the sound an animal makes when it's been gravely injured.

He pushed the door open and shone the light from left to right. All he could see was bright fabric and dark wood. Arnie set the flashlight down on the porch. Gripping his gun tightly, he reached around with his other hand and felt for a light switch. Finding it, he flipped on the overhead light. Arnie stepped through the door, looked around, and froze.

A young woman lay on her back in the middle of the room staring upward blankly. Blood flowed from a clotted mess on the side of her head. She moaned again and tried to lift her head to face him, but was unable to support herself. When the woman's head smacked down on the rug with a wet thud, Arnie saw her left temple had been caved in.

The woman began to shake violently, uncontrollably flailing her arms. Arnie started toward her, but stopped at the sound of tires crunching on the road outside. He prayed it was his back up as he ran to the door.

Another cruiser pulled up behind his, and Deputy Mike Tremblay hitched up his pants as he climbed out.

Arnie waved frantically and shouted, "Call an ambulance!"

When he turned back to the woman, she was pointing repeatedly toward the back of the trailer.

"It'll be alright, ma'am," he reassured her. "Help is on the way."

She poked her finger insistently at the rear of the trailer and then her hand dropped. She gave a final shudder and was still. Arnie knew the woman was dead.

What had she been trying to tell him?

Was her attacker still in the trailer?

Arnie raised his pistol and moved cautiously toward the back. Behind him, Tremblay stepped into the trailer with his gun drawn. The deputy quickly assessed the situation and then went to attend to the woman on the floor.

Arnie inched toward the bedroom. The front sight of his pistol quivered as he squinted down its barrel.

"Anyone in there?" Arnie said in a voice so strong it surprised him.

He hesitated in the doorway. The room was empty except for a crib against the far end. Above it, blood dripped from the blade of an eight-inch chef's knife that had been driven into the wall.

Oh Jesus!

Arnie moved slowly toward the crib with rising dread. He gasped in horror at a sight that would follow him to his grave.

A little girl of about two lay on her side, dead from multiple stab wounds. Her face in profile looked almost serene as if she hadn't been the victim of an unimaginable crime but had just gone to sleep peacefully.

Arnie slumped beside the crib. Gripping its bars, he sobbed uncontrollably, vaguely aware of a fog-muted siren in the distance.

THREE hours later in the tiny kitchen of the mobile home, Sheriff Roy Huggins handed Arnie a shot of bourbon in a Styrofoam cup.

Huggins was a big man whose face was flushed from the extra weight he carried. The twinkle in his gray eyes, gone long ago, had been replaced by a cynical weariness, and his prominent nose was laced with small red lines—a map of years of heavy drinking.

Arnie's hand shook and the bourbon made his stomach roil. He ran outside and vomited in the garden next to the trailer. When he returned, Roy had refilled his cup. Arnie swirled some of the alcohol inside his mouth to kill the acid taste.

"If you're looking for reason in all this," Huggins sighed, "don't."

"But ... a child ..."

Huggins held up a hand to stop him. "It doesn't make any sense. That's all there is to it."

Arnie numbly swallowed the rest of the bourbon.

TRACES of the woman's blood and hair were on a baseball bat the county detectives found behind the sofa. The crime lab later matched a clean set of prints on the handle to her boyfriend, a lowlife named Robert Hooper. Hooper was a mean drunk and a brawler who was well known to the sheriff's department.

Speculating that Hooper was likely sleeping it off somewhere, the detectives expected to make a quick arrest. They searched the county, but never found him.

The monster had disappeared.

MONTHS later, the case was marked **INACTIVE** and filed away along with all memory of the mother and child who had been murdered. In the years that followed, the case faded into the miasma of accidental and intentional deaths that every police force experiences.

Arnie Voxx had been sheriff of Sunset County for almost twenty-five years now, and in all that time he'd never given up hope he would someday bring Robert Hooper to justice, even though the odds told him Hooper was most likely long dead. Regardless, Arnie vowed never to forget the mother and child and the vicious way in which they had died.

Their ghosts were always with him.

TWO

Pine, Michigan, present day

A bullet might be an act of hate or an act of love.

The barrel of the gun pressed tight under his sleeping father's chin shook as Mark Barnard wavered between these two emotions. All he had to do was pull the trigger to end the suffering. He hesitated, looking at the old man's face peaceful in sleep. Mark shut his eyes and increased the pressure.

Just a gentle squeeze.

Death would be a sweet release for them both. His father's dementia had progressed to the point where there was nothing left and Mark, devoted to his father's care, would be released from his servitude. The .45 slug would rip out what little remained of the old man's brain.

As if his father had somehow sensed Mark's desire, he released a loud shuddering gasp and was still.

Did he stop breathing?

Maybe God had answered his prayer and sent the Angel of Death to take his father. Then came a soft wheeze and his father's chest rose and fell. Mark wanted to scream. He gripped the pistol so tightly that he almost squeezed the trigger involuntarily.

Almost.

If his father had been conscious, the bastard would have sneered at his son not having the courage to go through with it. That was the old man for you, nasty to the core. If their positions had been reversed, Mark knew his father wouldn't have hesitated to fire.

This was the thumb Mark Barnard had lived under for thirty-two years. Mark had tried to escape the ceaseless, grinding demands from a parent who had no admiration for his only son by joining the army and serving in Iraq. He'd lived a lifetime in eighteen months of chaos and horror. But even after he returned from that shit-show, his father still showed no respect.

Robertson Barnard had once been a robust man with the features of a Renaissance statue. Now shriveled and ancient, his face had collapsed in on itself and his translucent skin was dry to the point that it flaked away at the slightest touch.

Robertson Barnard stirred in his sleep once again. His son dropped the pistol onto the floor and wept in frustration at his lack of courage.

Mark stepped back from the bed and thought about how close he'd come to killing his father. No matter how intense his rage, there was still a spark of love that kept Mark from veering into patricidal madness.

He took another deep breath and grimaced at the stench of camphor and stale urine, although at this point he hardly noticed the odor. Mark had smelled worse—much worse.

The day was fading into twilight. Soon his father would wake up and, like Dracula, would again start sucking the life out of his son with a barrage of insults and demands.

Mark picked up the gun and stuck it into the back of his jeans. The pistol tucked against his spine reminded him of just how close he'd come to ending his torment.

Age had not made his father this way. It was how he'd always been—self-centered and detached. He believed the whole universe swirled around him. And for a long time, it had.

Mark's father was a real American hero. In Korea, he'd saved his platoon during a violent firefight with the Chinese. The old man never let anyone forget how brave he'd been, and his Medal of Honor was only the beginning. He'd turned a single act of bravery into a best-selling memoir and leveraged his fame into a long senate career.

Robertson Barnard was a larger than life character who left his son and his wife deep in the background. They became props in his father's campaign literature and were trotted out at rallies with admiring smiles plastered on their faces.

Living with the black hole that was his father, Mark Barnard struggled to find his own light, but had failed under the inevitable comparisons to his father—another reason Mark had been driven into the military where a single tour overseas had left him psychically shattered.

It took eighteen months in the psych ward of a VA hospital before Mark could go home. During that time, his mother, the one anchor in his devastated life, died suddenly of a stroke. Or so they told him. Mark Barnard believed his mother had just tired of his father's constant need for care and attention. And then his father's health began to fail and Mark found himself in purgatory, unable to resolve his own trauma while stuck caring for his father.

With resentment boiling inside him, Mark turned away from his father's bed. As he looked out the window, the timed floodlights illuminated the yard signaling feeding time was at hand. He sighed deeply and quietly left the bedroom, careful not to wake the old man.

MARK Barnard went to the kitchen and put the Colt .45 1911 on the counter. He knew it wasn't a smart idea to keep the pistol around. The VA doctor had warned him about firearms, and Mark shivered when he thought how close he'd come to killing his father.

He looked down at the gun, another prop his father had used through the years, and promised himself he would unload it and drop it down the well when he finished feeding the cattle.

Mark pulled on his father's waxed-cotton barn coat, the faint scent of gasoline and hay surrounding him. Six inches taller than his father, the jacket was too short and the sleeves rode up no matter how often he tugged them down.

Crossing the yard to the barn, Mark Barnard inhaled the rich fragrance of the damp carpet of fallen leaves. Their earthy smell was a harbinger of winter. Noting they needed to be raked, he mentally added that chore to his to-do list for the morning.

At one time, Barnard Dairies had the biggest dairy herd in this part of Michigan. But when his father got ill, Mark was unable to care for the herd himself and sold off most of the cattle. Now there were only six cows left and, like everything else on the farm, they were his responsibility—a responsibility he did not want.

His father's lawyer had explained that Mark's power of attorney would allow him to sell the farm if he wanted to. Mark Barnard had been thinking about it, but couldn't imagine what life would be like without the only home he'd ever known.

AFTER he finished with his chores, Mark turned out the lights inside the barn and slid the door shut.

Bang!

Marked ducked instinctively.

A brilliant flash of light from his father's bedroom window was followed by another loud bang.

Ambush!

Mark Barnard's training kicked in and he reached for his rifle but it wasn't there.

Where the fuck is my gear?

Confused, he grabbed for his sidearm.

The bedroom strobed again, punctuated by yet another bang.

Gunshots!

Mark covered his ears and pulled himself into a protective ball.

They're over the wire and inside the camp!

Huddled against the barn door, he waited for the final vicious assault. Instead, everything went dead silent. The Iraqi desert faded away, and he was back on the farm in Michigan.

But danger was still there.

The kitchen light went out, and Mark crawled into the shadows to watch. A few seconds later, the door opened and a figure glided out. Mark strained his eyes, trying to penetrate the darkness so he could get a better look.

The figure moved from the shadows near the house out into the backyard. He could see it clearly now and gasped.

Mark Barnard was looking at something from one of his childhood nightmares—a bone white face, red tears, and the jack-o-lantern smile of a clown.

In stunned silence, he watched the clown twirl down the gravel driveway like a terrifying dervish. Only when the clown disappeared did he exhale.

Was it a hallucination?

Doctors at the VA hospital had warned him that he might experience them.

No, it was real!

Dread washed over him.

"Dad!"

He sprinted from his hiding place and ran to the house.

ROBERTSON Barnard's body was twisted unnaturally, sprawling halfway off the bed. He'd been shot three times at close range and the right side of his head was gone. Blood and brain matter dripped from the wall and curtains.

In a daze, Mark stooped and picked up his father's .45 from the carpet where it had been dropped and sat down in the armchair across from where his father lay.

Cradling the pistol in his lap, Mark Barnard began to sob.

THREE

WHAT a bitch of a morning!

The day had started off badly when her car refused to start. The vintage Austin Healey 3000 was notoriously fickle in anything but perfect sunny weather. Even then Molly couldn't depend on her car. The Healey was like a bad boyfriend—a source of endless sorrow but with fantastic sex.

"DEMOCRACY is messy."

Costas, the fry cook and owner of the Silver Birch Diner, leaned against the counter pontificating in his thick accent.

Deputy Sheriff Molly Parsons looked up from her breakfast.

"But isn't Greece still a mess?"

Molly dabbed a piece of rye toast into the center of her poached egg to make the yoke bleed.

Costas frowned and then smiled brightly.

"Greece was the birthplace of democracy," he said proudly. "We were democratic while America was still overrun with Indians."

Molly winced and looked around, hoping there were no Native Americans within hearing distance.

Costas wore one of her campaign buttons on the right strap of his apron—**MOLLY PARSONS FOR SHERIFF**. In the interest of fairness, he also wore a button for her opponent Kenton Sharpe.

The campaign for sheriff had been a whirlwind of debates, town meetings, and baby-kissing. Molly hated every minute of it, but this election was personal to her. She detested Kenton Sharp, who she had once worked under when he was chief of the Sunset Police Department. Sharp had made her life hell until he found a pretext to fire her.

Luckily for Molly, she was a damn fine cop who got results, which is what had led to her current job with the Sunset County Sheriff's Department. Sheriff Arnie Voxx had hand-picked her to succeed him now that he'd decided to retire.

So far, the campaign had been rough. The county political machine hacks who supported Kenton Sharpe wanted to make the sheriff's department *great again*, whatever the hell that meant, though Molly was certain it involved violating the Constitution.

Molly had some well-connected supporters of her own and had given Sharpe a run for his and his supporters' money. Going into the final ten days of the campaign, they were now in a virtual dead heat.

But all the electioneering bored Molly. She detested the endless cycle of fundraising, campaign dinners, and delivering the same canned speech night after night. Truth be told, Molly had been desperately hoping for a distraction—a murder or other serious crime—where she could exercise her investigative skills and take a break from the campaign trail.

The only real work she'd been doing recently was as a liaison with the state police in an on-going investigation involving the cover-up of sexual molestation of young boys by the basketball coach at the Pine Academy. She was helping by interviewing some of the victims, and the entire experience had left her feeling miserable and angry.

Other than this case, Arnie Voxx had been adamant that Molly focus on the campaign and leave the work of the department up to the other officers.

Oh well, in ten days it'll be all over.

Then she'd either be Sunset County's first female sheriff, or she'd be looking for a new job.

"Coffee please, Costas."

Molly turned to see Paul Booster standing behind her.

Once aligned with Sharpe against her when they'd worked together, Paul ended up becoming disillusioned by the Chief's machinations and pettiness. When the town council forced Sharpe to resign, Paul took his place on a temporary basis. Now his position was just as tenuous as Molly's. One of the things Kenton Sharpe had campaigned on was the elimination of the Sunset Police Department as an expensive redundancy. If Sharpe won, Paul would be out of a job as well.

Costas set a steaming cup down in front of Paul.

"Thanks, Costas." He blew across the rim to cool the coffee. "Cold out there, and it isn't even Halloween yet."

Molly nodded, recalling the crunch as she walked across her front lawn that morning.

"Anything happening?" she asked expectantly, even though she knew there wasn't.

"Just the usual—bar fights, break-ins, and drunk drivers." He smiled. "It's under control."

She thought about looking up a cold case for diversion, but Arnie would find out and give her shit.

Focus!

It was going to be a frantic day of campaigning. She had a Rotary lunch at the Great Northern and All-Candidates Meeting in Boyle later that evening.

Boyle.

Molly shook her head and wondered why she'd agreed to the All-Candidates in the first place. Boyle didn't count. It was the meth capital of the state. The only voters down there were either cookers or users, and she was sure Kenton Sharpe had their support all sewn up.

Molly's cell phone buzzed.

"Hey, Molly."

She recognized the voice of Kurt Harbou, the department's crime tech.

"Thought you might like to know that I'm on my way to Pine. Someone just shot Robertson Barnard."

Molly hadn't heard Barnard's name in a long time. In fact, she thought he was already dead. A quiver of excitement ran through her.

"Who's handling it?"

Kurt hesitated. "Jeff Cunningham caught it. But Arnie's not in yet, so it's technically up for grabs."

"I'll see you up there in half an hour."

Kurt gave her the address on a side road outside Pine.

Molly gulped the last of her coffee as she stood up.

"Gotta go, Paul." She threw a ten-dollar bill down on the counter. "It's on me."

Paul looked at it and smiled. "Hey, you can't buy my vote that cheaply."

"And I thought you were a cheap date, Paul," Molly said with a smile.

She waved goodbye to Costas as she raced out the front door of the diner and jumped into her Austin Healey.

FOUR

Florence, Colorado

IT was a routine traffic stop.

Jason Wildman of the Colorado State Patrol noticed a silver Escalade having a tough time staying in its lane as it went north on Interstate 50. Trooper Wildman pulled the Cadillac over just before Exit 115. The Caddy rode up the embankment and slewed to a stop.

Wildman turned on the flashing lights and stepped cautiously from his vehicle, his hand firmly on the butt of his sidearm. As he approached the car, the driver's window glided down.

The trooper pulled his weapon reflexively.

"Please keep your hands on the steering wheel where I can see them."

Through the open window, Wildman got a glimpse of gray hair and estimated the well-dressed driver was in his mid-seventies. He relaxed a little and lowered the gun to his side, keeping it out of sight below the level of the window.

The driver blinked and turned away when the trooper shone his flashlight into the car.

"How are you this evening, sir?"

"I'm all right."

Even though he was three feet from the driver, Wildman could smell the alcohol.

"Have you been drinking tonight?"

The old man looked directly at him, an overwhelming sadness filling his face. Then he turned and stared straight ahead.

"Would you please turn off the ignition and step out of the car." It wasn't a question; it was an order. Trooper Wildman stepped back to allow him to open the door.

The man stumbled as he got out of the car and grabbed for the door handle as he went down.

Wildman shook his head, holstered his pistol, and helped the drunk to his feet. Then he handcuffed him and read him his rights before putting him in the back of the cruiser.

The man slumped forward, staring silently at his lap.

WHEN he came off shift, Wildman learned he'd struck the jackpot. Even though the man's license was in the name of Gavin Ricks, his fingerprints had identified him as Robert Hooper, wanted for a double murder in Michigan.

Wildman recalled the grim expression on the old man's face when he'd booked him. Ricks, or Hooper, or whoever he was, had looked strangely relieved.

FIVE

"IT'S a mess in there," Sheriff's Deputy Jeff Cunningham warned Molly.

Jeff stood next to his criuser parked outside the farmhouse. Molly pointed at the handcuffed young man sitting in the back seat.

"Who's that?"

"Victim's son. He called it in. When I got here, I found him on the porch holding this." Jeff held up an evidence bag containing a large pistol.

It looked like a Colt 1911, a real old-fashioned gun.

"Keep him here. I'll be out in a few minutes."

IT was a typical crime scene with the victim as the star attraction surrounded by a photographer taking high-resolution pictures from every angle and crime scene techs marking the locations of bullet casings on the floor.

County Coroner Ronnie Kolmenn, measuring an exit wound with a pair of calipers, paused and looked up at Molly.

That's strange.

Typically Kolmenn would make some ghoulish joke about the victim or the nature of the injuries. It was his way of dealing with the horror of death. Today, however, the coroner worked with quiet efficiency.

Molly noted there were distinctive black rings around each of the entrance wounds and offered Kolmenn another opportunity to make a joke.

"Point blank?"

He nodded. "The gun was no more than two inches from the victim's head."

She turned to Kurt. "How about the son? Did you do a GSR yet?"

"Yup. First thing. Looks clean, though there was a tiny bit of residue. But that could be consistent with picking up the gun after the murder had been committed."

Kurt showed Molly a pair of evidence bags. Each held a leather glove.

"Found these in the son's jacket pocket. His coat was hanging in the mudroom. The right one smells like gunpowder."

Kolmenn motioned to the EMS guys who had been waiting patiently outside the bedroom. "You can take him now." And the coroner grimly followed them out the door.

She turned to Kurt in surprise. "What the hell's wrong with him?"

Kurt shrugged. "I don't know. He's been this way for a couple of weeks now."

Kolmenn was a strange little man at the best of times. He was also a damn good coroner who produced excellent work that was difficult for defense lawyers to pick apart. Molly forced herself to put Kolmenn out of her mind for now. Considering his uncharacteristic behavior would have to wait until later.

Molly looked at her watch. It was almost 11:00. The campaign event at the Rotary Club was at noon and she had to get moving. She asked Jeff Cunningham to take Mark Barnard back to the station where she would question him later that afternoon.

SIX

SHERIFF Arnie Voxx stared at the empty space on the wall where his photograph would eventually hang alongside the lawmen who had preceded him.

His hand shook as he gripped the phone while a state policeman in Colorado explained what they'd discovered. Arnie's blood pressure rose to a pounding crescendo in his ears.

Arnie gazed at the photograph of his mentor, Roy Huggins, and remembered the night he'd found the mother and her daughter in the trailer. Roy, a tough, old-fashioned lawman, had displayed an uncharacteristic tenderness toward Arnie, a rookie deputy who was forced to cope with an unbelievable horror.

Roy had been gone for many years now, his life cut short by a cerebral hemorrhage that had felled him at the very desk Arnie now called his.

Arnie smiled grimly at Roy's photograph.

They finally caught that bastard Robert Hooper.

The toddler in the crib would have been in her fifties by now, probably with at least a couple of grandkids. Arnie liked to imagine she would have led a happy life, the kind of life denied to her by Robert Hooper.

Every few months Arnie took out the open case file and carefully went over its contents hoping he would find something, anything, that would lead him to her killer. Now, just a few weeks before he left office, he would finally get to stamp PAID on that account.

Arnie glanced at the clock and saw it was almost time to leave for the campaign event at the Rotary Club. But first he needed to call his travel agent and book a ticket to Colorado.

MOLLY was running late. She had stayed too long at the farmhouse and hadn't left enough time for the drive back to Sunset.

On the way, Molly reminded herself for at least the one-hundredth time how much she hated campaigning. She was tempted to just drop out of the race and let Kenton Sharpe have it. But the thought of his vengeful smirk was enough to re-energize her.

As Molly pulled into the parking lot, she remembered Robertson Barnard was on the list of Pine Academy board members. After she talked to his son, she would have to drop by and see Les Caulfield, state police lead on the Academy cover-up investigation.

THE first course had been served by the time Molly slid in the back door. She looked around at the Rotary Club members, all male and mostly white, and knew she wasn't going to sway them.

Sharpe was already busy working the room, moving easily from table to table, shaking hands and sharing laughs.

Arnie waved Molly over to a table near the front. She sat down and introduced herself to the men seated there. Their lack of enthusiasm told her all she needed to know.

Arnie looked at her reproachfully. "What's going on?"

Molly leaned in close and told him about Robertson Barnard's murder.

"Sounds like an open and closed."

"Yeah, it looks that way. I'll talk to the son this afternoon."

She remembered Mark in the back of the cruiser. He'd had the look of someone whose life had just spiraled out of control.

"Don't get bogged down with it. You've still got another week of campaigning and you can't afford to take your eyes off the ball."

She nodded and ate her salad. When finished, she looked over at Arnie. He was smiling to himself.

"What's up?"

Arnie's smile faded. "I'm going to be out west for a few days, so I need you to keep an eye on things. Might as well get used to being in charge."

Maybe when this damn campaign ends.

In his element, Sharpe shot Molly a smug smile from across the room. He'd been sharing a laugh with Ben Dorsett, the owner of funeral homes all over the county. Maybe they were planning a funeral for her.

Molly looked away.

She didn't understand how any reasonable person couldn't see through Kenton Sharpe's lies and distortions. The answer stared back at her in this room full of white, middle-class, middle-aged men.

SEVEN

MARK Barnard hadn't as much as twitched for the past five minutes.

In fact, Molly was positive Mark hadn't blinked since they'd brought him into the interview room.

Jeff Cunningham cornered her outside the room before the interrogation. He was concerned about Mark's mental state.

"I called the Vet Center in Traverse City. They confirmed that he goes there twice a month for counseling."

"What for?"

He frowned. "They wouldn't say without a court order, but I'm guessing PTSD."

Post-traumatic stress disorder was something Jeff Cunningham had first-hand experience with.

As a soldier in Afghanistan, Jeff had been part of a convoy that had come under attack in Kunduz Province. His Humvee had been blown up and he'd escaped death by crawling over the mutilated corpses of his friends. Jeff was still getting counseling for the trauma caused by that horrifying experience.

While Molly worried about Jeff and his ability to cope with the stress of the job, so far she had no cause for concern.

"MARK?" she said softly.

Mark Barnard looked up at her.

Molly found his gaze disturbing. He was staring beyond her into a dark place. She shivered and wondered just what Mark been through in Iraq.

"Could you tell me what happened last night?"

"My father died." His voice was devoid of emotion.

"Did you hurt him?" Molly kept her tone unthreatening.

Mark Barnard shook his head slightly as if he was clearing his mind. "No … I was in the barn. I heard the shots and came out."

"Did you see who fired the shots?"

Mark blinked.

"No, I didn't. There was someone in the house. He was gone when I reached my dad's room."

"Who was gone?"

"My dad's killer."

His nostrils contracted and his eyes shifted down to the left.

Molly knew he wasn't telling the entire truth. She decided to try another tactic.

"But he was shot with your pistol."

Mark shook his head. "It's Dad's army pistol from Korea."

"The only prints on it are yours. Can you explain that?"

Mark shifted. "I had it out last night."

"Why did you have the gun out, Mark?"

"I don't know. I …"

"Was it to shoot your father?"

Mark looked as if she'd hit him in the face. His eyes dropped again and he traced a finger along one of the gouges in the top of the table.

"Yes," he said in a voice so quiet Molly had to lean forward to hear him.

"Why don't you tell me what happened to your father."

He looked up and fixed his gaze on her, his eyes filled with emotion. Molly could see that Mark was barely holding it together.

"I took out the gun and loaded it. I've done it before, loaded the gun and put it against my father's head." Mark's eyes darted at the recollection. "You don't know what it was like with him. All his demands. He didn't care about anyone else. Nothing mattered if it didn't center around him. I was so tired ..."

"Are you saying you killed him?"

Tears rolled down Mark's cheeks and his nose began to run. He made no attempt to wipe them away.

"I thought about it for years. I imagined pushing him down the stairs, or putting rat poison in his oatmeal, or just blowing his fucking head off!"

Mark slammed his fist down. "But I couldn't do it."

Jeff Cunningham opened the door and slipped into the room, prepared to back up Molly if the prisoner got violent. Jeff shut the door and leaned against the wall.

"Well, someone did, and right now you're the only person who had a motive and access. Plus your fingerprints are all over the murder weapon. Tell me, Mark, how do you think that looks?"

Mark slumped forward. "Bad," he whispered.

"CAN you handle the Boyle crowd tonight without me?" Arnie asked Molly when he popped into Molly's office a few minutes later.

Just thinking about the town hall in Boyle gave Molly a headache. The meeting was sponsored by the Boyle Business Improvement League, which was a laugh considering that Boyle's core business was crystal meth.

Arnie's airline ticket had arrived. He was scheduled to fly out to Pueblo via Chicago late that evening and was shoving files into his briefcase.

Molly picked up one. Once bright yellow, the folder had faded into something closer to jaundice.

A stark black and white crime scene photo showed a bloody handprint near the bottom of the refrigerator door just below where a couple of child's drawings were fastened by a magnet. Molly riffled through the other photos and grimaced when she saw the toddler in her crib.

"Glad they got the bastard," she muttered.

"Yeah, so am I." Arnie took the file from her, put it in his briefcase along with his ticket.

"When you get him back here do you want me to handle the interview?" She already knew the answer but asked anyway.

He shook his head and Molly saw the pain in his eyes. Arnie Voxx had spent a lot of sleepless nights thinking about this case and about the monster who'd eluded him for fifty years.

Well, that monster was finally going to face justice.

She was glad Arnie was going to bring closure to this case at last.

"What about our guest? You going to charge him?"

Molly nodded. "The DA's preparing charges right now. We'll arraign him in the morning."

"Good, then you can get back to the job of being elected."

"I don't know, Arnie. I might take another look at the farmhouse. Something doesn't feel right to me."

He frowned. "Molly, don't go wrapping yourself up in an investigation just to get out of campaigning. If you want my job, you have to prove it to the voters."

"But this entire election is bullshit."

"Maybe, but that's the way it works. No matter how good you are at doing your job, you still must convince the good people of this county that you can handle the responsibility. After all, you've got big boots to fill."

"And a big hat as well," she added with a laugh.

He chuckled and then let his smile fade.

"Kenton Sharpe is not going to show you any mercy. He knows this is a fight to the death. When it's over, one of you will have to get out of Sunset, and I don't want it to be you. So hold your nose and finish the campaign. Then you can get some real work done."

Arnie swept up his briefcase and strode out of the office. Molly stayed behind for a few minutes to look at the photographs of his predecessors—all men.

It was time to change that.

EIGHT

INSPECTOR Les Caulfield of the Michigan State Police rose slowly to his feet as Molly entered the room.

Molly motioned for him to take a seat. She set a thick stack of files on his desk. "I talked to Lowe and Black. Their statements are in here."

The folders were full of venom. They contained her interviews with two abuse victims who, after all these years, still carried horrible scars from their experiences.

The interview with Marty Black had been especially unnerving. Black was eight years old when Greg Akron, the basketball coach at the Pine Academy, had raped him. Black resented that he had to tell his story again about a crime that would go unpunished.

The case was a foul one, the kind nobody wanted to get involved with—the sexual molestation of children. Molly was thankful she was only working the periphery of the investigation, interviewing victims and witnesses.

Les Caulfield was the lead investigator charged with putting together a criminal case against the board of directors and the administrators of the Pine Academy for criminal negligence.

He was trying to prove the directors and the administration had enabled Akron to commit his atrocities by not investigating the allegations when they were first raised against the coach. Les believed these two groups had swept the accusations under the rug because Akron had been a much admired and winning coach.

Molly could see this cesspool of an investigation was taking its toll on Les. Hell, her own peripheral part of the investigation kept her up nights. She even found herself sobbing on the way back from her interview with Marty Black. She had no idea how Les could live with this horror day after day.

But Les Caulfield took it all in stride, as he had most of the parts of his life. Molly found his soft drawl—he'd been born and raised on a farm in Tennessee—had a soothing effect on both her and the victims they interviewed.

Still, there was a toughness to him that she admired. It masked the pain he must have been feeling since his wife died from breast cancer ten years ago. To counteract his grief Les, a star investigator for the MSP, had taken difficult and complex cases all over the state.

At sixty-two, Les had experienced another personal tragedy after he stopped to help a stranded motorist and was hit by a drunk driver. His injuries left him in crippling pain that qualified him for a generous state disability pension. Being a lawman was the only life that Les Caulfield knew and he begged to be allowed to keep working.

Lansing gave him the Pine Academy cover-up investigation which was wrought with political danger in the hope that it might discourage him.

The case was a formidable task. It made sense to the state brass that Les be the one to take it on. He had a reputation as an excellent investigator and if the case went sour, his superiors could claim it was due to his injuries.

While Les Caulfield looked over the files Molly had delivered, she casually glanced at the wall of his office where photos of the Pine Academy board members and former administrators were pinned.

Les put notes under each picture as evidence was uncovered. The first job was to prove that a cover-up had even been committed.

The accused perpetrator, Gregory Akron, had an entire section of the wall to himself. His picture had been taken courtside just after the Academy's senior basketball team won the Midwest championship in

2000. Akron was smiling broadly. Of course, he didn't know he was only four years from a fatal heart attack, also at courtside.

In the eyes of Central Michigan basketball fans, Coach Akron had died a hero.

But soon after his death, ugly rumors of his sexual predilection for young boys started to surface. A reporter from the Detroit Free Press did an investigative piece which eventually won him a Pulitzer Prize.

Although Akron was beyond the reach of the law, those who may have enabled him were not.

Because many of the board members were well-liked and politically-connected, the cover-up investigation was conducted in secret. It was essentially a one-person show to minimize any potential blowback.

The deeper he dug, the more Les was convinced these were not misguided people but were truly evil individuals. They'd been more concerned with shielding the glorious reputation of the Academy's basketball program than protecting the children in their charge.

The cover-up had begun almost from the day Akron had arrived at the school in 1983. It continued for the next twenty years as the powers-that-be looked the other way while their prize-winning basketball coach molested young boys.

Lansing had appointed a special prosecutor, Ami Silver, to handle the case and prepare the indictments. Silver pushed Les to make certain they had an airtight case. Smart and tenacious, she knew this prosecution could be a career maker or breaker.

And, like Coach Akron, Ami Silver didn't like to lose.

Les had arranged the pictures of the Academy directors and teachers who'd been targeted by his investigation along one wall in linear order. A line indicating the years Akron had been at the school ran across the wall above them. Molly studied the pictures and pointed to one on the left, a photo of a much younger Robertson Barnard.

"You can take that one down."

"Oh yeah? Why?"

"He was murdered last night."

Les grimaced and hobbled to the wall next to Barnard's picture. There were very few notes under it.

"He was only on the board for a year after Akron came to the school. I had pretty well ruled him out."

"Well, you can rule him out *permanently.*

Les reached for the picture and then hesitated. He left it in place and turned away from the wall. He couldn't stand to look for too long at all those smug faces he'd grown to hate.

Molly glanced at the clock on the wall. It was almost 5:30. She needed to be in Boyle for the town hall in an hour and it was a forty-five-minute drive.

"Les, I've got to go. I have to be in Boyle for a town hall."

"You mean they still haven't wiped out that vipers' nest?"

Molly smiled and shook her head. "What, their respected business community? They're like cockroaches. They're hard to kill. Believe me, we've been trying for years."

"It's a disgrace that they can operate with impunity."

"We'll nail them. Someday."

Molly knew Arnie was reluctant to stir up too much trouble in Boyle because his elderly aunt lived there. Molly believed Arnie didn't want to risk a reprisal against her if they shut down the meth trade.

However, Molly had no qualms about slamming the door on Boyle and had made it very clear during her campaign. Boyle was a blight on Sunset County and she was dedicating herself to bringing it down. This should make for an impressive town hall.

ARNIE looked out the plane's window at Chicago far below. They were on the final approach. He gripped the armrest as he always did when the engine pitch lowered and the flaps went down.

To distract himself, he thought about Robert Hooper. He would be close to Arnie's age now, in his early seventies.

How the hell had Hooper managed to stay hidden for so long, and what had he been up to?

Arnie was disappointed that Hooper had enjoyed fifty years of freedom. At least now Hooper would die in prison, but somehow that wasn't enough.

Hooper's picture was clipped to the inside of the case file. He'd worked odd jobs around Sunset for several years before becoming involved with the victim.

From every account, Elsie Maranello had been smart and well-liked and had a decent job as a teacher. Sadly, her husband died in Viet Nam a few months before their daughter was born.

Elsie's little girl June was the only thing that kept her going—that and booze. The consensus of those who knew her at the time was that Elsie was an alcoholic. That's how she'd become involved with a low-life like Robert Hooper. They met in a dive bar and clicked—and her life spiraled downward. Her compounding misery inevitably led to that fateful night when, in a drunken rage, Robert Hooper had caved in her skull with a baseball bat and stabbed her child to death.

Arnie was so involved with his anger he hardly noticed the plane's perfect landing.

As soon as it was safe, he pulled his overnight bag from the overhead bin and marched into the terminal. He had forty-five minutes before his connecting flight to Pueblo.

Arnie continued to simmer in the departure area. He saw little June in her crib and tried to reconcile that image with the conversation he'd had with the police chief of Florence. According to the chief, Robert Hooper was a prominent and well-respected member of the community. The town had been shocked when his past came to light.

Arnie opened the file and looked at Hooper's picture once again. The booking photo had been taken after Hooper's arrest for a bar fight a few months before the murders. Even with a black eye and bloody nose, Hooper stared at the camera in arrogant defiance, a smirk playing across his swollen lips. Arnie tapped Hooper's picture with his index finger, his rage flaring up again.

Spending the rest of his life in prison was not bad enough for Robert Hooper. Not bad enough by a long shot.

NINE

MOLLY was boiling in the oppressive heat of the Boyle Moose Lodge.

The outside temperature had dipped as evening approached, so the caretaker had turned up the ancient oil furnace. The building was at capacity, and the heat from all those bodies raised the temperature another ten uncomfortable degrees.

From the small stage, Molly stood behind a podium and looked out over the room.

The good citizens—though she preferred to think of them as denizens—had turned out in force. She hadn't seen so much corruption in one place outside a cemetery.

The future of law enforcement in Sunset County was the number one concern in Boyle. The stakes were high here. Kenton Sharpe had made it clear that things would stay status quo if he were elected. Molly, however, responded that she would be keeping a keen eye on their little community and was determined to erase the meth trade that drove its economy.

It wasn't just the meth cookers who stood to lose if Molly was elected. The entire business community's livelihood depended on the wealth the drugs produced. At the center of this circle were the Atkinson Brothers—Sammy and Tom—who owned the most lucrative auto dealership in this part of Michigan. Crank cookers had a real affinity for luxury pickup trucks, and the Atkinson Brothers made a fortune scratching their itch.

While Tom was thin and quiet, and comfortable remaining in the background, his older brother, Sammy, could be politely described as corpulent. Sammy was also the public face of the dealership, waddling around the sales floor, slapping backs, and making deals.

As Kenton Sharpe made his way toward the stage, Sammy Atkinson embraced him in a huge bear hug. Sharpe looked around uncomfortably. And no wonder, Sammy was sweating profusely from the heat. When he finally released Sharpe, Molly smiled. The front of Sharpe's dress shirt was soaked.

Her eyes narrowed as she saw another figure slink into the room through the back door—Taylor Mead, the undisputed boss of Boyle.

On the surface, Mead was a respectable businessman, the owner of the ValuRama chain of liquidation stores. The main store located on the edge of town was huge and had become a destination for bargain-hungry shoppers from all over the Midwest. Truth be told, however, it was just a huge washing machine for the drug profits that Boyle's meth trade produced.

Mead controlled all the drugs, from manufacturing to distribution. He'd found a way to funnel hundreds of millions of dollars out of the country and into off-shore banks safely out of reach of the IRS and DEA. There were rumors that Mead also used his pipeline to help other criminal organizations launder their cash and took a significant percentage in return.

Locking eyes with Mead was like staring down a cobra. The old man was cadaverous, with a thinly cruel mouth that curled into a knowing sneer. Mead preferred cheap black suits that draped listlessly on his frame. He was the personification of death, like a corpse who had climbed from his coffin when he decided it was not his turn to die.

Mead leaned against the back wall next to Tom Atkinson to watch the proceedings.

Tom and Sammy had been bikers before Mead reached down and offered them respectability. In addition to their dealership, they also served as Mead's two main henchmen. It was common belief that Tom would likely take over from Mead when the old man retired or died.

Molly fixed Taylor Mead and Tom Atkinson with a glare.

Scumbag and Scumbag Jr.

While the criminal element had the community firmly in its grip, there were still many hard-working, tax-paying citizens living in Boyle who just wanted to live in a decent town and raise their families. These people despaired about what Boyle had become when the bad guys moved in. This the only reason Molly had agreed to the town hall in the first place. She wanted to send a firm message to them that their community had not been forgotten and she was determined to clean it up. The town hall's moderator was one of these people.

Adam Gmerek, Boyle's mayor, had lived here all his life. He was frustrated that his hometown had been overrun by criminals and had resolved he would initiate change. To his dismay, he discovered that making changes in Boyle was a Sisyphean task. But he was determined to keep fighting. He owed it to his community.

Molly felt sorry for Adam and wondered how long it would take his idealism to metastasize into cynicism. She watched as he struggled to get the crowd's attention.

Hang in there, Adam, the cavalry is on the way.

The crowd quieted down and Adam introduced the two candidates. Molly thought she detected a hint of scorn when he said Kenton Sharpe's name.

The first question was for Sharpe. It came from Brad Seymour, a guy Molly recognized from his mug shot.

"Mr. Sharpe, could you explain to us what your approach to law enforcement is?"

Good question.

Kenton Sharpe looked out at the audience and smiled.

Here come the lies.

And for the next four minutes, Sharpe took the basic libertarian position that law enforcement should focus on catching the bad guys and not interfere with law-abiding citizens. Sharpe's subtext was clear—he would keep his investigators far away from Boyle.

Much to Sharpe's joy, when it was her turn to answer the question, Molly stumbled around a bit. She cursed under her breath for not being better prepared.

"I believe that everyone deserves the full power of the law. If you're innocent, it should protect you. However, if you're guilty, you should expect that it will come down on you like a ton of bricks."

Molly's unwavering gaze was aimed squarely at Mead.

"I don't want anyone to think they're above the law because times change."

Mead returned her stare and began to clap his hands mockingly. Heads turned toward him and his minions joined in. Molly saw some citizens watching nervously. They were not clapping.

The meeting went on like this for the next hour and a half with wild applause for Kenton Sharpe and more muted reactions to Molly.

Fear and intimidation were palpable in the room. Molly had expected the attendees would only be from Mead's camp, so she was surprised to see how many citizens had shown up. Adam Gmerek had worked hard to convince them to attend.

Maybe Boyle wouldn't be a write-off after all.

OUTSIDE the Moose Lodge, someone had scratched a profanity in the side of Molly's cruiser. She looked at the word, shaking her head in disbelief.

"I don't agree with that," Kenton Sharpe said from behind her.

Molly turned to face him.

Sharpe was standing next to his silver pickup.

"Thanks, Kenton, I appreciate that."

Sharpe gave a cruel chuckle. "You don't actually think you're going to win, do you?"

"Well, I could say something cliché like that's up to the voters, but I won't because right now I can't say for sure."

"There's still a week left, and that's an eternity in politics," Sharpe replied with a smug grin.

"Well, at least I'm not jumping into bed with Taylor Mead and his collection of deplorables."

Sharpe scowled at her, barely contain his anger. But somehow he managed to hold it in check and smiled again.

"Molly, you should mind your language. I don't need to remind you about what happened to the last politician who ranted against 'deplorables'."

They locked eyes for a few moments before Sharpe glanced away. When he looked back, his cheeks were flushed.

"The very first thing I'm going to do when I'm elected is to fire you. And then I'm going to figure out a way to throw your ass in jail."

"Fine, Kenton, but you have to win first."

"That's not going to be a problem. You'll be history in about a week."

This kind of threat was typical Kenton Sharpe bullshit. Molly didn't take the bait.

Without another word, Sharpe got into his truck and pulled away.

Molly thought back on his arrogance and had second thoughts. Maybe Sharpe wasn't bluffing.

Did he have an ace up his sleeve?

Molly looked at the Moose Lodge and saw Taylor Mead standing by the half closed door to the kitchen, a sliver of light spilling over one side of his thin body. Even from this distance, Molly could feel his malevolent stare.

She returned his look.

Your ass is mine, fucker.

TEN

ARNIE white-knuckled it all the way into Pueblo.

The tiny commuter jet glided down the side of a mountain, tossing in fierce updrafts, and landed hard. Several of Arnie's fellow passengers gasped loudly, and Arnie held his breath as the jet skidded to a stop on the short runway. The rapid deceleration forced him forward, his belly pressing painfully against the seatbelt.

When the jet reached the gate, Arnie was the first one off. Even though he wasn't wearing his uniform, a young state trooper walked straight up to him as he entered the small terminal.

"Sheriff Voxx?" Arnie nodded.

The trooper extended his hand. "Jason Wildman."

Arnie smiled. He might have mistaken the trooper for a teenager if not for the uniform. Wildman took Arnie's overnight bag in his huge hand and led him through the airport.

"You made the arrest?"

"That's right, sir. He was weaving and I pulled him over to check if he was DUI."

Jason had a broad, enthusiastic smile, with one front tooth overlapping the other. From his build, Arnie guessed Jason Wildman spent a lot of time outdoors.

"I understand you've been looking for the suspect for a long time, sir."

Arnie nodded. "Since I was about your age. How was Hopper when you arrested him?"

Jason frowned. "It was strange, sir. He acted relieved, like he'd been expecting it."

They got into Wildman's vehicle at the front entrance of the terminal.

IT took almost half an hour to reach the state patrol office in Florence.

Winter had come early in southwestern Colorado. Two feet of snow lined the highway, and Arnie wished he'd brought a heavier jacket and boots.

Jason introduced Arnie to his sergeant, Carl Tibbets.

"Could you take Sheriff Voxx over to the Best Western, Jason?"

Arnie stopped him. "If you don't mind, Carl, I'd like to see the prisoner."

"Let's talk for a few minutes first." Tibbets motioned toward a conference room.

Arnie gratefully accepted the cup of coffee offered by the state policeman. They sat down at a long table and Arnie took a sip.

"I just want to give you a little context, Sheriff. I've known Gavin Ricks and his family for almost twenty years. We serve together in our church. A lot of people in town, including me, are having a tough time reconciling him with the man you say he is and with the crime he's accused of."

Arnie opened his briefcase and slid out a file. Flipping it open, he pulled out a black and white shot of little June dead in her crib. He pushed it across the table.

"The medical examiner said she had been stabbed seventeen times."

Tibbets picked up the photo. His eyes tapered in sorrow and he set the picture down gently.

"The man you know as Ricks was born Robert Hooper in some crappy little village on the Pennsylvania/West Virginia border. He never graduated high school, just floated from place to place like a piece of shit until he ended up in Sunset County. He left that baby and her mother dead."

Tibbets shook his head. "You just never know I guess."

"I understand he's waived extradition. I've got us booked on the first flight out of Pueblo in the morning."

"Yup, we've got all the paperwork ready. I should mention that his son Colin is a pretty well-known attorney around here and is making a lot of noise about this."

Arnie leaned forward, concerned. "But we're okay to go, aren't we?"

"Yes, sir, the judge has signed off on the paperwork. I expect that Colin will likely come along with his father when you take him back to Michigan."

"That's fine." Arnie leaned back in his chair.

Just as long as he keeps out of my way.

GAVIN Ricks didn't look up when Arnie stood outside the tiny cell.

"Well, Robert, I guess we've come to the end of a long road." Arnie tried to keep the bitterness out of his voice.

Tibbets stood next to him, averting his eyes from the man who had been his friend for twenty years.

Ricks remained mute and continued to stare at the floor of his cell.

"You're going to find that some things have changed in Sunset since you were last there. We have a new jail. It's a lot like this one. And we have a new judge who will be pleased to throw your ass in the state prison for the rest of your natural life."

Tibbets was shocked at Arnie's bitterness but didn't interrupt.

As Ricks continued to stare at the floor, Arnie's anger mounted. He expected some reaction from Ricks—pleading his innocence, or perhaps hostile denial. Instead, Ricks remained stoically silent.

Arnie turned from Ricks's cell.

"I'll pick him up at 6:00," he told Tibbets and strode away.

Tibbets hesitated. He thought about saying something, but the picture of the little girl's body flashed through his mind. He couldn't make sense of any of it, so he just walked away.

ELEVEN

MOLLY couldn't sleep.

Not too long ago, she'd been afraid to go to bed. The night had held terrors for her. But over the past six months, she gradually had fewer bad dreams.

Tonight it wasn't nightmares that prevented Molly from sleeping. She kept going over the town hall meeting in her head, contrasting Taylor Mead and his henchmen with Adam Gmerek and the other honest citizens of Boyle. Along the way, someone had sold them a bill of goods and they'd bought it. Before they realized what was happening, a wormlike Taylor Mead had taken over.

Molly didn't understand why Arnie had left that part of the county alone for so long. She knew about his aunt Ida who lived there but couldn't believe Arnie would bow to that sort of pressure. She had a fleeting thought about a payoff but immediately buried it. There was no way in the world that Arnie would ever do that, and she was ashamed for even considering bribery.

Well, no matter what the situation was, if she was elected, Molly was going to bring down Taylor Mead and his cronies.

Molly shifted her thoughts from Boyle to Robertson Barnard's murder. On the surface, it was straightforward patricide—sons had been killing their fathers since before Oedipus. The voice of reason, which sounded very much like Arnie, told her there was nothing more to the killing. Prints on the gun, apparent motive, and no alibi all pointed at Barnard's son Mark. Still, for some undefinable reason, she had a feeling that Mark Barnard was telling the truth when he said he hadn't killed his father. The son was hiding something. Molly was sure of that. But whatever it was, it was not his innocence.

Molly took this thought a step farther. If Mark Barnard had not killed his father, who had? Again Molly heard Arnie warning her to leave the case alone, it was cut and dried, focus on winning the election. But her doubts about Mark's guilt continued to pester Molly. There was something missing, and she was determined to find out what it was.

Since there were no campaign events planned for the next day, it was a good opportunity to go up to Pine and nose around.

Once she'd made the decision, Molly was able to float off to sleep.

PINE is located on Lake Michigan in the northwestern part of Sunset County. Several shoals a few miles offshore posed a significant hazard to ships heading north to the Straits of Mackinaw. So after the Civil War, the federal government erected a lighthouse on a point of land outside of town.

In November of 1898, a vicious storm washed the lighthouse away. The government rebuilt it in the center of town, reasoning that putting the lighthouse a quarter of a mile from the lake would protect it. The engineers selected a small rise at the top of Burns Street in downtown Pine and constructed the building from locally-milled wood and, in the nautical tradition, painted it white with red stripes.

In the 1970s, the light was automated and the Coast Guard hired a local electrician to oversee its maintenance. Although GPS and advanced navigation systems made the lighthouse pretty, the town of Pine continued to pay for its upkeep because it drew tourists.

In a small town where the tallest building is three stories high, the Pine Lighthouse can be seen for miles. The light is turned on each night at dusk and, when there's fog, the horn is activated to warn passing vessels.

Molly saw the lighthouse as she crested the hill a mile out of town. She had left Sunset before dawn, deliberately skipping breakfast because Pine had an excellent diner on the main street.

THE front window of the Foghorn Diner had a professionally carved pumpkin in the window. Black paper bats hanging from the ceiling stirred to life as Molly came in the front door.

Halloween!

Molly had completely forgotten about it. For the past few years, she had lived on Shadow Lake outside of Sunset and trick-or-treaters never came there. A few months ago, she'd moved into town and that meant there would probably be a stream of costumed kids knocking on her front door.

It was after 9:00 and the restaurant was almost empty. Molly was headed for a table by the front window when she saw the familiar face of Rita John, Dean of the Pine Academy, sitting by herself in a booth.

As part of Molly's investigation with Les and the state police, she had interviewed Rita about the Coach Akron cover-up. Rita had been appointed to help put a positive face on the ongoing scandal that had consumed Pine Academy.

Molly felt a kinship to Rita. They were around the same age—rubbing up against forty—and both had difficult, demanding jobs. But while Molly pissed off a fair number of people, Rita had an easy-going personality that naturally defused tension.

Molly approached her table and Rita waved at the seat across from her.

"Please join me."

She sat and picked up a menu.

"God, I'm starving," Molly said cheerfully.

"What brings you back to our fair town?"

Molly leaned forward in the booth and looked around nervously.

"You heard about Robertson Barnard?"

Rita nodded. "I heard that his son shot him."

"It looks that way."

43

"But you're not sure?"

Molly shrugged. "Did you know him?"

"Robertson? Or his son?"

"Well … either, or both …"

"Robertson came to our annual dinner last year. He was a former board member. He seemed like a nice man, though he talked a lot."

"Yeah, I'd heard he was a tangent talker. Apparently, he always liked to bring the conversation around to his favorite subject—himself."

Rita laughed. "That's true. One of the teachers joked that you could tell when you'd reached the forty-second mark in a conversation with him. That's when he would start talking about his past glories."

"Do you know Mark?"

"I met him once. Mr. Barnard sent him around to pick up some files about a year ago. He told me his father needed them for something he was writing."

"Did you give them to him?"

"No, of course not. All our files are sealed under court order." A cloud passed over Rita's face.

"Any idea what he was working on?"

Rita shook her head. "His son said it was some sort of history of the institution. The stuff he was looking for was from a much earlier time, the '50s and '60s. That was long before Akron arrived at the school."

"You don't happen to remember what specifically he was looking for do you?"

"He had a list that he left with me. I still have it back at the school. If you want, I can dig it out for you."

"Yeah, that would be great. I'll run you over to the school if you like."

"That's not necessary. I'm parked out front."

"I'll get the check then."

Rita smiled and Molly stared after her as she left the diner.

The next few years were going to be tough ones for both the Academy and the town. Strong leadership at the school would be essential, but Rita was the perfect person for the job. The legal bills were going to be crushing from the class-action suit brought by the boys who had been molested. They were looking at tens of millions in settlements which wouldn't leave much left over for keeping the school running.

Molly knew Rita was single and couldn't understand why. She thought Rita was beautiful with her radiant, unlined skin and emerald eyes. Molly considered herself ordinary by comparison.

The face in the mirror that looked back at her most mornings appeared weary. Years of stress had taken their toll. Molly, to her dismay, had noticed tiny notches starting to radiate from the corners of her eyes and her auburn hair had lost its luster and was starting to show some gray. Age was merciless.

A lot of it was attitude. Molly had grown cynical since her husband's death. While she still had a sense of humor, it had become caustic. Rita, by contrast, bubbled with enthusiasm. She used her natural wit to masterfully to defuse many stressful situations.

TALL maples lined the long driveway leading up to the front of the Pine Academy. The trees were naked now, ready for winter after losing their leaves in a burst of color.

The school came into view and Molly grimaced. Even with the wide porch running the full length of the front, the building was severe. With its imposing limestone walls, it resembled a prison more than a school.

Flanking the main school building were two wings that served as the student and staff residences. A few hundred feet farther down the road was a small arts and crafts style cottage where Rita lived.

Although it wasn't visible from the road, Molly knew there was a barn-like gymnasium behind the main building. It was there that Akron committed most of his assaults—in his office or the shower room. Molly felt a touch of nausea recalling the interviews she'd done with his victims. One had described how Akron had pinned him against the wall of the showers and raped him. Remembering the victim's toneless voice, Molly could still feel his pain.

MOLLY looked at Rita and thought about the challenging work she was doing to erase some of the institution's shame. It was going to be a struggle to keep the Academy open. Many people in Pine wanted it razed to the ground, buried, and forgotten.

Rita searched her desk for Barnard's list of files. Molly gazed out the window at the campus. Uniformed students casually walked across the lawn.

In the 1930s, when the school had first opened, it was not much more than a glorified orphanage. Through the years, troubled and special-needs children were stockpiled in its austere dormitories. From the accounts Molly had read, it was a cruel and hostile place, more like a reformatory than a school.

Today, the Pine Academy housed disadvantaged children who deserved a quality education. Academically it was gaining a reputation on par with many exclusive preparatory schools.

"No luck?"

"I thought it was here." Rita closed a desk drawer and opened another. "I'll keep on looking."

"Thanks. Is there anyone you can think of who knew Barnard?"

Rita continued rummaging through the drawer.

"William Vandermeer was on the board around the same time as Barnard. You might talk to him. He owns a sports shop in town."

Molly went through the motions of writing Vandermeer's name down. In truth, she already knew exactly who he was—Vandermeer was on Les Caulfield's wall.

Rita slammed the drawer in frustration.

"I don't know where the hell it went. I know I put it in a file with his name on it."

"It's okay, Rita. If you find it, please fax me a copy."

A doorbell chimed when Molly walked into the SportsStop at the Pine Mall.

Baseball bats and gloves had been put away for the season and were replaced by racks of hockey equipment. On a shelf behind the sales counter was a row of trophies, most of them for basketball.

A woman in her mid-fifties looked up as Molly approached the counter. The woman was built like a fire hydrant, with closely cropped hair and a faint 5:00 shadow on her upper lip. Her smile gave Molly the creeps.

"May I help you?" Her voice was husky.

"I'd like to speak to William Vandermeer." Molly flashed her badge and ID.

"He's in his office." The woman pointed to an open door behind the counter and shouted, "Bill!"

Molly's first impression of Vandermeer was of an older gentleman in remarkable shape. He had to be at least seventy-five but had the build of a much younger man. He walked with precision, carefully factoring every step. He smiled broadly as she held up her ID for him to inspect.

"Sheriff's department? Better come in the back then. We can talk privately in my office." Vandermeer opened a gate at the back of the shop and motioned Molly to follow him.

In his office were more trophies and framed photographs of athletes. Molly knew she needed to tread lightly with Vandermeer. He'd been on the Academy's board while Akron was coaching the basketball team. Les believed Vandermeer was the leading suspect in the cover-up.

"I was wondering when you'd get around to talking to me."

His demeanor was arrogant.

"Oh, why is that?"

He shrugged. "There've been rumors about a state police investigation into the whole Greg Akron mess."

Molly shook her head and lied. "I wouldn't know anything about that."

He smiled sardonically. "Of course."

"I'm investigating the death of Robertson Barnard, who I believe you knew."

"Sure, I knew Robbie. We were friends for almost fifty years. What's to look into? His son killed him, didn't he?"

Molly opened her notebook and flipped to a blank page.

"Did his son have any reason to kill him?"

"Sure, he was nuts. Got his head all scrambled up by the Taliban."

"When did you last see Mr. Barnard?"

"I stopped by to see him about a week ago. He was failing fast. I got the feeling he wasn't going to last much longer."

"What was his state of mind?"

"Robbie needed someone to talk to. He was pretty confused though. Kept asking me if I'd seen his wife. She died years ago. It's understandable that he was muddled like that."

"Why is that?" Molly asked politely.

Vandermeer regarded her with scorn. "He probably went looney cooped up in that house with his son Mark the mental case."

"Do you think he could have been depressed?"

"What? Depressed enough to shoot himself in the head *twice*? From what I heard, the first shot pretty well painted the walls with his brains, so I don't think he committed suicide."

Molly blinked remembering the splattered walls of the bedroom.

"Maybe he asked his son to kill him."

"I don't think so." Vandermeer was growing visibly angrier by the minute. "Robbie Barnard was my oldest friend. Believe me, if he had wanted to go that way he would have asked me to pull the trigger, not that psycho son of his."

"Did he?"

"What?"

"Ask you to kill him?"

Vandermeer stood up, his face flushed red. "How dare you suggest such a thing." He was shaking with rage. "Leave now," he ordered.

Molly casually closed the notebook and put it into her pocket. She let Vandermeer fume for a few more seconds before standing up.

"If you think of anything that could help our investigation, please give me a call."

She placed one of her business cards on his desk and walked out.

Behind her, Vandermeer picked up the card and crushed it in his fist. He tossed it into the garbage pail next to his desk.

As she left the store, Molly was again conscious of the woman's stare. She felt creepy, as if she was being eyed by a predator.

TWELVE

OIL, stale beer, and piss.

The smell was overwhelming, but Frank Brighton didn't give a shit. He hadn't given a shit in a long time. His auto repair garage was decrepit. If a customer was offended by the place, fuck 'em. They could just take their car somewhere else for service. His customer service philosophy seemed to be paying off. There hadn't been a patron all day, but Frank Brighton was okay with that. Dealing with customers cut into his drinking time.

Brighton had once been a pillar of the community, a respected citizen who had owned the most successful Ford dealership in all central Michigan.

With its gleaming showroom and three service bays, his dealership was always busy. But success had a price, and in twelve short years Frank Brighton went from being the light of the social scene to being an alcoholic outcast. In the process, Brighton lost his business, his wife and kids, and his respect.

All he had left was this dump of a garage by the side of a blue highway. If he was lucky, ten cars a day passed his business. And if he was really lucky, someone might even stop for an oil change, or to have a signal light replaced. But it had been seven months since he'd done his last brake job and almost a year since he'd rebuilt an engine. Now he spent most of his days drinking cheap beer and napping.

Brighton had passed out late in the afternoon and woke with a nasty headache and an attitude to match. When his eyes finally focused, he saw it was night. He stumbled to his feet. Time to close up.

The service bay was barely wide enough to fit a compact car because of all the junk scattered around there. It was so crowded that Brighton had to use the mechanic's pit to store his beer. He couldn't use it for anything else because the hoist leaked hydraulic fluid.

Brighton locked the door and headed to his tiny office in the back. He popped open another beer and pulled a Hungry Man Swiss Steak dinner from the freezer compartment of the tiny fridge. When he turned it on, the microwave made alarming clunking sounds until the bell dinged. The food was only half-thawed. Brighton shrugged and popped open another High Life and settled into a lawn chair to eat the unfrozen portion.

He turned the small space heater on high to chase the chill from the room. The oil tank hadn't been filled in a while, and he wondered when it would run out. He thought about calling Richardson Fuels in the morning and then considered the cost of a fill-up. Fuck it. If it ran out, he'd drag out the electric heater. It would carry him through the winter, or until they finally turned his power off.

As it got hotter in the tiny room, Brighton unzipped the front of his coveralls and opened another beer. A few minutes later he fell asleep in his chair.

BRIGHTON woke up feeling queasy. According to the Pennzoil clock on the wall, it was almost 11:00. The remains of his dinner had slipped from his lap and spilled onto the oil-stained floor.

Brighton crushed the empty can of Miller he clutched in his fist and stopped breathing for a second.

What the fuck was that?

A soft tinkling came from the glass panes of the service bay door. Brighton pushed himself out of the rickety chair and stood, waiting for the nausea to roll back down his throat. Then he staggered into the garage, careful to avoid the pit. Brighton turned on the exterior floodlight to illuminate the broad gravel entrance and looked through the rolling glass door.

The lot was empty.

As he turned away, a movement caught his eye and he froze in horror. Through the streaked glass of the service bay door, he saw something colorful twirling at the edge of the spotlight's spill.

Brighton rubbed one of the panes of glass with his sleeve so he could get a better look.

Jesus!

He jumped back from the window and almost tumbled into the mechanic's pit. Flushed from the burst of adrenaline, his heart hammered in his chest.

The image was vivid—a bone-white painted face slashed with a broad crimson grin, eyes circled in rosy greasepaint, and nose the color of fresh blood. The ghastly face was capped off with a yellow wig.

Brighton fought to catch his breath as he took short, hesitant footsteps back to the glass and forced himself to look again.

The clown was gone.

He searched the entire parking area for any sign that what he'd seen was real.

Thank God. It was only a hallucination.

Brighton had them all the time—imaginary rats or snakes crawling out of his brain after a five-day binge. But this was unusual, he'd only drunk six beers all day and felt perfectly sober.

Brighton gazed through the window again. There was nothing there, nothing at all, but he felt sick to his stomach.

Nothing that a little High Life won't cure.

Brighton swore under his breath and flipped off the front light. The parking area was dark again. He walked back to his office and sat down so hard that the lawn chair almost buckled under him.

Of course, it had to be a clown.

When he was a kid, he'd had an irrational fear of clowns. He thought he was over it, but his fear had obviously just been dormant, like an unexploded bomb waiting for the right time to shatter his sanity.

This waking nightmare was his penance for all the years of alcohol consumption.

Fuck it!

Brighton pushed the image of the clown from his mind. It was time to sleep. He got up and went to the cot. As he was about to lie down, there was a soft tap on the door at the back of the office.

"Frank …" The voice was high-pitched and grating, like every clown he'd ever heard.

It's not real!

The metal doorknob turned slowly counter-clockwise, its rusted innards squeaking as it moved.

Brighton, still flushed with adrenalin and his head throbbing, tried to combat the rising terror. He shut his eyes to block out the vision, convinced it was more of the delirium tremens. He cursed loudly because there wasn't a can of beer close by to chase them away.

"Frank …"

"Who's there?" he moaned.

The knob stopped moving.

Wrapped in silence, Brighton felt surreal, trapped in a fever dream. No one was there. The terror was just in his mind.

Look, I'll prove it.

Brighton grabbed the doorknob and yanked the door open so hard it banged off the cinderblock wall.

A huge clown filled the doorway.

Brighton screamed and fell backward, landing hard on the cement. The room above him swirled. He got up after a few minutes and crab-walked back from the door.

The clown towered a thousand feet above him, leering down, its mouth frozen in a wide, rictus grin.

Brighton desperately tried to shuffle away, but the clown was fast and seized him. Brighton looked away, trying to will the terrifying image out of existence. His head smacked the cinderblock wall as the clown pinned him against it. The room swirled from the explosive pain and Brighton tumbled into merciful darkness.

THIRTEEN

WITH a final sickening lurch, the Piper Apache dropped a thousand feet in what seemed like seconds on its approach to the Sunset airport.

Landing in Sunset was a skill. The runway was short and the glide path steep, hence the sudden drop just before landing. Pilots explained the situation and told the passengers not to be alarmed, but the warning never helped.

They were on the last scheduled flight of the day—Pueblo via the twin cities on American and then a puddle jumper into Sunset.

Arnie sat in the aisle seat with Gavin Ricks/Robert Hooper handcuffed to the armrest beside him. During the seven-hour trip, Ricks remained mute. This suited Arnie just fine, the last thing he wanted to do was make small talk with a monster.

The plane taxied to a stop fifty feet from the terminal. The flight attendant lowered the ramp and eight passengers filed out, careful to avoid looking at the sad old man in the bright orange jumpsuit. When they were gone, a sheriff's department cruiser pulled up next to the plane. Jeff Cunningham jumped out and opened the rear door.

Arnie unhooked Ricks. "Let's go."

Gavin Ricks would be formally arraigned on two counts of capital murder in the morning.

Arnie had traveled a great distance, in miles and years, to see that justice was done.

"GODDAMN it, Molly, you're supposed to be focused on the campaign!"

Arnie looked tired. Molly knew he hadn't gotten back until late the previous evening.

Molly had dropped by to see Ricks in his cell. She was curious to see what this monster looked like. It didn't surprise her that he looked ordinary. Most real life monsters do. The ugly ones are only in Frankenstein movies.

"Vandermeer is a big deal in Pine, and you managed to royally piss him off."

Molly took a bite of cheese Danish. "He's an arrogant prick."

"Maybe, but he has considerable clout in a town where you need the votes. Why are you stirring things up? Robertson Barnard's son killed him. End of story."

"I'm not so sure about that."

Arnie held up his hand in exasperation. "Look, I know that you hate campaigning and all the election bullshit, but stop trying to make a simple homicide into some kind of conspiracy. You can't afford the distraction. There's only a week left before the election. Just focus on that."

Molly frowned and started to formulate a comeback but stopped. Arnie was right, of course. She was bored and grasping at straws.

"If you need to piss someone off, piss off Kenton Sharpe. The polls are close. We need to shake him up. Force him off his game. I don't want to wake up next week and find that the good people of this county have elected that asshole."

Arnie got up and grabbed a folder from his desk. Molly didn't need to look at it. She knew it was the Gavin Ricks AKA Robert Hooper case.

"I've got to get to court," he said curtly and left.

Molly picked at the remaining Danish and thought about what Arnie had said.

She had to make the rounds of the local diners at noon, shaking hands and asking for votes. That evening she was going to be interviewed by Channel Seven for the 11:00 news. TV always made her look old. She flashed back to Rita and her eternally youthful appearance and wondered if there was time to have her hair done.

VINCENT Rainer gripped the wheel and prayed Mazda would make it to town. Its fourteen-year-old engine had begun to shake alarmingly, like it was coming off its mounts.

Rainer swore at the car again and pounded the steering wheel.

Damn! Shit! Fuck!

The manager of the Pine Country Market was waiting impatiently for the fresh eggs in his trunk. He had to get them there on time.

Up ahead he saw Brighton's garage. If he were sober, Frank Brighton would be able to patch whatever was wrong with this piece of shit and get him on his way. And Brighton wouldn't charge an arm and a leg either.

Rainer pulled the violently shuddering car into the lot in front of the garage. He sighed in relief and got out.

"Frank? Where are you, buddy?"

No answer.

Rainer frowned. The service bay was dark.

He's probably out back sleeping it off.

Rainer tried the door that led to the service counter on the side and was relieved to find it unlocked.

That's a good sign.

"Frank?"

Still only silence. Rainer entered the office and looked around. Fingers of ice began to crawl up his spine.

Where the fuck was the old man?

Rainer stood in the doorway looking into the service bay. It was pitch black. With the lights off and the windows so crusted with grime, no sunlight could penetrate.

He felt along the wall next to the door until he found a switch panel. Rainer flipped one up and an overhead fluorescent light buzzed and flashed to life. A piercing whine from the direction of the mechanic's pit drew his attention.

Frank Brighton was sprawled on the floor with his head lolling over the edge of the pit. To his horror, Rainer saw the car hoist coming down fast, like a guillotine. He flipped the switch up and down frantically, but the lift kept on descending.

A loud, wet crunch was followed by Brighton's body jerking upward. It hung suspended in mid air for a few seconds before slamming back down to the concrete floor and rolling to one side. Blood fountained out of the severed neck and sprayed across the floor.

Vincent Rainer's vision swam and he knew he was going to be sick. When he was finished vomiting, he screamed until his throat was raw.

FOURTEEN

THE transformation was incredible.

The stylist had convinced Molly to let him re-color and sculpt her hair, add blush to accentuate her cheeks, and use a base to mask the dark rings beneath her eyes.

She looked ten years younger and the fresh look appealed to her ego. While she admired herself in the mirror, Molly thought she would look good on television.

Smiling to herself, Molly gave the stylist her credit card and pulled on her jacket.

Her phone vibrated and she checked the caller ID—Kurt Harbou.

"We've got a weird one, Molly." The crime tech's voice was strained.

"Define weird."

"I think you'd better see for yourself."

VINCENT Rainer, sitting in an ambulance huddled under a Mylar blanket, was in shock. Molly couldn't imagine what had traumatized the poor man.

Violent death was part of her job. Molly had seen it in most forms, from horrendous car wrecks to willful homicide. Death was always depressing, but occasionally it could also be horrifying. What was waiting for her inside Frank Brighton's garage definitely fit the latter category.

Blood spray was the first thing that caught her attention. It fanned out almost ten feet across the garage. Blood still dripped from a rack of oil filters against the far wall. Molly traced its path back to a narrow point to where the corpse lay under a rubber sheet next to the mechanic's pit. The outline of the corpse ended abruptly at the neck.

"Where's the head?"

Dr. Kolmenn, dressed in a white Tyvek suit, climbed out of the pit and nodded curtly at Molly.

Kolmenn pointed at the pit. "Down there. He was decapitated by the hoist. His head was crushed beyond recognition." The coroner frowned and turned away.

It was uncharacteristic of Ronnie Kolmenn not to make a sick joke when confronted by a horror like this. Molly was convinced there was something wrong with the coroner, but right now she didn't have time to think about it.

"We got an ID on the vic?" she asked Kurt.

"Frank Brighton. This is his garage."

"Was it an accident?"

Kurt shook his head grimly and pointed to a panel by the entrance to the bay. "Someone tampered with the switches. The power was rerouted from the hoist switch to the light switch. When the light switch was turned on, it activated the hoist."

Ronnie Kolmenn looked up from his notes.

"Plus, there's a large contusion on the side of his head. Someone knocked him out first."

Kurt agreed, nodding toward the office.

"It appears that he was dragged from back there. Whoever did it, took care to position him directly under the hoist so when an unsuspecting soul flipped on the lights …"

Molly thought of the traumatized man sitting in the ambulance.

"You're saying someone went to all *that* trouble to kill him? Why not just bash his head in?"

"Maybe the killer didn't want to get his hands dirty," Kolmenn said.

VINCENT Rainer was still shaking badly. When Molly questioned him, Rainer began to sob loudly. He told her about turning on the lights and how the lift came down. Rainer's cheeks flushed when he described what had happened next.

"Was there another vehicle out front?"

Rainer shook his head. "No, and I didn't see anyone either."

Molly closed her notebook and put a hand on Rainer's shoulder. She wasn't good at giving comfort. It wasn't in her nature. But in situations like this, she had to try.

"It wasn't your fault."

Rainer wiped his eyes. "Yeah, well, that's not gonna help me sleep."

He broke down again and Molly left him to the paramedics. They sedated Rainer and took him to the hospital.

Once Kolmenn cleared the scene and Brighton's body and head were loaded into the morgue van, Kolmenn stripped off his coveralls and climbed in.

"I'll do a post this afternoon, but it's pretty clear what happened."

"WHEN you've got a moment, Molly, could I speak to you?" Kurt asked.

"How about you come by my office tomorrow morning around 9:00."

He nodded. "I should have some of this evidence processed by then." Kurt paused and then smiled. "Nice look, by the way."

MOLLY hesitated before she got into her cruiser.

Why would anyone go to all this trouble to kill a down on his luck mechanic?

Maybe he'd given someone a bad brake job.

In a peculiar way, she was relieved that Brighton's murder had happened. Arnie wouldn't be able to pull her off this case. Right now she was the only experienced investigator the department had and this was a clear-cut case of murder—a real who-done-it, just the kind of investigation that was perfect for her.

Molly would have to squeeze in the election around it. Anyway, the only campaigning left before the election was the TV interview that night and the final debate on Saturday evening. After that, it would all be over except for the waiting once the voters went to the polls on Tuesday.

With luck she might have the murder investigation wrapped up by then. Cracking this case would be a huge boost for her campaign.

Molly grimaced.

Christ, I'm turning into a politician!

JUDGE Harrison Pomm had a full docket in the morning but agreed to fast-track Gavin Ricks's arraignment.

The proceeding was over in a matter of minutes, with the two counts of murder being read into the record and Judge Pomm asking the prisoner if he had representation.

Ricks shook his head.

Arnie stood against the back wall of the courtroom, alternately glaring at Ricks and watching a younger man who sat near the front making notes on a yellow legal pad.

Judge Pomm instructed the prisoner to obtain legal counsel and then put the case over for three weeks, at which time he would entertain a plea. An officer took Ricks from the courtroom. Since the county jail was over capacity, he would have to remain in a cell at the sheriff's headquarters.

Arnie left the courtroom. At the same time, the younger man slipped his legal pad into a leather messenger bag and followed him.

The man caught up to Arnie on the street outside the courthouse.

"Sheriff Voxx?"

Arnie turned to face him.

"I'm Colin Ricks, Gavin's son."

Arnie looked at him in surprise followed quickly by annoyance.

"I've got nothing to say to you, sir." Arnie turned abruptly and started to walk away.

"My father deserves a fair hearing, Sheriff."

Arnie paused and said over his shoulder, "If he wanted that, he should have stuck around fifty years ago."

MOLLY didn't let the TV interviewer shake her as they sat side-by-side in Molly's office.

"Kenton Sharpe says you lack maturity and experience to do the job. What do you think?"

Molly smiled serenely. "I've been in law enforcement for almost fifteen years. As for my lack of experience, there are bad guys in jail right now who could tell you about that."

Arnie stood in the hallway watching the interview on a tiny monitor next to the producer.

Molly was doing well. She hadn't taken the interviewer's bait but rather turned it into an opportunity to reinforce her record as someone who put "bad guys" in jail. That should appeal to the law and order bunch.

The interview had been televised live on the evening newscast. She knew the interviewer was a hack who'd thrown his support behind her opponent, but Molly had interrogated enough suspects to know how to avoid being blindsided by loaded questions. In the interview, she presented herself in a reasoned, confident, and unflappable manner she knew would connect with the voters.

When it was over and the TV crew had left, Arnie wrapped an arm around her shoulders.

"You're a natural politician."

"Please, don't accuse me of that," she laughed.

"MIND if I look?"

They were back in Arnie's office, and Molly had picked up the case file on Gavin Ricks.

"Haven't you got enough to do right now?" he said gruffly.

Arnie took the file back and slid it into his top drawer. Then he tapped her preliminary report on the Frank Brighton murder.

"What's happening up there in Pine? Did someone put something in the water?"

"It's just a coincidence as far as I can tell."

Molly wondered if she should be looking at a link between the two killings. On the surface, there didn't appear to be any. The well-to-do Barnard was evidently murdered by his son in a psychotic rage and Brighton was a broke, burned-out alcoholic.

She couldn't get over the strangeness of the mechanic's murder. Who would go to that amount of trouble when a simple ball peen hammer to the skull or knife to the throat would have done the job? Something else nagged at Molly, but she couldn't quite define what it was. Still, she had an uncanny feeling that somehow there was a connection.

On the surface, the only parallels between them were that the two victims were both from Pine and were approximately the same age. Molly wondered if they had known each other, or if their paths had intersected in the past.

"SHERIFF, you can't keep me from seeing my father."

Arnie and Molly looked up in surprise.

Colin Ricks stood in the doorway of Arnie's office. He was visibly upset.

"I don't have to do anything for you, sir. Or your father," Arnie responded coldly.

"But I'm an attorney …"

"Yes, in Colorado. Do you have a license to practice in Michigan?"

"If I could just talk to him."

"Visiting hours are over for today."

Molly could see Colin Ricks was desperate and turned to Arnie. "I could take him back and watch over him for a few minutes if that's okay?"

Arnie started to protest and then shrugged. "Sure. Whatever. But he only gets five minutes."

Colin smiled gratefully, and Molly led him back to the cell block.

"YOUR boss certainly hates my father."

Molly and Colin Ricks were outside the heavy steel door leading to the cells.

She nodded. "He has every right to. He'd only been on the job for a couple of weeks when he found that mother and her child. It's eaten at him for over fifty years. No one wants to see the murder of a child go unpunished."

"But my father isn't like that. He would never hurt someone."

"That's your perspective. I've seen the pictures. It was horrific."

Colin paused. "I haven't seen the pictures, or any of the other alleged evidence for that matter."

"You don't want to."

Molly unlocked the door to the cell block.

"Please stand behind the red line on the floor. You've got five minutes."

Ricks nodded gratefully and entered the cellblock. Molly shut the door behind him and locked it.

A monitor next to the door displayed each cell in a tiny frame. With only a video feed, Molly could see Gavin Ricks sitting on the cot in his cell but couldn't hear what Colin was saying. From the younger man's posture, it was clear he was pleading with his father. The old man pointedly turned away from his son and faced the cinderblock wall.

After five minutes, Molly unlocked the cellblock door and Colin Ricks shuffled out. He looked like he was close to tears. She felt sorry for him. She could only imagine what impact the revelation of this shocking crime must have had on the Ricks family.

Molly locked the door again. Gavin Ricks stared at the wall while Colin continued to look at his father with concern.

Molly put her hand on Colin's shoulder. "Look, it's dinner time. Why don't we get something to eat."

JENNIE Summerville led them to a quiet table at the back of The Villager. The waitress was six months pregnant and starting to show.

Jennie's father Hank, owner of The Villager, was pumped at the prospect of becoming a grandfather for the first time.

"So how are you feeling?" Molly asked Jennie.

Jennie smiled. "Like I'm ready to have this baby."

Molly put a hand on Jennie's belly and felt the baby move under her palm. Her joy for Jennie was muted by sadness as Molly remembered how she'd lost her baby the same night her husband died.

The proud grandpa-to-be ambled over and joined them.

Hank pointed at the front of his restaurant. "I hope you noticed that I only have your campaign signs in the window."

"Aren't you worried about losing customers?"

"As far as I'm concerned, Molly, anyone who supports Kenton Sharpe can find another place to eat!"

He said it loud and looked around to see if there had been any effect on the other diners. No one appeared offended. Satisfied he turned back to Molly and Colin.

"In fact, I'm expanding," Hank said brightly. "We're taking out the wall next weekend."

Molly looked across the narrow dining room at the wall dividing The Villager from the store next door. Hank had finally convinced the owner to sell. Now he could double the size of the dining room, and Hank needed the extra space. During the summer he had to turn away almost as many customers as he served. Even in the off-season, The Villager was always crowded.

As much as he loved his restaurant, Hank loved his daughter Jennie even more. She was his pride and joy. He'd also come to love his new son-in-law Andrzej, a baker who worked in the kitchen. Andy's baked goods were so popular that his bread was being sold to other local restaurants.

Colin Ricks picked up a menu. "What's good?"

"Everything but the pizza," Molly replied with a smile. "I usually have the whitefish."

"Sounds okay. I'll have that as well."

Jennie took their order.

"By the way, thanks," Colin said to Molly after Jennie had left. "I appreciate you doing this."

"I'm sorry it wasn't under better circumstances."

Colin Ricks's youthful ruggedness was just starting to give way to paunchy, middle age. His hair had receded like a glacier to the middle of his head. What remained was tied back in a long, salt and pepper, ponytail that fell to his shoulders.

The aging hippie look.

Molly wondered what kind of lawyer he was.

Criminal?

"This is all so surreal. I can't get my head around it."

Molly shifted uncomfortably.

Ricks looked at her sincerely. "My father is a good guy. He's kind and loving ..." he stammered and Molly was afraid he was going to lose it.

Colin Ricks took a few seconds to regroup.

"And you had no hint about any of this?"

Ricks released a long breath. "Up to last week, things were normal. Dad doesn't drink. He was gentle and kind, he never so much as even raised his voice to us. Everybody loves him. He gives so much back to the community."

Because of guilt?

Molly held her tongue. The morgue photo of the dead child came back to her in stunning relief and the image tempered her sympathy. Maybe Gavin Ricks *had* redeemed himself and gone on to live an exemplary life in Colorado. But the fact remained that here in Sunset he'd brutally taken two innocent lives, and now he'd have to face the consequences.

Her phone buzzed. The caller was Ronnie Kolmenn.

"I have to take this," Molly apologized and walked to the small stage at the back of the restaurant away from the other diners.

Molly gazed absently at the stage and a shiver raced along her spine She recalled Desirée Platt, the last singer who performed here. Desirée had been a talented singer but her song had ended badly. Very badly.

Molly chased the memory from her mind and concentrated on what Ronnie Kolmenn was saying as he rattled off the preliminary report of his autopsy on Frank Brighton.

"He suffered head trauma including multiple contusions before decapitation. Like we suspected, the victim was unconscious before he was dragged to the hoist."

"Any idea what he was struck with?"

"A fist from the look of it. The blow caught the victim across the temple. And there was a streak of white across his cheek."

"White?"

"At first I thought it might be paint, but it's smeared. I gave Kurt a sample, and he was going to run an analysis. It might be a lubricant, maybe white grease."

"Anything else?"

"He didn't have much to eat last night. And from the level of alcohol in his blood, he was legally intoxicated. But apparently that wasn't unusual. He had a reputation as an alcoholic."

"Sounds like you know … knew him."

"No, not really. Friends of mine up in Pine do. Brighton used to be a big deal in the community until his drinking caught up with him. I'll fax you my final report in the morning."

Molly was going to remind him there was this thing called e-mail and it would be much easier to send a PDF, but she didn't want to go there with him again. Ronnie Kolmenn was a stubborn Luddite.

DINNER was on the table when she came back. Colin Ricks hadn't touched his food. He was politely waiting for Molly. She apologized, and they ate in silence. When they finished, she remembered what he'd been saying before they'd been interrupted.

"You said your father never drank."

"That's right. In fact, my dad wouldn't have any kind of alcohol in the house. He told us his father had been an alcoholic and he was dead set against it. And then last week he suddenly started drinking."

Ricks frowned.

"He called me at home and was rambling and slurring his words. I rushed over to his house. I thought he'd had a stroke or something. There was an empty bottle of bourbon on the kitchen counter and a couple more empties in the garbage. It didn't make sense to me and when he tried to explain, he just started crying. I finally got him to go to bed. But I was pretty shaken up. The next morning he refused to tell me what was going on."

"Maybe he couldn't stand the guilt any longer. Guilt can be like that for some people. It's a disease that just eats away at them until they have to relieve the pain."

Ricks leaned back in his chair.

"Sorry, but I refuse to believe that my father was capable of what you say he did."

He put a couple of tens on the table and stood up.

"Colin, I can only imagine how you're feeling right now but if you want to help your father, you should find him a good lawyer."

"I've already contacted an attorney in Traverse City. He'll be coming up to speak to my father tomorrow. Hopefully, he can get more out of him than I did." Anger flashed in Colin Ricks's eyes. "My dad is an innocent man."

Molly wanted to tell him the evidence said otherwise but held off. She could see how much torment Colin Ricks was feeling.

They parted outside the restaurant without another word. Colin strode along Main Street toward the Great Northern Resort where he was staying, and she climbed into her cruiser.

Molly thought about going home, but she was restless. So instead, she drove back to the office. She had paperwork to finish up and needed to prepare her talking points for the final debate on Friday night.

Molly wondered if Arnie had left his top desk drawer unlocked. She wanted to get a look at the Gavin Ricks file.

FIFTEEN

DELORES Marsh woke in a blind panic.

She'd dreamed of the children in the pit again, their pleading, upturned eyes still burned indelibly into her mind. It was hard to catch her breath, and for a moment she feared she was having a heart attack. But she knew she wasn't. She was suffering the burden of memory.

Delores lay in her narrow bed and listened for traffic on the distant highway. It had rained during the night and now, in the hour before dawn, there was a steady drip outside her bedroom window.

She thought of the dream and cursed in Polish.

It didn't matter that they were children. They were not innocent. They were only subhuman like all who lived in the pit—Jews, gypsies, the feeble-minded—they were all the same, less than human.

They deserved to be there, just as she deserved to stand above them on the rim of the pit and watch over them with her rifle. That had been a long time ago and now was forgotten thank God.

Delores crossed herself and whispered a prayer of thankfulness that she had been given another day. But what sort of day would it be? There would certainly be more rain. The drop in barometric pressure burrowed behind her eyes like an ice pick in her sinus cavity. In addition to that agony, both her knee joints were on fire. She desperately needed something to dull the pain, but Delores had forgotten to put her vial of Celebrex on the bedside table the night before.

She thought again about the girl she'd once been—a prime young woman with her rifle and prisoners to guard. She'd been cute when she was barely twenty. All the German boys had courted her, wanted to be with the beautiful Polish maiden who worked alongside them in the camp. But that beautiful young maiden was a distant memory. Somehow she was now eighty-three and barely had enough energy to get out of bed and face the day.

Once she was able to, Delores pulled on a thick cotton robe that kept the cold out. After a few painful steps, her knees eased up a little and she hobbled to the bathroom. She swallowed her medication and waited for its warm glow to diffuse throughout her body and make the agony go away.

Aging was insidious. It had twisted her fingers and etched deep crevices under her eyes and across her cheeks. Delores hardly recognized the face staring back at her from the mirror.

Delores knew she had to eat soon, or the medication would upset her stomach. It was a good thing she'd left oatmeal warming in the Crock-Pot overnight. The oatmeal would be good, especially with a slice of toast and honey followed by a cup of strong tea.

All thoughts of breakfast scattered at the distinct sound of a creak. Delores's head shot up and she listened intently.

Age might have dulled her eyesight and other senses, but her hearing was still remarkably keen. She tensed at another sound, closer this time. Someone was sneaking down the hall toward the bathroom. That was impossible, of course. She was just an old woman and had nothing of value.

Delores tried to scream in an attempt to frighten whoever it was, but it came out as a weak croak because her throat was constricted with terror.

And then there was another sound, closer but different.

The swishing of cloth on cloth.

Delores stared into the bathroom mirror at the empty doorway behind her. Whoever was in her house was right there in the hallway shadows.

She needed a weapon.

Scissors!

As she reached for the medicine cabinet, Delores froze in horror. A large shape filled the doorway.

Delores squeezed her eyes shut to block out the reflection. It wasn't real. She was still dreaming. This was something the children had sent to her. But when Delores opened her eyes, the figure was still there.

She smiled at the absurdity as darkness spun around her.

Yes, it is a delusion.

The clown deftly caught Delores as she fell forward.

FIFTEEN cases of long neck Bud in the back of his pickup were making one hell of a racket as Clark Benjamin pushed the truck up to fifty on the Old Pine Highway. He thought about slowing down in case the ragged road smashed some of the bottles.

Fuck it!

Benjamin was pissed at being dragged from his warm bed because someone at the Warsaw Corners Elk Lodge had forgotten to put in their beer order last week.

As the sky started to lighten in the east, Benjamin saw potholes ahead. He slowed the truck to forty. The fucking shocks were nearly shot, and he couldn't afford a new set right now. Once past the rough stretch, he opened up his speed again. They wanted him there by 7:00.

Who the hell needs a beer at 7:00 in the fucking morning!

On the Ford's satellite radio, Greta Van Susteren was railing against the proposed gun control legislation New Jersey was considering. The new law would require ID to purchase ammunition. Thank Christ he kept his NRA membership paid up, not that the state government here would ever try shit like that.

Benjamin wished he'd stopped for coffee, but there would be time for that, and breakfast too, once the delivery was done. With his thoughts focused on bacon and eggs and bullets, Benjamin pushed the truck up to sixty.

A hundred feet ahead, something emerged from the woods next to the road. Benjamin barely had time to register what it was.

A clown?

He stomped down on the brake pedal—and immediately realized his mistake when the brakes locked and the truck slewed sideways.

As he slid by, Benjamin caught a glimpse of a clown. The painted bastard bowed with a flourish.

Son of a bitch!

Benjamin lost control of the pickup and it rolled, spewing cases of beer in its wake. The inside of the cab was like a blender. Even though Benjamin wore his seat belt, he was still tossed from side to side. Excruciating pain shot through his right arm as it snapped in two places, and he let out an agonized scream. Benjamin's head slammed against the side window, knocking him unconscious.

The truck continued to tumble along the road until, after two hundred feet, it came to rest on its roof.

When he came to, Clark Benjamin hung upside down with blood flowing over his face from a gash on his chin. He swiped at his eyes to clear them.

The truck was making an ominous clicking sound as white hot metal cooled. At first, Benjamin thought he smelled gas, but it was just beer. The cab was awash in the shattered remains of his cargo.

With great pain, Benjamin turned his head so he could see the side mirror reflecting the road behind him. A trail of broken bottles littered the highway.

Benjamin tried to make sense of what had just happened. And then he gasped. Off in the distance, the clown was dancing down the road, its image becoming smaller and smaller as Benjamin drifted in and out of consciousness.

Less than a mile away, Davy Snider heard the commotion. He briefly wondered what it was before deciding he didn't care. Draining the PBR clutched in his hand was more important. He sucked out the last of the beer so hard the sides of the can collapsed. Snider tossed the empty over his shoulder and picked up the PSE Brute X compound hunting bow he'd left leaning against a stump.

Christ, it was an ugly bitch. But *Field and Stream* gave it an excellent review, so he'd plunked down four hundred large for it.

The remaining cans of beer hung from their plastic rings tied to his belt.

Only two left.

Snider considered having another, but decided that too much beer might impair his aim. He was determined to get himself a deer today, no matter what.

Snider's sneaker caught a root. He lurched to one side, wishing he'd worn rubber boots. The woods were still wet from the rain last night, and it was hard to walk in a straight line because of the rough terrain, not to mention all the beer he'd drunk. Snider slipped and fell, soaking the ass of his cammo pants.

Fuck it.

He turned on his MP3 player, a cheap one he'd picked up a K-Mart, and selected *Cat Scratch Fever*. Ted Nugent was a guitar god. He was also a bow-hunting god.

The Nuge don't take shit from nobody.

Snider dialed up the music so loud it felt like his headphones were going to vibrate right off his ears.

And then nothing mattered.

Through the trees, Davy Snider saw the unmistakable tan hide of a deer. He advanced a step.

Holy shit!

There it was—a big buck just standing in a clearing.

Snider notched an arrow and brought his bow up, pulling smoothly back on the string. He let the arrow fly and almost jumped for joy when it slammed into the buck's chest.

Surprised the large animal didn't go down right away, Snider quickly strung another arrow and let it fly. This one connected with another satisfying thump.

Son of a bitch!

He stepped forward cautiously. The deer hadn't moved. And it remained upright. Snider watched it from the edge of the clearing.

Fuck!

It was a fake deer!

Who the hell did this?

He thought it was likely one of those animal rights groups Ted Nugent was always bitching about. Those fuckers would do anything to embarrass hunters.

Maybe they're filming it for the internet.

Snider looked around for a video camera but couldn't see one. When he turned back to the deer, blood dripped from where his arrows had pierced the hide of whatever this thing was.

What the fuck! Had those assholes filled the damn thing with paint?

He walked closer and touched the red liquid.

The deer moaned and Snider jumped back in surprise, falling on his ass again. A can of beer came loose from his belt, hit a rock, split open, and sprayed him with foam.

This is not my fucking day!

Snider staggered to his feet and nervously prodded the fake animal. Another muffled groan accompanied movement inside the deer. He poked again, and a seam along the belly ripped open. With a gush of blood, a body tumbled out.

Snider screamed in shock as an old woman hit the ground at his feet. One of his arrows stuck out of her neck. The second had been driven through her stomach.

The old lady opened her filmy eyes, gave a final shudder, and died staring at Davy Snider's muddy shoes.

SIXTEEN

MOLLY read the Gavin Ricks file three times.

Then she copied the contents of the file so she'd have a copy for herself. It was after 2:00 in the morning when she finished and put the file back in Arnie's top drawer.

It felt like a betrayal, or disloyalty at the very least. However, Molly couldn't shake the feeling that Arnie's rage had blinded him to the possibility that Gavin Ricks might be innocent.

On the surface, Ricks certainly looked guilty, and the fact that he hadn't said anything in his defense didn't help. But Molly knew she had to dig deeper into this case.

Arnie would be furious if he discovered what she was up to. He would likely accuse her of ducking out on the campaign to chase rabbits down a hole.

Molly had to admit, there was a grain of truth to this. She should be using every spare minute to fight for votes. As Arnie kept pointing out, the election was close. But Molly couldn't see the voters electing Kenton Sharpe. Even a child could tell he was unfit for the job. Still, it wouldn't be the first time Michigan voters were hoodwinked into voting for an incompetent candidate.

And look where that had led.

THE dream was terrifying, like a creased and stained faded black and white photograph.

Molly was cowering in the trees outside the trailer waiting for what she knew was going to happen. Then she was inside on the floor with Gavin Ricks standing above her, baseball bat raised over his head, a crazed look in his eyes.

"Leave the baby alone," Molly pleaded.

Gavin Ricks lowered the bat and sank down beside her, wrapping his arms around her and pulling her close. He smelled of cigarettes and beer. Molly could feel the man's anguish as he held her tight.

MOLLY sat bolt upright in bed at the sound of a high pitched whine coming from the side of her house. She relaxed when she saw her neighbor Fred in his driveway tinkering with his snow blower.

Molly got out of bed and pulled on her robe. She went to the kitchen window and waved at Fred. He returned her wave and turned off the machine. He and his wife Bernice owned an antique business in Detroit and only came up to their house in Sunset on the weekends. Molly went to the door and opened it.

"Sorry, Molly, I'm just getting it ready for winter."

"No problem, Fred. I needed to get up anyway."

"Why don't you come over. Bernice has coffee on."

"Sounds good. Give me a few minutes."

Fred smiled and went back to working on his snowblower.

Molly was walking back to the bedroom when the phone rang. It was Jeff Cunningham and he was out of breath.

"Molly, you're not going to believe this."

DAVY Snider was sitting on a fallen tree drinking coffee, lots of coffee, and trying to shake the image of the old lady out of his head.

Jeff was standing next to Snider.

"What's the story?"

Jeff pointed across to the clearing from where they stood. Next to the crumpled remains of a deer costume was the body of an old woman.

"Well, near as I can gather, Davy was drinking beer and playing William Tell out here in the woods. He spotted what he thought was a deer and shot it with a couple of arrows. Unfortunately, the lady over there was inside the costume at the time."

Molly grimaced.

Kolmenn stood up and pulled off his gloves. If there ever was an occasion for his sardonic humor, this was it. Instead, the coroner scowled.

"She was shot in the neck first. The second arrow pierced her stomach. It took her at least a couple of minutes to die. It would have been a very painful death."

Molly looked over at Davy Snider again.

Kurt had bagged his hunting bow and was filling out an evidence label. The crime tech smiled grimly at Molly.

"What's wrong with him?" she said angrily. "Can't he tell the difference between a reindeer costume and a real deer?"

"He was likely pumped up on the thrill of the hunt and a half dozen Pabst. He's pretty low on the evolutionary ladder."

"He doesn't even look like he believes in evolution."

Molly turned toward Snider who stood up as she approached, distress written all over his face.

Jeff Cunningham held Snider's arm just in case the little man tried to make a run for it.

"I didn't know she was in there," Davy whined. "I thought I was shooting at a deer. Honest."

Molly looked down at the can of Blue Ribbon still hanging from his belt.

"A deer? I'd say you're on the bad side of a six pack, Mr. Snider. Looks to me like your judgment was impaired."

"Well ... I had a few brews for breakfast, but I ain't drunk or nothing. I really thought she was a deer."

Weaving back and forth as he spoke contradicted his words.

"This is an accident, right?" Fear raised the pitch of his voice.

"Maybe. But I could also push for negligent homicide or manslaughter."

"*Manslaughter*? But she's a woman!"

Molly shook her head at the man's stupidity.

"Show me your license."

Snider looked at his feet.

"Add bow-hunting without a license to the charges," Molly said making a note. She looked up at Snider. "Now tell me exactly how this happened?"

Snider gave Molly a rambling account of the morning's adventure right up to the point when he called the sheriff's department.

At least he'd called it in. That was something in his favor. Many others might have just left the body and run.

"Have you ever been convicted of a crime, Mr. Snider?"

"No, ma'am … Well, I was charged with a DUI once."

Snider looked at her hopefully, but she ignored him and put her notebook away.

"Seems to me you should be looking for whoever put her in that thing." Snider pointed at the costume.

He was right of course. Someone had deliberately put the woman in an outfit that could have been mistaken for a deer at a distance. The killer was probably hoping a sap like Snider would come along and finish her off.

Just like Brighton's murder!

Molly rubbed her face as she thought about these seemingly unrelated events. In both cases, the murderer had set up the victim to be killed by an innocent third party.

Murder by remote control.

"Okay, Mr. Snider, I'm going to write up my report for the DA. I think the circumstances are unusual, and I expect he probably won't press charges. However, I think the DNR will want to talk to you about hunting without a license."

"Do I get my bow back?"

"I don't think so. It's evidence, and then Natural Resources will probably keep it."

"Damn! That thing cost me a lot."

"And it cost this woman her life."

Kurt was still holding the bow when she joined him.

"Any idea who she was?"

Kurt shook his head. "No idea. She was in a nightgown and robe though, so I don't think she was out for a walk."

Molly nodded and turned to Jeff Cunningham.

"Check the houses around here, Jeff. See if anyone knows her."

Before the attendants bagged the woman's body, Jeff took a photo of her face with his phone.

Ronnie Kolmenn joined them.

"Well, she was alive inside that thing until she was shot. Probably unconscious though. Looks like someone slugged her pretty hard."

"Same MO as Brighton," Molly said.

"Yeah, looks that way."

Kolmenn turned to Kurt. "She had a small grease stain on the shoulder of her robe. It might be the same stuff that Brighton had on his face."

"I'll check it out."

Kolmenn nodded to them and started hiking back toward the highway. They watched the tiny man limp away.

"What the heck's going on with him?" Kurt asked.

"I don't know. In the past, Ronnie would have been jumping up and down with glee and making sick jokes."

Dr. Ronnie Kolmenn had been the coroner in Sunset since the early 1960s. He did excellent, unimpeachable work but had a sense of humor that went way beyond gallows.

"Maybe he's growing up," Molly suggested.

"More like growing old."

Kolmenn was of an indeterminate age. Molly guessed he was pushing ninety. She was worried about him. Kolmenn was acting strangely out of character. Molly wondered if their coroner might be suffering from dementia. She hoped not, but his recent behavior certainly pointed in that direction.

Molly turned to Kurt.

"You wanted to get together this morning, right?"

He shrugged. "It's not that important."

"Come on, I've got time now. Let's go back to the cars and talk."

MOLLY and Kurt sat in the forensics van a few minutes later.

Kurt, usually confident and forthright, was struggling to get the conversation going.

He was a big man and kept himself fit with an almost religious workout schedule. If she had to describe Kurt in a single word, it would be *massive*. But she would say *gentle* as well.

They'd known each other for over five years, but Molly had to admit she didn't know much about him. Over the years, all she'd learned was that Kurt was a great forensics technician and a strict vegetarian.

"Molly, I'm getting married."

"Wow, congratulations. Who's the lucky ..."

"His name is Lawrence."

"That's wonderful," Molly said without hesitation.

"You're the first person I've told."

"I'm honored. When's the big day?"

"Aw, Molly cut it out. We both know how complicated this is."

She sighed. "In a town like Sunset, it might be. But people will get used to it. And if they can't handle it, well fuck 'em."

"Look I wanted to tell you now before the election. We're going out to Seattle next month."

"You're moving?"

"No. Lawrence's family lives there, and we're going to Hawaii afterward for our honeymoon."

"Then what's the problem, Kurt?"

"The problem is that if Kenton Sharpe becomes sheriff ... Sorry, Molly ... I know that isn't going to happen. But if it does ..."

"If Sharpe wins we'll all be out of work. At least you can claim sexual discrimination." She took Kurt's hand. "Just know that as long as I'm in charge, you'll have a job in this department—unless you fuck up evidence or something."

He chuckled. "Thanks, Molly. I appreciate it."

She patted his shoulder.

"Right now we need to find a killer."

SEVENTEEN

INTENSE pain in his arm woke him from a drug-induced sleep.

At first, the boy had no idea where he was. High up on the walls, windows bathed the ceiling in bluish light.

The boy remembered then.

He'd been climbing a tree on a dare from Billy Hollis and fell.

The boy broke his arm so bad that his wrist bone had ripped through the skin, its end all jagged and red.

The boy had passed out from the hellish pain.

When he awoke, he was in the infirmary and the doctor had finished setting the bone. His arm was immobilized in a plaster cast.

Whatever they had given the boy for the pain made him barf. Luckily, the nurse had held a steel pan to catch it.

The doctor smiled down at him, displaying a row of twisted yellow teeth.

When he spoke, the doctor sounded like Count Dracula.

"It vill hurt for a while, but you are big boy, aren't you?"

The doctor may have been grinning, but his eyes glittered with cruelty. Wiping the crook of the boy's undamaged arm, the doctor injected him with a brownish liquid.

The boy hardly felt the prick and then slipped back into a semi-conscious state. Somewhere nearby, the boy heard a rhythmic squeaking sound. He strained to open his eyes, but his eyelids were too heavy, and he finally gave up.

The unusual sound was coming closer.

He had to see. He fought against the drug and was finally able to open his eyes a crack.

There was a movement in the corridor outside his room.

The boy rolled over on his side to face the doorway, trying to make out some detail of what was in the hallway. Even though he lay still, the room continued to spin and he grabbed for the railing on the bed to stop the dizziness.

Consciousness was slipping away, but from somewhere in the back of his head a voice shouted that the boy had to bear witness.

And he slid down into a gentle darkness.

But the squeaking sound came to him like a rescue rope. He frantically grabbed hold of it and hauled himself back into reality.

Whatever they had given him wasn't enough. The room around him was more lucid now and the noises more intense.

The boy jumped up, but that was a mistake. He was on the carousel again, whirling out of control. He slumped forward, dropping his head between his knees and breathing deeply to still the air around him.

The sound was louder and closer.

The room still swayed in front of his eyes, but he had to see. The boy lifted his head as the shadows in the hallway congealed into solid shapes.

A clown pushed a stretcher along the corridor.

The boy gasped in terror.

His gasp caused the clown to turn in surprise, and the boy's insides turned to jelly.

"Quiet," the clown whispered.

But the boy was beyond reason, he screamed and tried to throw himself out of the bed.

The clown stepped into the room.

"Go back to sleep," the clown ordered.

"Yeah, don't be scared silly," his sister Darcie's voice, full of beatific joy, came from the stretcher.

"Clowns are funny," she said.

The boy felt a warm sensation in his pajama bottoms as his bladder let go.

The clown didn't seem to notice. He walked back to the stretcher and continued to push it along the corridor.

Full of shame, the boy lifted his head

He had a brief glimpse of his sister's smiling face.

She was so loving, so innocent.

That was the last time the boy ever saw his sister.

EIGHTEEN

HALFWAY back to town Molly remembered who the woman was.

As if he were clairvoyant, Jeff Cunningham called a minute later to confirm her fear.

"Molly, I think I have an ID on the victim. You were right. She lived nearby. A neighbor told me her name is Delores Marsh."

Delores Marsh.

She definitely recognized that name and felt a twinge in her gut.

"I'm at her residence securing the scene now. Kurt's on his way."

Jeff gave Molly directions to the house.

"I'll call Judge Pomm's office and rustle up a search warrant," Molly said.

BY the time Molly reached Delores Marsh's home, the Judge had sent a PDF of the search warrant to her phone.

The small house was located on a side street on a little lot surrounded by thick woods. Molly parked on the road and walked up the driveway. A six-year-old Nissan sat in the open garage.

Jeff paced anxiously on the front lawn.

"The back door's wide open."

They walked around to the rear of the house and saw the screen door swinging leisurely in the gentle breeze.

"Go around front and wait for Kurt."

Molly pulled on a pair of protective booties and disposable gloves before entering the house.

The kitchen was from another era. While the appliances were modern, the décor was a time capsule from the 1950s with rose pattern wallpaper, multiple knitted wall hangings, various collector plates, and an ancient thermometer mounted to the window frame.

An old lady's kitchen.

Molly wondered if her home would look like this when she was the murder victim's age. God, she hoped not.

If I start collecting knick-knacks, just smother me with a pillow.

Delores certainly liked to keep things neat. There were a single teacup and saucer on the counter. Molly guessed Delores was frugal and wouldn't wash the cup and saucer until she had enough dirty dishes to fill the sink.

A sharp ticking from the clock over the door reminded Molly she had work to do.

Searching Delores's place wouldn't take long. The house only had a combination living/dining room, two small bedrooms, and a single bathroom.

As with the kitchen, the rest of the house was immaculate, except for the unmade bed in the back bedroom. There were no obvious signs of a struggle and nothing appeared to be out of place.

In the living room, small ceramic figurines of cute children in European dress were arranged neatly on wooden racks next to the fireplace. Molly turned one over. **HUMMEL** was stamped on the bottom. She looked sadly at the ornament. It was as if the old woman's reason for living had boiled down to these figurines.

After a perfunctory examination of the room, Molly moved to the hallway where there was an antique fold-down desk. She opened the lid and leafed through papers that had been carefully sorted into pigeon holes. Gas bills, cable bills, electric bills, Sears credit card statements—just day-to-day paperwork. Molly felt a twinge of envy at Delores's organizational skills. Her own bills and bank statements were jammed into one of her dresser drawers.

Something caught Molly's eye—Delores Marsh's latest pension statement. It wasn't the amount that attracted her attention, it was Marsh's former employer, The Pine Academy. Molly slid the document into an evidence bag and sealed it.

She carefully searched both bedrooms and found nothing exciting. *So, Delores, where do you hide the juicy stuff?*

In the basement, Molly hit pay dirt in the form of two shoeboxes shoved into the rafters in a corner. One was jammed with small notebooks bound in deteriorating elastic bands. The other held an assortment of documents in a foreign language. One of the documents was an old passport. Molly lifted an eyebrow in surprise at the hammer and sickle embossed on its cover. She flipped the passport open and saw a picture of a much younger looking Delores Marsh. The expiration date was August 11, 1953.

Kurt came down the stairs and she showed him the passport.

"What do you think? Is it Russian?"

"No, the characters aren't Cyrillic. It looks like a Slovak language. Czech maybe, or Polish."

Together they laid out the contents of the box on the top of the washing machine. Along with the official looking papers, was a metal insignia from a uniform and a small disc on a chain. Molly put them back in the box.

"I think I'll show them to Balthazar. He might be able to tell me what language this is."

Polish immigrant Balthazar Piotrowski had made quite a name for himself in Sunset as a renovator of classic buildings and homes. Although in his mid-forties, Balthazar brought an old-world craftsman's expertise to any project he took on.

If the language on Delores Marsh's papers was Polish, Balthazar could save the department a lot of time by not having to go outside to get the documents translated. If the language wasn't Polish, he might be able to identify what it was. Molly decided she'd drop by The Villager where Balthazar was working on the restaurant's renovation and ask him.

"Maybe Delores Marsh was a sleeper agent planted here during the cold war," Kurt joked. "Perhaps she was feeding the Commies the most sensitive secrets of Sunset County."

Molly chuckled at the thought. But she couldn't escape the feeling that something wasn't right here. If someone wanted Delores Marsh dead, why go to all the trouble of staging her murder? It would have been easier and faster to just stab or shoot the frail old lady.

Molly had an uncomfortable feeling that as farfetched as Kurt's spy scenario was, the truth might be even stranger.

Delores Marsh was turning out to be more interesting than she first appeared.

LES Caulfield was working on the chronology of the crimes at the Pine Academy on his laptop.

The timeline was a long one, and he'd been working on it for the past week. When it was finished, the chart would show the full extent of the horrors that had been committed by Coach Akron. The chronology would also be fully searchable making it easier to cross reference names and events.

Les smiled when Molly walked into the conference room.

"Hi there, stranger. I heard you're up to your ass in alligators. Two murders. Wow, that's got to be a record."

Molly grimaced.

"Did a Delores Marsh come up in your investigation?"

Les thought for a few seconds and then tapped her name into his laptop.

"Yes, she worked there from the mid-'50s until the early '90s. She ran the kitchen at the school and taught courses in home economics."

Home economics?

From Molly's experience, home economics was a fancy term for learning how to sew, or bake muffins.

Do they still teach that in school?

Probably not. Training girls to be proper little housewives went out with saddle shoes.

"Delores Marsh was on a list of former staff I was going to talk to, but she didn't have anything to do with Akron or the cover-up."

"Maybe she knew more than you think."

"No, her timeline is wrong. She retired just after Akron came to the school."

"Still, she might have known something."

Les nodded thoughtfully. "It's worth taking a look at I suppose."

"How about Frank Brighton? Ever come across him?"

"Nope, not at all."

"Mind taking a look?"

Les nodded again and typed the name into the computer.

"Nothing."

"Oh well," Molly sighed, "it was worth a shot."

He waved at the photographs covering the walls.

"Well, not everyone in Pine is involved in this."

She stared at the picture of Vandermeer.

What an arrogant looking bastard.

Molly wondered if he knew Delores Marsh and Frank Brighton. She also wondered if it was worth the risk of pissing off Arnie to find out.

"Give my offer any more thought?" Les asked.

Molly pulled herself back to the here and now.

"About working for the Staties if I lose? Sorry, I've been kind of busy."

Les smiled. "I could sure use you on this full time."

She nodded unenthusiastically. Molly saw what this investigation had done to Les Caulfield. This case had aged him ten years.

Anyway, the investigation was almost at an end. Les would soon be turning it over to the District Attorney and the Grand Jury. Once the case found its way into the courts, there would be tears, recrimination, shock, and grief. A lot of innocent people would be hurt by ripping open these wounds once again.

Rita John for instance. She'd inherited this mess and was now giving her heart and soul to keep the Academy going. By the time the investigation was over, the Pine Academy would probably be history, one more ugly footnote in Sunset County's past.

IT was nearly 3:00 when Molly left the state police post. She drove through Pine on her way to the highway. Kids were just getting out of school, and many were wearing costumes.

Halloween—shit!

She'd forgotten to pick up candy. She wondered what sort of tricks they would have in store for her that night.

NINETEEN

BALTHAZAR Piotrowski was caked in bone-white dust.

He and his workers had been busy. Molly was impressed with the progress they'd made renovating the old store next to The Villager restaurant.

"Can we go outside for a minute?" she asked Balthazar. The dusty air was tickling her sinuses.

On the street, Balthazar slapped at his coveralls and a cloud of dust rose around him. When it cleared, he no longer looked like the Pillsbury Doughboy.

Molly admired the gregarious Pole, though he'd nearly driven her crazy with his fastidiousness and careful attention to detail when he renovated her house a few months ago. At the time, she just wanted Balthazar to be finished and out of her hair.

But houses like hers were the reason Balthazar had come to Sunset. Molly owned one of a handful of architectural gems designed by Earl Andrew Young in the 1930s. It was a unique style that only existed in Sunset.

Young's eccentric and whimsical homes had at first incensed the town's more prominent citizens. They preferred a much more conventional and conservative type of architecture. But in the years that followed, Young's houses had come to be hailed by critics around the world as unique treasures.

Molly certainly felt that way about her house. Known as Lane's End, hers was an excellent example of Young's work. From the outside, Lane's End resembled a place where Bilbo Baggins would feel right at home. But the inside had needed a lot of work and Balthazar had begged her for the opportunity to do the job. He'd seen pictures of Young's homes in Poland when he was a student and instantly fell in love with them. The chance to work on one had been the realization of a life's dream and, when Balthazar finally finished, he'd lovingly returned Lane's End to its original form.

In Balthazar's mind, he owed Molly much more than he could ever repay. Over the past few months, he'd flourished. His reputation for doing excellent work had led to a steady stream of renovation contracts, and Balthazar had to hire a small crew to help him keep up with the work.

"Balthazar, I need your help."

He nodded and waited as she took the passport from the box. He looked at the cover and frowned.

"We think it's a Slovak language, Czech or Polish. I thought maybe you could tell."

"It's Polish but very old. From another time." He tapped the hammer and sickle on the cover. "A bad time."

Balthazar flipped it open and looked at the picture.

"Doloreta Bagno," he pronounced the name carefully for Molly. "She must be old now."

"She was, but her name wasn't Bagno. It was Marsh, Delores Marsh."

"This makes sense. Bagno means marsh or swamp. Why are you interested in her?"

"She was murdered this morning."

Balthazar's eyes widened in shock.

Molly showed him the shoebox full of documents.

"Would you be willing to look through these and give me an idea of what they say?"

"I can help, but these papers look from time before I was born."

"There are diaries as well. I'm hoping they'll give me some clues about Delores."

"Give me few days."

Molly was tempted to hand him the stack of documents and diaries right then, but considered the chain of evidence protocol—it had to remain in her custody from the scene of the crime to the evidence locker. And she had no backups.

"I'll have copies made for you and have them dropped off at your house this evening. Is that okay?"

Balthazar nodded.

"If you see anything unusual, please call me right away."

He brushed more dust from his coveralls. "Yes, and now I must get back to work."

After Balthazar had gone, Molly was surprised by a couple of trick-or-treaters who came around the corner. One was dressed as Batman and the other as a clown.

Molly glanced at her watch. It was almost 5:30. She might have just enough time to get to K-Mart and back home before irate trick-or-treaters egged her house.

BY 8:00 the parade of costumed kids had trickled to a few stragglers who were mostly teenagers out to score free candy, so Molly turned off the porch light.

She warmed up a piece of day-old fried chicken and added a generous helping of coleslaw to her plate. She carried her food and a bottle of Wolverine beer to the dining room table and sat down to go over her notes for the candidates' debate on Friday evening. It would be her last real chance to get her message across to the voters. The local radio station would be broadcasting it live and, based on what they saw, the local newspaper would give its endorsement in the Sunday edition. Arnie was reasonably sure they would endorse her.

But will the paper's endorsement be enough?

Kenton Sharpe had blanketed the county with signs as well as taking large ads in all the local papers. But Arnie's nephew, who was running her campaign, had mobilized his workers and matched Sharpe's sign and ad blitz.

We will fight them on the sports pages, we will fight them on the front lawns.

The campaign had been brutal so far, and Molly relished every opportunity to poke Kenton Sharpe in the eye. This combativeness was the only part of the campaign that inspired her. Molly knew she'd make a hell of a lot better sheriff than Sharpe, and she trusted the voters to see it the same way.

But no matter how it went on voting day, Molly was satisfied she'd run a good campaign. And she was confident she was going to win.

Molly raised the beer in a mock toast to herself.

ARNIE Voxx had been sitting at his computer for more than an hour listening to the recording over and over trying to decide what to do with his nuclear option. Recorded with a concealed listening device planted in a toy elephant on Sammy Atkinson's desk, this would blow the election apart.

No one in the department, including Molly, knew what Arnie had been up to in Boyle. Months before, the DEA had taken him into their confidence. The agency had set up a special task force to bring down the meth empire headed by Taylor Mead and the Atkinson brothers, cagey bastards who trusted no one, not even each other. So it had been impossible for the DEA to plant an undercover agent inside their operation. Any strangers in Boyle would be immediately suspect. But Arnie had a unique connection to Boyle—his aunt lived on a farm just outside the town limits. The bad guys knew this and didn't pay much attention when the sheriff visited her now and then.

During one of these trips, Arnie had smuggled in a pair of DEA agents and their equipment. They'd set up a listening post in his aunt's attic and got lucky when Arnie turned a backwoods lowlife named Scott Ginger into a confidential informant.

Ginger was up to his neck in Mead's meth operation by providing a pipeline to launder their money. Ginger had been the one who planted the listening device right under Sammy Atkinson's nose. And the bug had hit gold when it picked up a conversation between Atkinson and Kenton Sharpe.

Though the sound was a little muddy, it was clear enough to understand the deal Atkinson had made with Sharpe—leave their meth operation alone in exchange for kickbacks. Sharpe had even been given a new quad cab as a signing bonus.

One of the DEA guys had made a copy of the recording for Arnie with a warning not to use it publicly because it might tip off their investigation, so Arnie had been sitting on it for the past four months. But that afternoon, the DEA agent called to let him know they were shutting down their investigation in Boyle and Arnie was free to use the recording any way he saw fit.

Arnie was pissed off that the DEA, which had dedicated so much time to the case, had just given up. It looked like the Atkinsons and Mead were made of Teflon after all.

Arnie was damned if he wasn't going to put this recording to proper use. He slipped a blank CD into his laptop.

IT was Halloween, and the clown was free to walk among the masses of costumed trick-or-treaters.

He did a little dance.

A child started to cry when she saw him. He felt sick. The last thing he wanted to do was frighten a youngster.

Children were precious to him, special like Darcie had been. He remembered her smile as she lay on the stretcher. It was an angel's smile, so perfect, so innocent.

The pain of the memory jabbed him. Tears stung his eyes. He should have protected her.

He paused in the shadows and looked through the front window. He saw someone move inside, someone familiar. The clown's inner pain turned to hatred.

Soon it would be time.

COLIN Ricks poured his fourth shot of vodka and scowled out the window of his room at the Great Northern.

Ricks tried to imagine what the main street was like at the height of the summer tourist season, because tonight it was bleak with half the shops shuttered for the winter. Still, the street had been crowded on this Halloween evening. Despite his melancholy, Ricks smiled at the parade of children in their cute costumes.

Ricks couldn't help but wonder if his father had been wearing a disguise all these years.

If the charges were true, and Colin Ricks had serious doubts they were, then Gavin Ricks's costume had been one of respectability, honor, kindness, and concern. Had his father hidden a darkness deep inside himself—a darkness that stretched five decades back to a mobile home on a foggy night? Had his father been capable of such savagery, this man who had held his hand and kept him safe, who had provided comfort and stability after his mother had passed?

Colin Ricks drank the fiery liquid and considered pouring another. He looked at the bottle. Is this what had let the beast out of his father?

Ricks set the glass down and put the bottle away.

BALTHAZAR Piotrowski set the first diary down and wept. The journal was a narrative of an old woman's recollection of a time and horrors that had long since faded.

He picked up a pencil and scribbled a few notes in shaky script. When finished, he reluctantly took the second diary and began to read.

KENTON Sharpe looked at the calculations he'd made on a notepad. He was surprised by the sum. He'd multiplied the amount by six, the number of years he expected to be in the sheriff's job, and smiled. His retirement was going to be very sweet.

The poll his campaign chair had shown him that afternoon had also been sweet. The race had been tight for most of the campaign, but now his numbers were moving up while Molly's remained static. He looked at the numbers again. There was only a small gap between them.

Sharpe resisted the temptation to get cocky. The election wasn't in the bag yet. The stakes were high and he couldn't afford to lose. And he certainly didn't discount the people working with Molly. Arnie Voxx had turned his campaign team over to her. They were experienced and pro-active. Even with her late start, they'd already blanketed the county with signs. Her name and face were everywhere.

Well, my team can take care of that. After all, it is Halloween, and we have plenty of tricks.

He smiled as he thought about making Molly's election signs disappearing and picked up the phone. Sharpe knew just who to call.

MARK Barnard lay on the hard cot in his cell. The drunk they'd brought in just before 11:00 had finally settled down, or, more likely, had passed out. The jail was frightening. He'd been scared in Iraq where the enemy seemed to hide under every rock, but this was a different kind of fear.

Even in death, the old man demanded to be the center of attention. His father had visited him in his cell, complaining about how much his head was hurting and put his index finger into a wound on his temple. Though Mark was sure it had only been a dream, he'd squeezed his eyes closed and prayed his father, or whatever it was, would go away.

While his father was annoying, the clown terrified him. Mark thought he heard the clown approaching with every footstep or rustle in the hall.

I need to tell them!

But if he did, Mark was convinced the authorities would put him in an even darker place, a place where the clown would be sure to find him.

The drunk began screaming again. Mark balled his fists into his ears to block out the sound and begged for the night to end.

ANXIOUS about the election, Molly lay in bed waiting for sleep. She was confident she would win, but then what would happen?

Molly had doubts she was cut out to be sheriff. She was an investigator, not an administrator. Fighting budget battles with the penny-pinching county board would quickly wear her down.

Right now, Molly's only responsibility was to catch bad guys. She loved the challenge of investigating crimes. There wouldn't be time for that once she was elected. She would spend all day clawing for every dollar the department needed to do its job.

Molly even questioned her motive for running in the first place. As much as she claimed to stand for effective law and order, the underlying truth was she was in the race for revenge.

When she'd worked for Kenton Sharpe, he made her life hell, and finally fired her for doing her job. Sharpe had even threatened Molly with arrest as she closed in on a killer. She'd embarrassed him and he hated her for it. Denying him the office he desperately coveted would be a fitting punishment for that.

Beyond winning the election, Molly didn't have a plan.

She shifted her thoughts away from the election to the murders in Pine.

What the hell was going on there?

Pine was a small town where nothing much happened, and yet in less than a week, it was suddenly the murder capital of Michigan. What were the chances that a town where there hadn't been a murder in almost six years would have *three* in that many days? And what about the strange circumstances of the murders? While it was obvious one of them had been committed by the victim's son, the other two were just plain weird. Who would set up their victims to be killed by innocent third parties?

Molly thought about the Pine Academy investigation she and Les Caulfield had been piecing together. Was it a coincidence that two of the victims were connected to the school? The strange thing was that the victim in each case wasn't even connected to the school when Coach Akron had committed his crimes.

Maybe they intersected at an earlier time in the school's history?

But that still left the mechanic. Frank Brighton had nothing to do with either of the other victims, or with the school. He was just an alcoholic one step away from sleeping on a park bench. Molly flashed back to his office with its cot, lawn chair, and half-eaten Hungry Man dinner that had spilled onto the floor. It smelled like motor oil, unwashed sheets, and a backed-up toilet.

There must be a connection.

Maybe it wasn't the school. Robertson Barnard was a decorated hero, and Delores Marsh would have been in Europe during the Second World War. Maybe Frank Brighton had been in the army with Robertson Barnard. Maybe they knew Delores Marsh from over there. But, that couldn't be right, because Barnard had been in Korea, not in Europe. Wrong war.

Molly hoped Balthazar would find something among Delores Marsh's papers that would make a connection between the victims. Or maybe the crimes were not related at all. Maybe they were just a tragic coincidence.

A painful tightening behind her eyes told Molly a headache was on its way.

And then there was Gavin Ricks. When she'd looked over Arnie's file on the case, everything seemed to be air-tight. Ricks's prints were on the weapon, he'd fled the scene, and so far he hadn't tried to contest the charges against him.

But Colin Ricks continued to insist his father was not capable of the crimes he'd been charged with. That was to be expected, of course. No loving son would ever believe his father was able to commit such a brutal act. Maybe Colin was covering up his own abuse. Had Gavin Ricks beaten his son as a child? Colin was certainly in a state of denial.

Molly squeezed back tears. She'd had some experience in that area and the memory was agonizing.

She cleared her mind.

Thinking about the case was costing her the sleep she desperately needed. She focused only on her breathing. Gradually the clutter in her mind began to recede and her body relaxed. After a few minutes, Molly turned on her side, curled into a fetal position, and drifted off.

TWENTY

MOLLY decided to start with Colin Ricks.

The next morning, she called Ricks at his hotel and asked if they could have breakfast together. He warily agreed.

COLIN Ricks sat in a corner of the small Great Northern dining room. Molly took a buttermilk biscuit and honey from the complimentary breakfast buffet and poured a cup of revoltingly bitter coffee from an urn.

Colin stood as Molly approached the table.

"Cold this morning," she said.

"Not really. We already have a foot of snow on the ground at home."

They made small talk for a few minutes while they finished their breakfast.

"Did you have a chance to look at my dad's case more closely?"

"I reviewed the file twice last night. To be honest, the case against him is very strong. There's physical evidence that links your father to the scene and the murder weapon. Plus, he hid for over fifty years and, to top it all off, your dad hasn't made a statement of any kind, or even denied the charges. You're a lawyer, you know how all this looks."

Colin nodded glumly.

Molly leaned forward and lowered her voice. "I have something to ask you. I don't want you to take it the wrong way, but I still have to ask. Did your father ever use violence against you or your mother?"

"Never. He didn't even spank me."

"And there's no chance your mother might have hidden it from you if she had been abused?"

Ricks shook his head adamantly.

Molly felt certain Colin Ricks wasn't covering up for his father and found this troubling. Typically, abusers don't stop. If Colin was telling the truth, and she believed he was, Gavin Ricks didn't abuse his family.

What about the time before the murders?

Molly knew Gavin Ricks had a record before he fled Sunset. There were a couple of arrests for assault noted in the file, but the details of those charges had long since been lost. Molly knew because she'd spent close to an hour in the records room trying to locate the arrest files.

She would have loved to take a closer look at those arrests.

BACK at the office, there was a note on Molly's desk from the crime tech asking her to drop by when she had a minute.

"What's up, Kurt?" she asked as she walked into his lab.

"I finished processing the evidence at the crime scenes. Grayling did a gas spectrometer on those weird white stains and got a match."

"Oil or grease?"

"Neither. It's white makeup. From the chemical composition, the lab guys are sure it came from a company called Mehron. They make theatrical make-up."

"Fuuuck ..." Molly considered what this nugget of new information meant.

"Here's the kicker. I found a trace of the same white shit at the Barnard scene as well. There was a streak of it on the gun's grip. They tested that sample and confirmed it was the same as the others."

Molly felt a shiver of excitement.

Did the same person commit all three murders?

She thought back to Mark Barnard. He hadn't said anything about another person being at the scene of his father's murder. And if the killer had left the same traces of makeup at each scene, then it was impossible for Mark Barnard to be the murderer. They had him in a cell when Brighton and Delores Marsh were killed.

"I also got a line on the reindeer costume. It was purchased at Bronners in Frankenmuth."

She'd seen the signs for Bronners along I-75. It was a huge store that sold nothing but Christmas decorations all year round.

"We need to find out who purchased it."

"I called them. Apparently that particular model was old stock and they cleared out a bunch of them last year."

"So, they could have been sold to anyone?"

"Yes. But ten of them were purchased by the city of Pine for their annual Santa Claus Parade."

The shiver of excitement Molly had felt before became a vibration.

MOLLY had Mark Barnard brought to an interview room. When he sat down, she turned on the recording system and informed him of his rights.

"Mark, I'll get right to it. I have evidence that you may not have killed your father."

Mark stared mutely ahead.

"I need you to tell me what you saw the night of your father's murder."

"Nothing," he said in a flat voice.

"I don't believe you."

Molly saw fear filling Mark's eyes.

"What are you not telling me?"

He began to shake his head violently.

"Nothing ..."

"There was someone else there, someone who held the gun. Someone who was wearing white makeup."

Mark's head jerked up.

"What did you see?"

"I didn't see anything."

"Yes, you did, Mark. You saw something that scared the hell out of you!"

Mark jumped up, tugging futilely against the handcuff anchoring his wrist to the table.

"Leave me alone! It wasn't real."

"What wasn't real?"

Mark Barnard slumped back into the chair, cradling his head in his hands, sobbing violently.

"It was a clown! I saw a clown. It was dancing outside the house. But it wasn't real … it wasn't real!"

After Mark was taken back in his cell, Molly considered calling the district attorney to inform him of the new evidence, but held off. Other than a few streaks of white makeup and the suspect's claim that he'd seen a clown, there wasn't enough evidence to warrant dropping the charges. And if there were a lunatic out there dressing up as a clown, it would be safer to have Mark Barnard in a cell.

Molly called Pine Town Hall and asked about the costumes. The clerk informed her they were stored in a Parks Department facility and arranged for someone to meet her at the building in an hour.

TWENTY-ONE

MOLLY was surprised to see Davy Snider leaning against a pickup parked outside the Parks Department warehouse.

"You work for Parks?"

"Yeah, part-time. I also maintain the lighthouse for the Coast Guard. I'm a certified electrician. Any word on my bow yet?"

Molly shook her head.

"Open it up, will you."

She wondered if he'd been drinking. It wouldn't surprise her. She had a vision of him drunkenly sticking his hand into a live electrical panel. It was probably only a matter of time before he did.

Snider opened the sliding door to reveal a cavernous room with a snowplow parked in the center.

"The parade shit's over here," he said and led Molly to the back of the warehouse which had been partitioned off with a plywood wall. A pair of doors were padlocked shut.

Snider fiddled with his key ring and then opened the lock. He reached in and flicked on the lights, a row of naked hanging bulbs above the storage space.

The place was hardly a winter wonderland. It looked and smelled more like a thrift shop. Battered Christmas props were jammed into cupboards along the side of the room, but Molly barely paid attention to those. Instead, she focused on a rack of musty costumes. Among them, she spotted reindeer costumes like the one Delores Marsh had been killed in.

Davy Snider looked at them in awe.

"Oh shit! This doesn't look good, does it?"

"Nope, not when you have easy access to this place."

Snider looked as if he were going to piss himself. Molly knew Snider wasn't bright enough to be the killer, but she let him squirm anyway.

There were only nine reindeer costumes hanging on the rack. She double checked to make sure the missing outfit hadn't been put in the wrong place. But there was definitely one costume missing.

"Who else has access to this place?" she asked sharply.

"The guy who runs the parade."

"Who's that?"

"Alfie … Alfie Iannarelli. He owns an art supply store on the main street."

Damn!

She knew the name. He'd joined the board of the Pine Academy after the scandal with Akron broke.

"He's a real hound if you know what I mean." Snider wiggled his eyebrows suggestively.

Molly ignored him.

"Anyone else have access?"

"I don't know for sure." Snider shrugged. "Probably though."

Molly looked at the costumes. There were some colorful clown outfits hanging there.

"Is there an inventory of all this stuff?"

Snider shrugged again. "If there is, I don't know about it. It's town property, so maybe the clerk keeps a record. Or, you could ask Alfie. He might know."

ALFIE Iannarelli did know. And Davy Snider was right, the art store owner was a hound.

When Molly entered the shop, Iannarelli stood near the back, holding court with a group of middle-aged women who hung on his every word. Molly could understand why.

Although in his early forties, Alfie Iannarelli was thin and lithe. He cut a fine figure in tight jeans and an even tighter shirt unbuttoned to his navel. Molly figured Iannarelli was quite a smorgasbord for the sexually frustrated housewives of Pine.

He passed around a sheet of paper, and each woman wrote down her contact details. Molly kept herself occupied by looking at the sample frames on the back wall.

After the women left, Iannarelli swaggered over to where Molly stood.

"Looking to frame someone, officer?" he joked as he offered his hand.

If he kisses my hand, I swear I'll shoot him!

Luckily for him, Iannarelli just shook her hand.

"What was that all about?" she asked pointing to the last of the women going out the door.

"They were signing up for a life drawing class I'm running in January. There's room for one more if you're interested."

He smiled so widely the corners of his eyes crinkled. This letch was about as subtle as an Adam Sandler movie.

"I understand you run the town's Santa Claus Parade."

"And the Independence Day Parade and the Easter one too." He sounded weary of it all.

Molly showed him a picture of the bloody reindeer costume. He wrinkled his nose and handed it back with a confused smile.

"It looks like the ones we use in the parade. Is this the one Davy Snider stalked and killed?"

Molly nodded.

"And you think it might be from the parade?"

"I think it is. I checked the costume rack in the warehouse and you seem to be missing one. Do you keep an inventory?"

"Yes, certainly. It's in my office."

Molly followed him into a small room at the back of the shop. There were several framed prints sitting on a workbench. One was of a clown.

She pointed to it. "Who likes clowns?"

"One of my customers collects Red Skelton prints."

Molly had a vague recollection of Red Skelton. He was an actor or comedian or something. She thought she'd seen one of his movies a long time ago.

"Which customer is that?" she asked casually.

Iannarelli tilted his head slightly. "Can't tell you. I respect my customers' privacy."

While Iannarelli was looking for the inventory book, Molly glanced at the print once again. A piece of scrap paper with a phone number was taped to the bottom of the frame. She memorized the number. When she looked back, Iannarelli was leafing through a file folder.

He pulled out a sheet. "Here's the costume inventory."

She looked it over and confirmed there had been ten reindeer costumes.

"You're missing one. When's the last time you used them?"

"Last Thanksgiving."

"Did you put them away yourself?"

He shook his head. "My costume coordinator did. She's in charge of all that. She takes care of finding the marchers and makes any alterations or repairs."

"Who's that?"

"Norma Cartier."

"Who else would have access to the costumes?"

"Besides myself and Norma, Bill Vandermeer I guess. He's in charge of the volunteer planning committee for the parade, and Davy Snider of course. I'm probably forgetting some people, let me think about it."

"You have a number for Norma?"

He smiled and pointed to the note taped to the clown print. "You already have it."

Iannarelli was sharper than she gave him credit for. Their eyes met and he smiled.

"Sure you won't reconsider that class? I think you'd be exquisite at it."

"I'll give it some thought." A blush warmed Molly's cheeks. "Right now, though, you could do me a favor and go over to the warehouse and do a count of all your costumes."

She handed him her business card.

"Please let me know right away if there's anything else missing."

"Certainly, I'm always happy to help out."

As she left the shop, Molly felt his gaze on her back and decided the feeling wasn't all that unpleasant.

TWENTY-TWO

MOLLY parked in front of the sporting goods store and went in.

Vandermeer was standing next to the hockey sticks. He scowled at her as she entered.

"I thought we'd finished our discussion, Officer Parsons," he said coldly.

"It's deputy. And I'm not here to talk to you. I want to speak to Norma Cartier."

"She's out right now. Maybe you could come back some other time."

"I'll wait," Molly said defiantly.

"That would not be very good for my business."

She ignored him.

"Please don't pester my customers for votes."

Molly had noticed the **Kenton Sharpe for Sheriff** poster in his window.

"I'm here on official police business, Mr. Vandermeer."

"From what I understand, you probably won't be official police after Election Day." Vandermeer grinned. "Do you have any plans for your future, Ms. Parsons?"

Molly considered a couple of nasty responses to his taunt, but refused to rise to the bait. She was further saved when Norma Cartier walked in the front door carrying a takeout food container and large pop.

"Norma, could we talk?" Molly looked at Vandermeer and added, "Alone."

"I got nothing to talk to you about."

"Yes, you do. I want to know how one of your parade costumes ended up with a dead body inside it."

Cartier hesitated. "Suit yourself, but I gotta eat my lunch."

She led Molly into the stockroom at the back of the store. Cartier took a thick clubhouse sandwich stacked high with turkey and bacon out of the container. Mayonnaise dripped from between her fingers as she clutched it and took a huge bite.

Apparently she isn't counting calories.

Despite her enormous appetite, Norma Cartier wasn't overweight. She looked as if she worked out—a lot. Short and squat, she would make a daunting opponent in a hockey game. If Cartier was enjoying her lunch, she didn't show it. A scowl remained fixed on her face.

Molly showed her the picture of the reindeer costume.

"That the one Davy Snider shot?"

Molly nodded. "Looks like it's one of the parade costumes. There's one missing from the warehouse."

"What can I tell you? We have a bunch of them. Everybody wants to be a reindeer. I haven't seen the costumes since I put them away last year."

"And you're sure you got them all back?"

"Of course, I'm sure," she said sourly. "They're expensive."

"Do you have a list of the people who were wearing them in last year's parade?"

"I suppose. It's probably somewhere at home."

"I need a copy of that list."

"I'll make sure you get one."

Cartier didn't sound all that convincing, and Molly hoped she wasn't going to have to go the subpoena route with this woman.

Molly couldn't figure out what was eating at Norma Cartier. She was overly hostile. Perhaps Cartier was just picking up her boss's vibe, but Molly didn't think so. Cartier acted like a woman who had an ax to grind.

"How about the other costumes, did you get them all back too?"

Cartier hesitated, her eyes shifting down to the right.

Bingo!

The movement was a sure sign of a lie.

"Our count is off by one. The guy who was wearing it swore he returned it, but I couldn't locate it."

"What type of costume was it?"

Molly had a sick feeling she already knew the answer.

"It was one of our clowns."

"Who was wearing it?"

Cartier scowled again and shook her head.

"Look we can't play at this all day. I don't know what your issue is, but unless you want to be arrested for obstructing my investigation, you'd better tell me right now."

Norma Cartier sighed. "Bill Vandermeer was wearing it."

"DEPUTY Parsons, I don't have to put up with your harassment."

"I'm not harassing you, Mr. Vandermeer. If you'd like, you can have your lawyer present and we can do this in a more formal setting like my office."

He shook his head.

"I had the costume dry cleaned first, and then I returned it to the warehouse."

"When was that?"

"A couple of days after the parade. You can check with the dry cleaner. They might be able to give you the exact date I picked it up."

Molly wrote down the name of the cleaners.

"When you dropped it off at the warehouse, where did you leave it?"

"I hung it on the rack with the other costumes. Norma noticed it was missing a week or so later when she was doing her final inventory. What difference does it make? It was a clown costume, not a reindeer."

Molly didn't answer him. She was determined to keep the information about the clown quiet for now. The fewer people who knew about it, the better.

But Molly moved Vandermeer's name up the suspect list.

"WHAT is it about the people in Pine? Are they all using peyote or something?" Molly said in frustration.

Les Caulfield snorted a laugh.

"I grew up there and I could never figure it out. The citizens of Pine are just unusual."

Back at Les's office, Molly had unloaded her frustration with Norma Cartier and William Vandermeer on him.

"Norma Cartier acted like I was the enemy when I tried to question her."

"Do you blame her?"

"What am I missing here?"

He waved an arm at the wall.

"You obviously haven't read the complete case file."

"I read the parts that concerned my witnesses. And what I read made me sick. Anyway, it's your case."

Les scratched his nose while he considered what to say next.

"Norma Cartier is, or was, Akron's wife. She believes we're trying to smear her husband's name."

Molly stared at Les in disbelief.

"Shit! I missed that. That explains why she's so hostile."

It also moved her into the suspect column alongside her boss. Norma Cartier was one more complication to sort out.

The clock clicked as the hand moved to 3:00. Molly needed to get back to Sunset. The debate would be starting in a few hours.

PAUL Booster slid behind the wheel of his Chevy Blazer and turned the key. The beast reluctantly roared to life. With winter coming, the Blazer needed a major tune up. It would be one more strain on the police department budget Paul was barely able to keep out of the red.

After Kenton Sharpe had resigned as police chief, Paul had been appointed temporary chief to buy the town council time while the question of who would be sheriff was settled.

When Molly and Paul had first worked together, they'd been close. Paul was right out of college and naïve, and Molly had shared the benefit of her experience with him. After the death of her husband, Molly had disappeared from Sunset for fifteen months without telling anyone where she'd gone. The bad times started after Molly had returned.

While Molly was away, Paul assumed her role as lead investigator and had done an excellent job. When she returned, Paul was forced back to being a deputy once again, and Kenton Sharpe had used Paul's resentment toward Molly to manipulate him.

Paul eventually came to his senses and realized how badly he'd treated her after she covered up an indiscretion he'd committed that could have cost him his job. While their relationship wasn't what it had once been, it was much better now. Paul had been trying to make amends to Molly for his behavior by feeding her any information that came his way. He also had a vested interest in helping Molly. If Sharpe won the election, it would likely mean the end of his department and his job.

Paul reached over and turned up the sound system. Instead of the Taylor Swift CD he'd been listening to that morning, something else was playing. Paul strained to listen to the voices which had been poorly recorded, but still clearly distinguishable. Paul didn't recognize the voice doing most of the talking. The other one, however, he'd heard almost every day for the past five years.

Kenton Sharpe!

As he listened to the conversation, Paul Booster began to feel sick to his stomach. When it was over, he ejected the CD from the player and put it on the seat beside him. Paul didn't give much thought as to how it had gotten into his vehicle. It didn't matter. He knew what he had to do with it.

TWENTY-THREE

SHERIFF Arnie Voxx snapped the pencil in half without realizing it.

God damn it! She can't leave things alone.

As soon as he opened it, Arnie knew that someone—Molly, he presumed—had messed with the murder file. Pages were out of order and staples had been removed from his original report.

She copied it!

As if the Pine murders weren't enough for her, now she had to poke her nose into his case. Molly was curious and stubborn, two qualities that made her an excellent investigator, but also led to innumerable conflicts.

Arnie flipped the folder open angrily.

Well, she won't find anything here.

Ricks was guilty as hell, and he was going to pay for his crimes. All Arnie needed was a confession.

Ricks's son had hired a hotshot lawyer from Traverse City. The attorney was on his way now to meet Ricks. Arnie figured he might have a half hour at the most. Once the lawyer showed up, the door might close forever. It wasn't a lot of time, but enough if Arnie played his cards right.

Gavin Ricks is going to talk, dammit.

He needed to hear Ricks admit to the slaughter of the mother and her child.

Arnie called Ben Connor, the deputy in charge of the cell block. Connor had once been a fine deputy, but too many cigarettes and fatty foods had led to a triple bypass which had restricted his duties.

Connor was hesitant when he heard Arnie's request and reminded the Sheriff the prisoner's lawyer was on his way. Arnie didn't have time to wait and coldly ordered Connor to bring Gavin Ricks to the interview room immediately.

GAVIN Ricks stared passively at his hands shackled to the table in the interrogation room. Ricks didn't bother to look over his shoulder as Arnie entered the room behind him. The prisoner's eyes remained downcast as the sheriff sat across from him and shoved crime scene photos across the table.

"This is what you did, you bastard!"

Ricks turned and stared at the wall. Infuriated, Arnie grabbed him. The sheriff wanted to wrap his hands around the man's throat and crush the life from him. Instead, Arnie jerked Ricks's head around and forced him to look at the pictures on the table.

Ricks's lifeless eyes looked at the grim photo of the tiny body in the crib.

"She was two years old and had her entire life ahead of her. You took all that away," Arnie screamed.

Arnie was aware the interview room door opened and someone entered, but he didn't take his gaze off Gavin Ricks's emotionless face. He desperately needed to hear the man confess, break down in remorse, and beg for forgiveness. But the prisoner remained mute.

Enraged, Arnie wrapped his hands around Ricks's neck and began to squeeze.

"Arnie, no!"

"Get out, Molly!"

"Not this way for God's sake. Leave it to the court."

"He doesn't deserve that."

"I know you've carried this for a long time, but it's over now. Please don't blow it. You don't want the case tossed out because you coerced a confession."

Arnie drew in a deep breath and then exhaled in a long sigh. He let go of Ricks's throat and put his hands on the table.

Molly put a comforting hand on Arnie's shoulder. She didn't need to look at him to see he was crying.

"KENTON," Paul Booster said sharply.

Kenton Sharpe turned to face him.

What the hell is this?

Sharpe didn't need to be interrupted right now. He was going over his talking points for the debate that was going to start in less than an hour.

"I'm busy right now," Sharpe replied curtly and gave Paul the kind of look he'd give dog shit on the bottom of his shoe.

Paul Booster had always been intimidated by Sharpe and had once allowed this fear to affect his better judgment. Now, Paul only felt scorn for his old boss. Sharpe was pathetic, all pumped up with his own hubris.

As if sensing Paul's disdain, Sharp sneered insolently.

"I suppose you're worried about your job. You'd better be, though if you kiss my ass I just might be able to do something for you, Paul. Once I'm elected, I'll need a new investigator and you'd be the perfect candidate."

Paul ignored Sharpe and took out his notebook.

"I've been going through the department's budget."

Sharpe froze and eyed his former deputy warily.

"When you were in charge, the department bought all its vehicles from the Atkinson Brothers' dealership, right?"

Paul saw Sharpe's complexion turn a shade grayer.

"So what? We got a good deal from them."

Paul Booster shook his head. "Not according to my calculations. We paid over list for our vehicles. At any other dealership, we would be entitled to a fleet discount."

"We got a good deal on the maintenance."

"That's funny because when one of my cruisers broke down last month, the mechanic told me it hadn't been serviced at all. Not even the routine stuff like oil changes."

"So, the Atkinsons did a shitty job. You should talk to *them* about it. I'm busy here. If you're finished discussing the department's vehicle maintenance records, I need to get back to work."

Paul laughed bitterly. "You know, once upon a time I had respect for you, Kenton. I thought you were a good guy. I don't blame you for the nastiness between me and Molly. That was my fault for letting you manipulate me. I always believed you had the best interests of the department in mind. But you're nothing more than a cheap crook."

Sharpe put a hand on Paul's shoulder and smirked.

"Well if you believe that, Paul, then don't vote for me."

A CD landed on the table beside him. Puzzled, Sharpe looked at it.

Paul pointed to the CD. "You should take a listen to this. Don't worry about giving it back. I've got plenty of copies so I can share it with the media."

Sharpe's eyes narrowed and he picked up the CD.

"What the hell is this?"

"Evidence."

KENTON Sharpe sat in his pickup listening to the CD.

Shit—where did this come from!

He tried to recall the conversation with Sammy Atkinson. It must have been recorded late last summer. There was a little interference, but his words were clear enough.

So it's hardball.

Sharpe almost admired Molly for this.

Well played, Molly.

He hit replay and listened to the recording again and grimaced.

Fuck! This is bad.

Kenton Sharpe tossed around possible strategies, but his voice made his head pound.

She was trying to throw him off his game. He would have to call off the debate. That's what she wanted., but it was too late. If he canceled now, he might as well kiss the election goodbye.

Bitch!

Sharpe clenched the steering wheel so tightly his knuckles hurt. And then he had a thought. Maybe this could be turned to his advantage. Sharpe hit the replay button and again listened closely to the CD.

Yes, there might be a way.

TWENTY-FOUR

MOLLY arrived at the Masonic Lodge with only minutes to spare.

This debate would be the final chance for voters to hear the candidates speak, and the place was packed.

Arnie and Molly had walked over from the office and the short walk had calmed him down after almost strangling Ricks.

Molly was anxious about her old friend and mentor. The one thing Arnie had repeated over and over was to never let your emotions impede your judgment. Molly flashed back to the murderous look on Arnie's face in the interrogation room and was shaken to her core.

To Molly, Arnie had already tried and convicted Ricks. In Arnie's eyes, Ricks was a monster and nothing she could say would deter him from this conclusion.

Her thoughts were interrupted by the debate moderator. Molly smiled confidently when her turn came.

God, I just want this to be over.

No more campaign bullshit. Let the people decide. She trusted them to see Kenton Sharpe as an opportunistic bastard who talked a good game but couldn't deliver on his grandiose promises.

With her guts churning, Molly tried to look relaxed behind her podium. She and Sharpe had each been given five minutes to outline their vision for the future of law enforcement in Sunset County.

Sharpe trotted out the same misleading statistics he'd been using throughout the campaign. While Sharpe spoke, Molly tried to gauge how well his remarks were going over with the audience. To her chagrin, people seemed to hang on his every word.

When it was her turn to give opening remarks, Molly succinctly highlighted her vision for modernizing the department and her plan to deploy innovative new technologies for law enforcement. She explained in detail how she would proactively target the high crime areas of the county for special attention.

When finished, Molly drew vigorous applause from the Boyle contingent at the back of the room led by their mayor. Regardless of the determination of good citizens like Adam Gmerek, Mead and his political hacks still controlled the polling stations in Boyle, and anything could happen there.

According to debate rules, Sharpe could now challenge Molly with a question. With a self-assured smile, he strolled nonchalantly from behind his podium and addressed the moderator.

"I would like to ask a slight indulgence to play something I think the audience might find enlightening."

Standing at the back of the room, Arnie Voxx's eyes widened in alarm as Sharpe and Sammy Atkinson's clandestinely recorded conversation thundered through the hall.

WILLIAM Vandermeer was working late in his office. Norma Cartier looked at her boss with concern. Vandermeer had been upset ever since that bitch deputy sheriff had stopped by at lunch. Cartier had no idea why Vandermeer was so troubled. She was the one the deputy sheriff had questioned. The bitch had tried to catch Cartier in a lie but she couldn't. Norma Cartier's story was solid.

Well, with a few tiny details missing.

But who gave a shit about those. Not Molly Parsons. That bitch was only interested in shitting all over her late husband's good name. The thought made Norma Cartier's blood pound in her temples.

If Greg hadn't died so suddenly, Cartier was convinced he would've cleared his name in a second. He would've nailed those ungrateful little bastards for the liars she knew they were. After all, he'd taken a mediocre bunch of kids and turned them into a powerhouse basketball team known all over the Midwest. And what had those little pricks done in return? They made him into a monster, a man who preyed on children. It was lurid.

Tears filled her eyes, and Norma Cartier pushed the awful memories away. Thank God, there were still decent people, like Bill Vandermeer, who believed her husband was innocent. He was one of the good guys, and Cartier didn't mind lying for him. Bill had supported her when the horrible lies about Greg had started circulating. Anyway, a missing clown costume was hardly the end of the world.

Cartier gathered her things and got ready to leave. She unlocked the front door and called, "'Night, Bill."

She heard him grunt in response.

Norma Cartier locked the door of the sporting goods store and got into her car. As she pulled away, she wondered how late her boss would be working tonight.

BALTHAZAR Piotrowski finished reading the diaries and was left feeling the world around him had been plunged into darkness where the only tangible emotion was pure evil.

The notebooks reflected a terrible period in Poland's history, when jack-booted storm troopers marched through the streets of Warsaw and no one was safe, especially the Jews.

Born in the late 1970s, Balthazar had experienced only the last few years of Soviet domination before the fall of Communism. He couldn't imagine anything like the Nazi tyranny Delores Marsh wrote about in her diaries.

A few minutes later Balthazar composed an email to his uncle who'd been a young man during the war. He lived in Jawor, the area Delores Marsh had written about. Hopefully, his uncle would reply by tomorrow, and then he would speak to Molly.

Right now, though, he needed a drink.

DEAFENING silence filled the hall when the recording ended.

Sharpe wheeled around and pointed at Molly with a melodramatic flourish. Before speaking, he glared at her, his mouth as thin as the blade of a combat knife.

"I cannot believe the Parsons's campaign would stoop so low. They know full well this is a crucial element of an undercover operation we're involved in. Leaking this recording for political purposes jeopardizes our entire investigation."

Arnie Voxx couldn't believe Kenton Sharpe's audacity. Sharpe had taken a damning piece of evidence and skillfully twisted it into a conspiracy. Sharpe had poisoned the well, and there wasn't a damn thing Arnie or Molly could do about it.

The press would be reluctant to run with the story without a lot of corroborating proof. That might take months, and by then they would've moved on to the next scandal. Meanwhile, Kenton Sharpe had planted strong doubts about Molly's credibility in the voters' minds.

Confused and blindsided, all Molly could do was hold her head high and let the controversy swirl around her. Arnie looked around the hall. Many people were having whispered conversations. The scene only lacked Kenton Sharpe shouting, "Have you no shame!"

Sharpe marched forcefully back to his podium and looked grimly at the audience. For now, he resisted the temptation to gloat.

That would come later.

HOW had the debate gone so wrong?

Hours later, Molly was still replaying the evening's events over and over in her head.

She knew nothing about the recording.

Who made it? How had Sharpe gotten his hands on it, and how the fuck had he managed to turn it on me?

There was a knock at the door. Molly peeked through a crack in the curtain. Arnie Voxx was standing stiffly on the front stoop.

"You want some coffee?" she asked after he'd taken off his coat.

"No thanks."

His voice was a soft whisper, the kind he used when he'd done something wrong. It was not a voice Arnie used often.

Right then, Molly knew where the recording had come from.

"Shit, Arnie, what were you thinking?"

The Sheriff shook his head.

"I had that asshole dead to rights. On tape no less, and he still managed to turn it on us."

"On me you mean."

Molly should have been furious, but she was too deflated. The debate had been her last chance to shine. Instead, Sharpe's maneuvering had cast her whole candidacy in doubt. In one bold stroke, Kenton Sharpe had reframed Molly as someone so desperate she would try anything, including breaking the law.

What am I going to do now?

Likely no one would stop to consider the underlying flaw in all this—why the hell would Paul Booster be conducting an undercover investigation in another town? In that context, Sharpe's accusation against her and her campaign didn't make any sense.

Molly sighed.

If anything, Arnie felt worse than she did. Molly could see it in the old sheriff's body language—head down, arms held tautly at his sides, hands balled into fists.

Arnie's heart was in the right place, but his paternal instincts clouded his judgment sometimes. Molly was like the daughter Arnie had wished for—intelligent, tough, and resolute.

After a few drinks one night, Arnie had revealed that he and his wife weren't able to have children. He and Betty had learned this devastating news the same week as the murder of the mother and her little girl.

Arnie inhaled deeply and straightened up, pushing his shame aside and replacing it with annoyance.

"You made a copy of the Ricks murder file."

Molly looked at him in surprise. It was obvious he was angry, but instead of defusing his rage, she drew on her own.

"I think you made up your mind about Gavin Ricks's guilt a long time ago. I don't see the harm in taking a fresh look at it."

"Look all you want, but that bastard is guilty as hell."

"I haven't found anything that disputes that logic so far. But we need to be fair and impartial."

"I'll be as *fair and impartial* as Ricks was when he stabbed that child twenty times and then caved in her mother's head with a *Louisville Slugger*."

Molly paused as the crime scene photo popped into her mind.

Arnie was clenching and unclenching his fists. He vibrated with the intensity of a tuning fork.

"You remember the first thing you ever taught me about being a good investigator?"

Molly let him consider the question, but Arnie remained silent.

"That emotion is the most dangerous thing in our work. It fogs up everything, so we can't see clearly."

Molly waited. Finally, Arnie's rigid bearing relaxed a little. He shook his head sadly as if coming out of a trance.

"Molly, you need to think long and hard about what the stakes are. I know you hate politics and campaigning, so you look for any way to get away from it. These killings are manna for you, a way to distract yourself.

"But if Kenton Sharpe wins next week, he's not just going to fire you. He's going to come after you so that you'll never work in law enforcement again. In fact, I wouldn't be surprised if he finds a way to bring charges against you."

"Charges? For what?"

Arnie sighed.

"That crooked son of a bitch will conjure up something vile. You can bet on it. His wrath won't just be directed at you. He'll come after me as well, and I don't really look forward to spending my retirement eating prison food."

Molly hadn't considered the ramifications of a Kenton Sharpe victory. Of course, that scheming bastard would take revenge on her. Sharpe was as vindictive as hell. She looked at Arnie, who seemed to have aged twenty years in the last ten seconds. The Sheriff was right, the stakes were high. So high, in fact, she could no longer afford to ignore them.

Then Molly cursed to herself.

Fuck Kenton Sharpe and the horse he rode in on!

Her responsibility was to the citizens of this county, and right now someone was out there killing with impunity.

As if reading her mind, Arnie Voxx threw up his hands, strode to the front door, and flung it open.

"Fine! Do whatever you please."

He slammed the door so hard the plaster cracked on the wall.

Molly stared at the crack. For a second she was tempted to peer into the fissure to see what hid in the dark cavity. There would be life in there, spiders, or mites, or something.

Finally, Molly looked away. Arnie's plea had not fallen on deaf ears. She would make as much time as possible between now and election day to get out there and work for votes.

But she also felt a deeper calling. Some victims needed—no, required—justice. With this thought in mind, Molly opened the desk drawer and took out her copy of the Gavin Ricks file.

She looked at the crack above the door once again and felt a tinge of regret. She and Arnie had disagreed from time to time, but not like this. This was serious, and she considered the possibility this rift might end their friendship. The likelihood of this loss made her feel sick.

Molly struggled to get her feelings under control. Objectivity was an investigator's most useful tool. Not rushing into judgment was what separated them from lousy cops like Kenton Sharpe.

MOLLY spent the rest of the night working her way through the case against Gavin Ricks. She was troubled by the lack of information about Ricks, or Robert Hooper, or whoever he was. There was nothing in the file about the man before he arrived in Sunset in the mid-'60s. It was if he had no prior existence. This absence of data bothered her, but Molly couldn't quite decide why.

She thought about the possibilities as she made breakfast. Once she'd finished her third cup of coffee, Molly called Colin Ricks.

Hopefully, he'd be willing to talk to her.

TWENTY-FIVE

COLIN Ricks looked like a jaundiced turd.

Reluctantly, Ricks had agreed to come over to Molly's house so they could talk. When he arrived, it was clear to Molly he hadn't slept, so Molly poured Ricks a cup of coffee and sat him down at her kitchen table. Ricks sipped the coffee gratefully while he rubbed the back of his neck to relieve the pain of his hangover.

"Looks like you had a rough night."

Ricks nodded and drank some more coffee.

"Can I get you something to eat?"

Grimacing, Ricks shook his head.

"I appreciate the coffee, but I'm not going to talk about my father."

Smart.

Ricks had also been smart enough to hire Earl Peckinpaugh who was the best criminal defense lawyer in this part of the state.

Molly knew that from hard experience. She'd been cross-examined a few times by Peckinpaugh, and she had a healthy respect for him as an adversary.

It was common knowledge in the law enforcement community that if you brought a charge against one of Peckinpaugh's clients, you better have a damn good case. If you didn't, Peckinpaugh would shred it to pieces.

Molly offered Ricks a disarming smile.

"I don't want to talk about your father's case. I just want to get a little insight into him before he arrived in Sunset."

Colin stared into his coffee.

"I'm not sure what I should tell you." "Just tell me what you can."

"What I mean to say is that I really don't know much. My father refused to talk about his past and growing up. He told us it was too painful."

"But you must have been curious."

Ricks continued staring the coffee, delaying while he considered what to say.

"After I finished law school and had been practicing for a few years, I hired someone to look into my father's background. I needed to know."

"Did you find anything?"

"Not much. My investigator discovered that Gavin Ricks had been born in Camden, New Jersey, in 1942 and died three years later, so my dad must have researched the birth and death records and adopted his identity. That was in the mid-'70s, before registrations were computerized, so it was a relatively easy thing to do. He applied for a replacement birth certificate and then built a whole new identity based on it. Before that, my dad is a total mystery."

"And you weren't interested to find out who he really was?"

"Of course I was, but I decided that if Dad had gone to all that trouble, maybe I didn't *want* to know."

"But you suspected he might have some dark secret in his past."

Tired and dejected, Colin swirled the coffee around in his cup.

"He used a lot of false IDs through the years. I don't know if we'll ever learn who he really was."

Molly agreed it might be difficult, but not impossible. There could be a way.

"How much do you want to know about your father's past?"

Colin looked up, sadness written across his face.

"As much as I can find out."

"Let's start with the first false ID that we know he used—Robert Hooper."

IT took Molly and Colin two and a half hours on the Center for Disease Control's National Vital Statistics System database to cross-match Robert Hooper's birth and death certificates.

The real Robert Hooper had been born in Saginaw in 1941 and died six months later. The records showed a duplicate birth certificate had been issued in 1967. While they had peeled away another layer, it only left them deeper in the dark.

GAVIN Ricks was sitting rigidly on his cot staring straight ahead when Molly and his son entered the cell. Molly leaned against the bars. Colin sat next to his father and put an arm around the old man's shoulders.

"Mr. Ricks, we know Robert Hooper is also not your real name."

"It's the name I chose."

Ricks spoke so quietly that Molly had to lean forward to hear him clearly. It was the first time she'd heard him speak, and his rich baritone surprised her.

"Why did you choose that identity?"

Gavin Ricks stayed mute.

"You were, what, twenty-one years old when you applied for Robert Hooper's birth certificate? Who were you before then?"

Ricks looked at his son painfully.

"What made you want to assume a different identity?"

"I died," Ricks whispered. "They killed us."

"Who killed you?"

Ricks shook his head, trying to block out the memory.

"The clown and the others."

Clown?

Ice congealed in Molly's chest, but she forced herself to speak calmly. "What clown, Mr. Ricks?"

But Gavin Ricks had lapsed into a fugue-like state. Ricks's eyes lost focus and his breathing became long and labored. Whatever he'd experienced in the past had driven the old man into a dark place. Molly knew she wasn't going to get anything else out of Gavin Ricks right now.

IT was Saturday and the Pine Academy campus was tranquil. The last of the autumn leaves had fallen from the maples lining the driveway. Molly parked her cruiser near the front entrance to the administration building. A few minutes later, she was sitting across the desk from Rita John.

"The board asked me to cooperate in any way I can with your investigation, but I have to admit I'm perplexed by your request."

When Molly had phoned Rita to make this appointment she'd given the school director a list of the records she wanted to see.

"From what I know, none of these records fall into the timeline of your investigation."

Rita held her ground nobly. She was determined to protect what little was left of the school's reputation.

"It's a related investigation."

Rita gave her a dubious stare. Molly felt like a student who'd been caught smoking pot in the washroom.

"Rita, believe me, it's important."

"Okay, I'll go out on your limb. We'll have to go over to the records storage room. That's Sara Lapeen's domain. She's the school's archivist. I'm not sure if I can find what you need today and Sara's away for the weekend."

"So let's see what we can find."

Rita led Molly through the silent corridors of the administration wing. At the far end of the hall, she used a large brass key to open a heavy door.

The weak fluorescent lighting barely penetrated the gloom of the storage room. The room was surprisingly spacious with rows of metal shelves filled with document boxes. Just inside the door, a gooseneck lamp sat on a wooden table. Rita turned the lamp on and picked up a three-inch binder. She began flipping the pages and stopped about halfway through the thick sheaf.

"Shelf number 7, boxes 46A and 46B."

Molly made a note of the numbers, then Rita led her to the back of the dim storage room. Together they wrangled the boxes from the shelf and carried them back to the table.

"Need my help?"

"No, I should be okay."

"Just leave the boxes where they are when you're finished. I'll be in my office."

Even though she only had to examine the male student files, Molly figured it would take hours to go through the two boxes. She couldn't be sure of the exact year, but guessed it would be between 1945 and 1955. The ten-year time span would mean she'd have to check over a hundred files. Molly knew she could eliminate all the non-Caucasian students, but she would still have a hell of a lot to go through.

Each file told a similar story—every child at the Pine Academy during the 1940s and 1950s had been treated with the same cruel, bureaucratic efficiency. They were referred to as "inmates" even though most of them had never committed a crime. When they'd been arrived to the school, each student had been fingerprinted and photographed mug shot style.

As much as this practice appalled her, Molly was glad it had been done. It would make her task easier. Over the next few hours, she collected fingerprint cards and photographs, making careful notes on which file each one had come from.

WHEN she finally finished going through the files, Molly walked back to Rita's office.

As she passed through the hallway, Molly noted the corridor was lined with framed black and white photographs and citations for the teachers and students who'd died in World War Two, Korea, and Viet Nam. As she got closer to the front of the building, there were color photos of students who had died in Iraq and Afghanistan. On the wall nearest the central corridor was a special tribute to a teacher who'd died in the 1960s. The woman's students had scrawled tributes to her on a poster under her photograph.

Finally, there was an empty glass case where Molly guessed the championship trophies from the Akron years had once been displayed. They'd been put into storage.

"That didn't take you as long as I expected," Rita said when Molly entered her office.

"I may have gotten lucky." Molly held up a few of the fingerprint cards.

"I'd forgotten about that." Rita frowned. "They fingerprinted and photographed every child until the late '60s."

"I'll have these scanned and bring them back next week."

"Take your time. They give me the creeps."

MOLLY tried not to think about the election as she drove back to Sunset. She knew she should be out campaigning to repair the damage Kenton Sharpe had inflicted with his accusations at the debate. Instead, Molly was thinking about the index cards in the file folder on the seat beside her. If her suspicions were correct, she would be able to confirm who Gavin Ricks really was.

"THIS had better be good."

Kurt Harbou was grumpy. The crime tech had had a busy week and was looking forward to an afternoon of beer and college football until Molly had called him in.

Molly passed him the fingerprint cards.

"How fast can you run these?"

He riffed the stack.

"There's about sixty of them. It should take about three hours," Kurt said glumly.

"Sorry."

The burly crime tech sighed. "If I had that new high-speed scanner I keep asking for it would only take twenty minutes."

Now it was her turn to grimace. When she was elected sheriff, Molly knew she would be inundated with equipment requests from Kurt and the other deputies.

God save me from budget overruns!

Kurt started scanning the cards.

"Let me know when you're through. I'll be in my office."

He just grunted in reply.

A day's worth of voice messages was waiting for Molly. She cleared them quickly but was surprised to hear William Vandermeer's voice on a message time-stamped early that morning.

"I understand you want to talk to me concerning Delores Marsh." His tone was belligerent. "Well, I can save you the trouble. I barely knew the woman, but I understand she was an excellent cook and was well liked at the school. And I suppose you want to talk to me about Frank Brighton as well. He was a drunk. There, I've saved you a trip."

What the hell was he talking about?

Molly hadn't mentioned questioning him about Delores Marsh's murder, and she certainly had no interest in talking to him about Frank Brighton.

Until now.

What was his relationship to Brighton? Had they been friends?

Molly had a thought and picked up the phone.

RITA John was still in her office at the school. Molly wondered whether or not the woman had a social life.

"I'll check for you," Rita replied after hearing Molly's request.

"Could you call me back?"

"Okay, it shouldn't take more than a few minutes. We have group photos in the staff room. They go all the way back to the founding of the school."

135

RITA called back fifteen minutes later.

"Got it—1959 through 1967."

Molly wrote the dates on a scrap of paper.

Bingo!

There was a connection between Robertson Barnard, Delores Marsh, and Frank Brighton.

"Are you still there?" Rita asked when Molly did not respond.

"Yes. Sorry, Rita. I'm still here."

Molly trod carefully. Everything seemed to intersect around the school.

"Could you do me another favor, Rita, and scan the staff pictures from 1958 to 1970 for me?"

"Certainly."

Molly gave her the department's fax number and hung up. Next she called Les Caulfield at home. A football game blared in the background.

"Les, it's Molly. I've uncovered something interesting."

"What's up, Molly?"

"I just found out that another one of the murders I've been investigating has a link to the school. Frank Brighton was on the board of directors of the Academy from 1959 to 1968."

"That's odd."

"I think something was going on there long before Greg Akron showed up."

"Oh, yeah?" he drawled. "What was that?"

"I don't know yet, but each of these deaths has a common thread, and that thread leads back to the Pine Academy."

"Molly, the Akron cover up is complicated enough. None of this ties into him does it?"

She thought about it for a few moments.

"But, Les, if something else happened there before Akron, it's been covered up too. We might be able to make a case that cover-ups are systemic at the school. You know, part of its culture."

"Well, that's an interesting theory …" Les sounded weary, the possibility of widening the investigation exhausting him.

Molly considered the possibilities. Les Caulfield was right to be hesitant. The last thing he needed was more complexity in his case. The investigation was enough of a political hot potato as it was. But there was something else involving that school. *Something* that had happened back in the late '50s or early '60s, something she couldn't quite define yet.

"Maybe I'm getting ahead of things," she admitted. "Sorry to bother you, Les."

"Molly," Les said with a note of unease, "you'll keep me up to date on anything you come across that involves the Academy, right?"

"Of course, Les. Don't worry. Take care."

Molly exhaled after he hung up. There was one logical direction she needed to go in next.

Vandermeer.

Vandermeer had a connection to each of the victims. If there were some dark secret, he would certainly know it.

Who else would have a better motive to make sure it never came out?

As distasteful as Molly found speaking to the man was, she needed to push Vandermeer about what had happened at the school during his time on the board.

Her thoughts were interrupted by the fax machine coming to life in the outer office.

Molly watched as the Pine Academy Board of Directors group photos came in. In the twelve-year span, only a few faces had changed. Molly wrote down the names listed along the bottom of each of photo. When she was finished, there were ten names on her list. She drew a line through Barnard's and Brighton's.

That left eight including William Vandermeer.

She called Rita to thank her for sending the photos. While she still had her on the phone, Molly read down the list of names and asked if she knew which of the others might still be around.

"I don't know for sure, but I can check if you'd like."

"Thanks, Rita, that would save me some time."

Right now, there was one name on that list of particular interested—William Vandermeer.

TWENTY-SIX

A star shell burst inside William Vandermeer's head.

Vandermeer had finally finished his bookkeeping, a task he performed every Saturday afternoon after his sporting goods store closed for the day. The start of hockey and basketball season meant extra profits for the shop, and this week had been no exception.

After he finished entering the figures into QuickBooks, he counted up the day's receipts, put the cash in the safe, and twirled the dial with a satisfied grin.

Norma Cartier had locked up out front, but he checked the door anyway. William Vandermeer was a careful man.

It was Saturday evening, and that meant dinner at the Bristol Country Club—a well-done strip steak with a baked potato and shrimp salad.

Vandermeer was still anticipating the steak while he closed the shop. Suddenly, he sensed movement in the periphery of his vision. Vandermeer twisted his head to see what was charging at him from the shadows. His frozen brain registered an impossibly huge, blood-red smile as large hands circled his throat and lifted him into the air.

I know you!

Vandermeer tried to say the name, but it only came out as a strangled gasp. He twisted frantically in the clown's grasp until he was swallowed by darkness.

WILLIAM Vandermeer floated in space.

The feeling was pleasant for a few seconds, like waking from a deep, satisfying, sleep. And then, like a mallet on a tough cut of beef, he snapped back to reality. Only this reality was one of pain. His head pulsed and his vision swam. What he'd perceived as floating was actually swaying. To his horror, Vandermeer found he was suspended from the ceiling with his hands tied together.

Where am I?

He was surrounded by huge panes of glass. Vandermeer twisted around. When he saw the powerful spotlight inches from his back, he grasped.

The top of the lighthouse!

Vandermeer could see the twinkling lights of Pine and, beyond those, the moon-stippled surface of the lake.

A loud clank from below snapped Vandermeer back to his present predicament. He struggled desperately against the ropes holding him.

The light was only inches from his naked spine. Whoever had put him here knew the light came on automatically at 10:00 every night.

Bile rose in Vandermeer's throat as he remembered the stories Bob Kerr the old lighthouse keeper had told of roasting whole chickens by putting them next to the light and letting the intense heat of the carbon arc lamp cook them "faster than a microwave oven."

DAVY Snider was sitting in Murray's Bar and Grill when his cell phone buzzed. Snider glanced at the screen and cringed. It was a text message from the Coast Guard. They'd been trying to call him for the past hour before giving up and sending him a text.

The light hadn't turned on as scheduled. Snider sneered at the message and cursed the government for being too cheap to put in new equipment.

With modern navigation systems on the lake freighters, why the fuck did they even need lighthouses anymore?

Snider looked at the six empty PBR bottles in front of him. A service call at the lighthouse was going to seriously cut into his drinking time. But he was under contract with the Coast Guard to be the emergency service technician for the Pine Lighthouse. They needed a certified electrician, and he needed the five-hundred dollars they paid him each month to be on call.

Snider staggered to his feet, and reluctantly headed for the door.

"Keep my seat warm," he shouted over his shoulder to Goose the bartender.

He stumbled to his van. Good sense told him he shouldn't be driving in his condition, but Davy Snider didn't pay any attention to good sense. He got into the van and put the key into the ignition, then noticed a state police cruiser crawling along the block.

Shit! Better not take a chance.

It was only a few blocks walk to the lighthouse and, with little luck, he'd be back in plenty of time to finish getting hammered.

Snider grabbed his tool kit from the floor beside him and climbed down. He locked the van and started walking down the street toward the lighthouse.

It was probably just the relay switch again. Those fucking things were ancient and tripped all the time. If that's all it was, Snider could snap in a replacement and be back at the bar in fifteen minutes.

FIFTEEN minutes later, Snider reached the foot of the lighthouse. He squinted up and saw it was out. The top of the lighthouse was a long way up, and Snider didn't look forward to climbing the spiral staircase if the problem didn't turn out to be a wonky relay switch. But what the fuck, that's what he was paid for.

Snider unlocked the main door and pushed it open. He hesitated at the threshold. This place always gave him the creeps. It was hard to believe that before the lighthouse was automated, the keeper used to live here full time.

He flipped on the lights, but nothing happened.

It has to be the relay switch.

Flashing a broad smile as he anticipated how the next beer would taste, Snider turned on his flashlight and headed to the large electrical service panel in the back. Inside the panel, to his satisfaction, he saw that all six of the breakers were showing red.

He loved it when he was right. One tiny thing troubled him though—all the breakers were tripped. Normally, the only breaker that was off was the one for the lamp, so why were all the switches off? Again, he cursed the Coast Guard and the antiquated system.

Snider pushed and held the first lever.

The room lights came back on, and he heard the reassuring hum from the system above. He snapped the next four switches and the capacitors energize. Snider let them charge as he hovered his index finger over the last breaker. The capacitors were supposed to take fifteen seconds to charge. If he turned on the lamp too soon, the entire system would shut down and he would have to start all over again.

Davy Snider waited thirty seconds just to be certain then pushed down hard on the final breaker, praying the system would initialize so he could get back to Murray's.

"Come on, light, you bitch," he muttered to himself.

BEHIND him, Vandermeer heard a screeching whine. He wasn't sure what the sound was, but knew it wasn't good.

He struggled, his spine banging painfully against the lamp housing behind him. The cycling vibration intensified and radiated down the ropes that bound his hands tightly together.

In horror, Vandermeer realized what was about to happen.

Jesus!

Enraged bees started buzzing inside his skull as the carbon rods in the lamp shrieked to life with 100,000 volts. An arc of electricity as bright as the sun jumped between the carbon rods and seared the skin on Vandermeer's naked back. The stench of roasting flesh and burning cloth enveloped him as he tried to break loose. But his desperate determination did no good.

He let out one piercing scream before his vocal cords melted.

DAVY Snider jumped as a scream reverberated through the lighthouse.

Holy shit! Is someone up there?

The Coast Guard safety protocols raced through his brain.

I didn't check the lamp deck before lighting it up!

Six beers rushed up his throat and sprayed across the open panel which exploded in a brilliant flash that threw Snider backward into darkness.

TWENTY-SEVEN

THIS is nuts.

Coming down the hill into Pine, Molly could see a cluster of flashing lights around the base of the lighthouse. There were so many vehicles in the vicinity that the streets were jammed, and she had to park two blocks away.

While the local media had covered the stories of the killings with intense interest, this latest murder had been picked up by the national press. Frayed by the travesty of national politics, the public was seeking distraction, and four murders in less than a week in a small town attracted CNN, Fox News, and the other major networks to Pine.

Molly pushed her way through a cordon of shouting reporters and producers. They were in a feeding frenzy as they jostled each other to get her attention. Molly ignored them and strode to the lighthouse.

Inside the building, a morose looking Davy Snider sat in a chair holding a coffee cup in his shaking hands, and Arnie was talking to Dr. Kolmenn. From the distressed looks on their faces, Molly knew the coroner and sheriff were stunned. Both men had seen more than their share of nasty crime scenes through the years, so this one had to be exceptionally dreadful to shake them up like this.

When he spotted Molly coming through the door, Arnie walked over and handed her a respirator.

"You should wear this. I didn't, and it's gonna take me a month to get the smell out of my nose."

"Who is it?"

Arnie shook his head. "We can't be sure. The body was pretty badly burned up."

Molly pointed at Davy Snider. "What's he doing here?"

"He turned on the stove."

She looked at Arnie uncomprehendingly, and the sheriff grimaced at his lapse in taste.

"Snider's under contract to the Coast Guard to maintain the light. He says some of the breakers were off, and when he flipped them the light came on and roasted the victim."

As she started toward the stairs, Arnie put a hand on her elbow.

"That's not a good idea. It still smells up there."

Molly pulled on the respirator and climbed the stairs.

The power in the lighthouse was dead, but the crime techs had set up portable lights so they could work.

Arnie was right. A haze of greasy smoke filled the air, and the respirator didn't completely mask the stench of burned flesh. Molly mentally blocked out the smell as she inspected the scene.

Scorched ropes dangled from a large metal hook screwed into the ceiling, and the corpse lay on the floor with a morgue sheet draped over it.

Molly stepped carefully around the body.

"Anything?"

Kurt Harbou shook his head. Even through the heavy mask, Molly could see the crime tech's eyes were troubled.

"Most of the trace got burned up by the light."

He shivered.

"It was a hell of a way to go."

"Any ID?"

"There was a wallet on the stairs. I don't think it fell out of the victim's pocket. I figure the killer wanted us to find it."

He handed her a brown leather wallet inside an evidence bag. Kurt had taken out the driver's license. Molly's heart jumped when she saw William Vandermeer's picture.

Kurt motioned to the body under the sheet.

"Kolmenn thinks he was alive for the first minute. I can't imagine what it must have been like, burning alive like that."

Despite the respirator, Molly could smell the faint odor of burned flesh. She gulped hard, fighting against nausea.

"Who the hell would do a thing like this?"

"I thought the other murders were bad, but this one really takes the cake." The crime tech paused, horrified at the analogy he'd inadvertently made.

Molly glanced at the ropes and the hook. This killing felt medieval, like an old-fashioned witch burning.

It's punishment!

Robertson Barnard was executed with two shots to the head like an army deserter.

Frank Brighton was beheaded like a French aristocrat.

Delores Marsh was bound up in a costume and shot like an animal.

And now, Vandermeer was burned up like Joan of Arc.

Molly was certain all these crimes were linked somehow. Mystified by the brutality of Vandermeer's death, she pondered the meaning of the killer dressing as a clown.

"Were there any makeup stains?"

"The body was too badly burned to show them if there were. I'll do a close examination of the ropes."

With a final glance at Vandermeer's body under the sheet, Molly went downstairs.

CHAOS filled the lighthouse.

Multiple voices demanded a statement. She and Arnie exchanged glances. Someone should talk to the press since they weren't going away. Arnie nodded in her direction.

Molly inhaled and strode to the door. Before she could face the media horde, however, another voice cut through the din. When Molly opened the door, she was surprised to see the reporters gathering around Kenton Sharpe.

"I would be happy to make a comment on the record," he declared. "As you know, this is the fourth murder we've had in the past five days. I think this demonstrates clearly the need for new thinking when it comes to law enforcement in this county. The current administration might be satisfied with their 'hug a thug' approach to law and order, but I'm certainly not.

"I won't allow Sunset County to become a haven for criminals."

Arnie took a menacing step forward but Molly stayed him with a hand on his shoulder. She glared at Sharpe in disgust.

"Let him make all the speeches he wants, We're still in charge here."

"We had a chance to nail him with that tape, Molly, and I blew it," Arnie said bitterly.

She squeezed his arm.

"And we'll have another chance on Tuesday. Let's trust the voters to see this for what it really is, exploiting a tragedy."

Arnie nodded grimly and pointed at Snider.

"You want to talk to him?"

Molly shut the door and walked to where Snider sat. She knelt beside him. He looked at her, his eyes rimmed with tears.

"It wasn't my fault," Snider said softly.

"I know, Davy."

"I couldn't save him. I tried."

He began to sob.

"I understand you got quite a jolt when the electrical panel exploded."

He held up his hands which had been dressed by one of the paramedics. Molly also noticed that Snider's eyebrows had been singed off.

"Can you tell me what happened?"

Snider sniffed. "I was at Murray's having a few drinks when I got a text that the light was down."

"From the Coast Guard?"

"Yeah, so I went out to my van and got my tools ..."

"You didn't take your van?"

Snider hesitated. "Nope. The lighthouse is only a few blocks away."

Molly knew Snider was lying. He was most likely drunk, but since Snider had a couple of prior DUIs, Molly figured that drinking hadn't stopped him from driving in the past.

Snider saw the skeptical look on Molly's face and cast his eyes down. "Okay, there was a cop car down the block, so I decided to walk instead."

"And walking took you ... what, fifteen minutes?"

"I didn't look at my watch, but yeah, that sounds about right."

"And did you notice anything strange when you got there?"

"Strange?" Snider thought for a second. "No. Nothing at all. Other than all the breakers had been tripped."

"And that was unusual."

"Yeah. Normally it's just the lamp breaker. It draws the heaviest load, and the equipment is from the '70s. I keep telling the Coast Guard to pony up for a replacement, but they say they don't have the budget."

"So how come all the breakers were off?"

"I don't know."

"Is it possible they could have been pulled manually?"

Snider bobbed his head. "Sure, it's like turning off the lights. You just flip the switch ... safety, y'know."

Safety was probably the furthest thing from Davy Snider's mind. Molly looked at the electrician's trembling fingers and blood-shot eyes and wondered how in the hell he'd dodged being electrocuted all these years.

As if sensing her thought, Snider straightened up with indignation.

"I'm not a complete fucking idiot. I follow safety rules."

"Like checking the lamp deck before turning the system back on?"

Snider deflated. "I figured it was safe. I mean who the hell would be up there at that time of night."

Molly waited patiently and let the implication of his last statement sink in.

Snider dropped his head into his hands and moaned. "This looks really bad ..."

Molly agreed. The fact that Davy Snider had been involved in two deaths in as many days looked really bad. Still, she felt sorry for him.

"Okay, why don't you tell me what happened after you reset the lamp?"

Snider spent the next few minutes taking Molly through the sequence of events leading to Vandermeer's death. The hapless electrician stopped periodically to wipe away his tears.

When Snider finished his statement, Molly asked one of the deputies to drive him home. She felt sorry for him. Davy Snider was going to have to live with the guilt of having unwittingly killed two people.

Frank Brighton's shabby little room littered with beer cans came to mind. Would Davy Snider end up like him?

Probably, he's half way there already.

IT was 3:00 in the morning by the time Molly left the scene. The reporters had gone and the streets of Pine were quiet as she walked to her car.

Molly paused next to the coroner's van, surprised it was still there. She thought Kolmenn had left hours ago. But Dr. Ronald Kolmenn was sitting in the passenger's seat staring out the window lost in thought. She tapped the glass gently and the window slid down.

"Everything alright, Ronnie?"

"Yeah, Molly. Just thinking."

"Hope you don't mind me saying so, Ronnie, but you look like you're off your game these days."

"Isn't my work satisfactory?"

"It's excellent as always, but a month ago, as horrible as the scene was, you would have made some sardonic remark about crispy critters, or something to break the tension."

He smiled wanly. "I guess I've grown up a little then."

The window went back up, ending their conversation.

Molly hesitated for a second and then moved on. The coroner's unusual behavior worried her. Something was going on with him. She just wished she had the time to learn what it was.

NEARBY, a figure stood in the shadows and watched her go.
Almost done, Darcie.
The clown smiled as Molly climbed into her cruiser and drove off.
Almost done.

TWENTY-EIGHT

THE rat inside Taylor Mead's brain clawed frantically for release.

Mead sat on his porch overlooking the Black River and drank a cup of freshly-brewed coffee. The gourmet blend, as thick and dark as molasses, took the edge off the crisp morning air.

Mead's house was a modest one, not much larger than a cabin, located at the end of a gravel road three miles outside of Boyle. He had no neighbors to share his view of the river and he liked it that way. Mead had lived on his own since he was thirteen and never felt the need for anyone's company.

He'd just finished his normal Sunday morning breakfast of buckwheat pancakes with link sausages and had moved to the porch to have his second cup of coffee.

The old man's hearing was starting to fail and, annoyingly, he found himself asking people to repeat themselves more and more these days. But despite his loss of hearing, Mead heard the growl of an approaching Harley just fine.

A few minutes later, Sammy Atkinson roared up the driveway and parked his beast of a motorcycle next to Mead's late-model Lincoln Navigator.

Atkinson was dressed in jeans and a leather jacket instead of the three-piece suit he usually wore at his dealership.

He must be slumming today.

Sammy Atkinson smiled broadly. "Morning, Mr. Mead."

Mead smiled back, masking his real feeling that Atkinson was a thug.

But he was a necessary thug.

Sammy Atkinson stomped onto the porch. Pointedly, Mead did not offer him coffee. Even though he was expecting Atkinson, he didn't want to encourage him. Taylor Mead suspected there would come a day in the not too distant future when Sammy Atkinson and his brother Tommy would turn into liabilities. If the DEA ever swept them up, the Atkinsons would squeal like the pigs they were. And that would be unfortunate for them.

"Tell me about the recording," Mead said quietly.

Atkinson looked petulant. "Sharpe handled it."

"For now. But it came from somewhere."

Sammy considered this while sensing the dangerous silence between them.

"I think Sharpe made it like he said. For his own protection."

Mead stood and set his mug down on the railing.

"And why would he need to protect himself? I thought we were paying *him* for protection."

"We are, but ..."

"Shut the fuck up!" Mead screamed.

Atkinson froze.

"He played a recording of you to a crowd of people and then announced it was part of an undercover investigation."

"I ... know how ... it looks ..." Atkinson struggled to get the words out.

Atkinson thought about the ancient Colt .45 tucked into the back of his jeans. He seriously considered putting a couple of slugs into the old man's face.

"And we got video recordings of Sharpe taking cash from us."

Mead glared at Atkinson incredulously.

"You really are stupid, aren't you? You and that retarded brother of yours. What, you've been documenting your crimes for *America's Favorite Home Videos*?"

Atkinson puffed out his chest. He wasn't about to let this old man push him around.

"Don't worry, they're tucked away in a safe place where no one will ever find them." Atkinson was tempted to add *"you old fuck"* but kept his mouth shut.

Mead's time would come, and when it did, Atkinson had a lead on a contract killer in Detroit who charged reasonable rates for his services.

He contemplated this happy thought while Mead glowered.

Finally, Sammy Atkinson held up his hand as if he were pledging allegiance to the flag.

"Look, the election is on Tuesday and, from what I see, Sharpe's got it in the bag. He's our boy, bought and paid for, and no matter what he says about secret investigations, Kenton Sharpe will come through for us."

Mead wasn't so sure about that. He sensed a change in the air.

The citizens of Boyle, who had been satisfied to sit back and suck off the tit of crime for years, were now starting to show a little backbone.

Mayor Adam Gmerek and his band of torchbearers were almost at the point of becoming a grave concern. Taylor Mead knew he would have to stomp on them before they reached critical mass. But others would undoubtedly follow.

Looking ahead to his future, Mead had the uncomfortable feeling he'd better start planning an exit strategy.

SAMMY Atkinson was still hotter than the exhaust manifold on his Harley.

That old fart Taylor Mead treated him like he was an idiot. But it was more than just Mead's attitude fueling Atkinson's rage. Atkinson didn't like the vibe he was getting from Taylor Mead. The old man had gravestones in his eyes, gravestones that Sammy Atkinson was certain had his and his brother's names carved on them.

When he got back to town, he was going to have a serious conversation about putting Taylor Mead back into the coffin he'd crawled out of.

TWENTY-NINE

MOLLY looked up and saw Balthazar Piotrowski standing in her office doorway looking very haggard.

Molly desperately needed some sleep. She'd been at the scene of Vandermeer's murder for most of the night and was thoroughly exhausted. But as tired as she looked and felt, her exhaustion was nothing compared to what she saw on Balthazar's face. Usually, he sparkled with enthusiastic optimism, but not this morning.

He collapsed into a chair facing her and pushed the photocopies of Delores Marsh's diaries across the desk. He couldn't wait to get rid of them.

"Anything interesting?"

"She write these diaries long after war. She was evil woman."

Molly leaned forward. "Evil? How?"

"It is story." Balthazar inhaled. "I have uncle from same city that she was born in. I sent him email. He was able to help fill in details.

"Most people in my country hated Nazis after they invaded. But some, like Doloreta Bagno, she love them. She volunteer to work with them."

"But she would have been a very young woman when the war started."

"She was twenty, but grew up believing all Jews were bad people. The Germans trained her to be guard in prison camp at Gross-Rosen.

My uncle told me camp inmates were mostly Jews and political prisoners. They worked in huge stone quarry there."

Balthazar shifted uncomfortably and stared into his lap.

"This was dark time for Polish people. Some Poles cooperated with Nazis so they would be treated better. She was not like that. She believed in evil things they did. She write about how Jews and Gypsies are subhuman, only suited for heavy labor. They did experiments …"

He struggled to continue.

Molly's impression of the Nazi death camps came mostly from scratchy black and white film of skeletal prisoners in striped uniforms. The single vivid image that had stayed with her was of the prisoners' haunted eyes devoid of any hope.

"They did experiments there," Balthazar continued. "To make sure they cannot have more babies."

"Forced sterilization?"

"Yes, to eliminate Jews forever. She write about master race and how proud she was to be part of it. This was a sick woman, Molly, and evil, very, very, evil. Toward end of war, she was not just guard anymore. She worked with doctors as nurse. She admired them for what they were doing right up to the end."

"And she wasn't captured or tried as a war criminal?"

"It was confusing time at the end. Many escaped when Russians come. She pretend to be refugee and fled from Poland. She went to Spain and got new identity papers. She come to United States in 1947. But she was smart and knew someone might look for her, so she come here. No one paid attention to her. No one cared."

"So that's it then? She worked in a concentration camp and then escaped to America?"

Balthazar shook his head.

"No, that's not all. Because she keep in touch with doctor from camp, a man she admired. I think she was in love with him. Dr. Martin Broder. He sterilized almost ten thousand people in camp and did other things I cannot even talk about."

"I wrote here," Balthazar held up a school notebook. "She get job as cook at school."

"The Pine Academy?"

"Yes, Pine Academy. She contact Dr. Broder. She tell him is safe place to continue experiments."

The room seemed to narrow into a dark tunnel leading directly to unspeakable horrors from the past.

"Doctor change name to Blanic. He come to school in 1953."

Molly wondered if there was anyone still alive who might remember the man, and then she had a thought.

A fire blazing in the hearth kept the chilly fall air at bay in Ronnie Kolmenn's study while he read Balthazar's notes.

The coroner had been in the job forever, well almost forever. Molly was certain Ronnie would know his fellow doctors in the county. With any luck, he might recall Blanic at the Pine Academy.

She gazed out the window at the row of tall oak trees that marched across the back of his property. It didn't help Molly's gloomy mood that the leaves were gone and the trees stood naked against the brooding autumn sky.

"Jesus," he sighed and closed the folder. "I remember that bastard."

"So, do you think she's telling the truth? Is it possible?" Molly asked

Kolmenn compressed his lips into a thin slit.

"Yes, there were lots of medical professionals at that time who believed in eugenics. Right here in Michigan we had the Race Betterment Foundation. Dr. Cornflakes founded it."

"Kellogg?"

"That's right. He and a lot of other right-minded people thought that if we could weed out the mental deficients, criminals, and the mentally ill from the all-American gene pool, we'd have a better society. Of course, a lot of natives and blacks were included just for good measure."

"Sounds like the master race without the death camps," Molly said, a worm twisting in her stomach as she imagined the horror of what he was telling her.

"They had sterilization programs in a lot of state schools and prisons. It makes sense they would do it in a school like the Pine Academy. In those days, it was a dumping ground for unwanted children."

"And the state allowed this?"

"Sadly, yes. In fact, they supported it."

"Even after they saw what the Nazis did?"

"Yes. If I recall, it was the '60s before Michigan banned hereditary sterilization. Toward the end, they used x-rays instead of the scalpel. It was a little more humane."

"Humane?"

The idea of forced sterilization of children was monstrous—science and sociology gone berserk. Sickened, Molly left the room without another word.

Kolmenn gazed at the papers he was holding. He was tempted to toss them in the fire, but resisted the impulse.

RITA watched from her office window as Molly's cruiser skidded to a stop in front of the administration building. When Molly had phoned earlier, Rita was surprised by the intense anger in her voice. Molly's determined stride and livid expression told Rita this visit was not going to be a pleasant one.

Molly paused at the entrance of the school. Her impression of the place had changed from one of tragedy to something deeply sinister. She pushed the door so hard it hit the wall with a bang that echoed along the corridor like a gunshot.

Molly slammed a sheaf of papers onto Rita's desk.

"Dr. Blanic!"

Rita's heart sank and she slumped in her chair.

Enraged, Molly leaned over, her fists hard against the wood surface and pinned Rita with a steely gaze.

"Dr. Blanic is ancient history."

Molly leaned closer. "Ancient history? What the fuck are you talking about?"

Rita pressed her fingers into the taut muscles at the base of her skull.

"Molly, please sit down."

Molly remained motionless for a few moments then sank into a chair.

"I heard rumors about Blanic when I first took over."

"Weren't you curious?"

Rita nodded and continued to rub her neck.

"Of course. I did some digging through old records. I was surprised I found anything at all. They'd buried it pretty deep."

"And you kept it quiet?"

"Like I said, it's ancient history, just more grief to add to our catalog. Anyway, Blanic isn't relevant to any investigation. He was gone from here by the early 1960s."

"Tell me what you found."

Rita shrugged and rotated her head slightly to ease the pain.

"Blanic was the school's physician from the 1950s until the mid-'60s. Some students died while under his care."

"Died? How?"

"Infection from a faulty instrument sterilizer in the infirmary."

"How many students died?"

"At least seven, maybe as many as ten. The board dismissed him."

"But it keeps with the tradition of the board covering up the sins of this place."

Rita shrank away, grief etched on her pretty face. Molly felt sorry for Rita. This wasn't her fault. If anything, Rita was another victim of the malignancy that was the Pine Academy.

Sensing Molly's sympathy, Rita straightened and shook her head stubbornly.

Her voice hardened. "You're right, this place does have a long history of mistreating the children in its care. Back in the 1930s, local factory owners used the students as free labor. There were rumors that some of the children were even used for prostitution."

Rita sucked in a noisy breath, fortifying herself to continue.

"A lot of wicked things happened here. Gregory Akron was only the latest in a long, sorry list of abuses."

"Sounds like you're making a good case to shut this place down."

"I expect the class action suit in the molestation case will do that. It's a shame, though."

"Why?"

"Despite what happened in the past, the students who are here today really need this place. It's the best chance most of them will ever have for a decent education.

"We can't go back and correct the awful things that happened in the past, but we can make the Academy stand for something good going forward."

Molly stood up. "Maybe …"

But Molly believed the Pine Academy was a lost cause. Nothing could redeem it. "But right now, I need everything you have on Dr. Blanic and the medical records of the children who were under his care."

MOLLY called Les Caulfield and asked to him to meet her at his office. When he arrived, Les looked at the pile of boxes stacked on the conference table and cocked an eyebrow.

"What the hell's all this?"

"Sit down, Les. I have a long story to tell."

When Molly finished, Les silently processed her account of the dreadful events involving Dr. Blanic and Delores Marsh. Then he glanced at the boxes. It would be a daunting task to go through all of them.

"I'm not sure how this ties in with the Akron cover up. Sure, the school's board has a long history of covering things up, but our investigation is only focused on Akron. The special prosecutor will freak out if we bring her all this."

"What are you saying, Les? We sweep it under the rug?"

Les shrugged and pointed at the stack of cartons.

"No, certainly not, but this is a whole separate thing. From what you said, this goes back into the 1950s. That's way beyond the scope of this investigation."

"I know, but it all ties in."

"You mean it ties into your murder case, not into my investigation."

"I think the killings are wrapped up in all of this. Barnard, Vandermeer, and Brighton were on the school's board of directors during the time Blanic and Marsh were carrying out eugenic procedures on the students."

"We don't know that for sure, Molly."

"Maybe not, but there seems to be a strong connection. Will you at least look at some of this stuff for me?"

His eyes narrowed cannily.

"Okay, but on one condition—you agree that if things don't go well for you on Tuesday, you'll come to work for me full-time on the Akron cover up investigation."

Molly smiled. "Okay, I agree to consider it. Hell, I'll need a paycheck from somewhere."

"That's good enough for me. I'll take a look."

Les looked over at the stack of boxes and shook his head wearily.

THIRTY

KURT Harbou slapped one of the fingerprint cards on Molly's desk.

"I'm surprised you're working on a Sunday."

"I was up all night processing the stuff from the Vandermeer scene, and I finished running the cards for you. I got a match on the fingerprints. Gavin Ricks birth name is Steven Praeger. He was born in Flint in 1946."

That made Gavin Ricks seventy-two years old. Molly picked up the phone and called his son.

"WE have a positive ID on your father."

Colin Ricks brusquely told her to hold off telling his father until he could get there.

While she waited for Colin to arrive, Molly debated whether or not to call Arnie and tell him.

Best not to stir that pot right now.

GAVIN Ricks finally broke his silence and began to sob when Molly spoke his birth name.

"Steve Praeger died a long time ago."

Colin sat on the bunk next to his father.

"Dad, please tell us. What happened that night?"

Gavin Ricks wiped away his tears and spoke haltingly.

"Elsie and I had been drinking a lot ... I blacked out ... When I came to, there was blood everywhere, and Elsie and June were dead. I would never have hurt them, but I must have. I loved them, but when I drank, I could get mean."

"Maybe someone else did it while you were passed out," Colin said.

"I don't think that's possible, son. I've had a long time to think about this, and I'm certain that I killed them."

"And you're going to pay for it," Arnie said coldly.

Colin Ricks and Molly turned to see Arnie standing by the cell door looking hard at them.

"I've waited a long time to hear you say that you killed them."

"Sheriff, I've said it to myself every day for the past fifty years."

"Too bad you weren't man enough to come back here and confess."

ARNIE was furious with Molly.

"I thought we had an understanding about Gavin Ricks," he shouted. "Instead you've been trying to prove that he's innocent."

"I was not trying to prove he's innocent. I was looking for as much evidence as I could find so a jury could decide."

"You don't think he's guilty then, even after he confessed?"

"I need to ask Ricks about the Pine Academy. He was a student there in the '50s."

Arnie inhaled deeply in an attempt to calm down.

"Why?"

"Because I think it might tie into my murder case."

"I don't believe it! Is everything a conspiracy to you?"

White with rage, her fists clenched at her sides, Molly stood and walked to the door.

Arnie hesitated and softened his tone. "Molly, I love you like a daughter, but you've got to stop doing this. You've got three, maybe four murders to solve, plus an election to win. Please don't interfere with this. Gavin Ricks is done. He's confessed and he's going to prison for the rest of his life."

"I still need to talk to Ricks about his time at the school, Arnie. He's the only person I can find who was there during that time period, and he might know something. It's my only link to the murders. Something evil happened at that school and Barnard, Vandermeer, Brighton, Blanic, and Delores Marsh are all tied up in whatever it is."

Arnie massaged his forehead with his fingers. Finally, he nodded.

"Okay, but I want Ricks to have his lawyer there when you talk to him. I'm not taking a chance on blowing the case because of some technicality or procedural error.

"We could already be in hot water by questioning him tonight. I'm just glad you had his son with you to confirm that Ricks's statement was voluntary. And, by the way, I'm hurt that you didn't call me before you talked to him."

She started to apologize.

"Molly you're a damn good cop, but you can be a major pain in the ass. Go have your talk with Ricks. I'm going to spend the rest of the day beating the bushes for votes. Hopefully, my endorsement might help overcome some of the damage from Friday night."

Molly looked at him out of the corner of her eye.

Damage you were responsible for.

"I'll give his lawyer a call."

"Now, please get out there and catch our murderer while there are still people left alive in Pine."

KENTON Sharpe had been busy since the Friday evening debate with Molly. He'd spent time working his influential contacts around the state, trying to see if anyone knew about any undercover operation in Boyle.

Someone made that recording, and Sharpe was certain it had been Arnie Voxx. Somehow that wily old fuck had planted a listening device in Sammy Atkinson's office.

Sharpe had managed to discredit the recording for now, and he would kill any investigation after he was elected. But his confidence eroded when he considered the possibility the recording was part of something bigger—the DEA perhaps. If they were involved, he was really fucked.

Still, if the DEA was involved, there was no way they would have allowed a recording like that to be played publicly. Not for the sake of a local election, that's for sure.

Sharpe smiled at this logic and its obvious conclusion.

Yes, this was Arnie Voxx's operation all the way.

From her reaction to the tape on Friday evening, Sharpe was sure Molly Parsons had been rattled by the recording. Sharpe smiled at the memory of her shocked expression.

He had messed up her smug confidence and knocked her off stride. *Sometimes the nicest gifts come wrapped in a blanket of shit.*

Sammy Atkinson had called an hour ago and asked for a meeting. Sharpe smirked. He'd been expecting Atkinson's call. He figured the events on Friday night had shaken up the car-dealing thug pretty good. *And Taylor Mead as well.*

Atkinson and Mead would be hard to placate, especially since Sharpe had put Sammy in the crosshairs. But the fat fuck could handle it. He just needed to reassure them that nothing had changed and, once he was elected, they would be able to expand their criminal enterprise beyond Boyle. All of Sunset County would be theirs.

SAMMY Atkinson stood next to his Harley which was hidden in a copse of oaks on an isolated side road outside of Boyle. Atkinson watched nervously as Sharpe got out of his pickup. Sharpe noted the sheen of sweat on Atkinson's face and was happy he had a pistol under his jacket.

To win his confidence, Sharpe flashed a grin.

"What the fuck did you do to me?" Atkinson moaned.

Sharpe shrugged.

"I was going to say the same thing, asshole. Don't you ever sweep your office for bugs?"

Sammy's mouth tightened, and Sharpe put a hand inside his coat.

"You told everyone that *you* made the recording."

"That was bullshit for the voters, Sammy. Arnie Voxx planted a listening device in your office."

"Yeah, we found it inside one of the elephants on my desk."

"So, who put it there?"

"We're looking into it. Meanwhile, my good reputation is in jeopardy. Everyone thinks I'm a crook."

Good reputation?

Sharpe took his hand from under his jacket and raised it in the air like he was taking an oath in court.

"This shit will go away, I promise. Once I'm elected, I'll track down Arnie's source in your organization and put a bullet in his brain."

Sammy Atkinson shook his head. "Naw, don't do that. Just let me know who it is. Whoever planted that bug has a date with my table saw."

Sharpe had heard rumors about Sammy Atkinson's penchant for shop tools. Apparently, Sammy liked to saw people up and feed them to his pigs.

Sammy Atkinson grinned when he thought back to his last meeting with Taylor Mead.

"Mead's having a shit fit over this."

Sharpe patted Atkinson's arm. "Well, I trust you can keep that old fart in line."

Atkinson nodded.

"I thought that after I'm elected, I might be able to toss the entire department's fleet budget your way. I could fix it so we will pay you a little over list, say fifteen percent. If I eliminate the department's mechanics, we could also move the maintenance contract to your dealership as well."

Atkinson smiled, already counting the profits in his head.

"That would be a real friendly gesture."

"Especially after kicking back ten percent."

Sharpe smiled to himself, satisfied that a potentially nasty situation was now under control. Sammy Atkinson needed him and his clout.

Once he was elected there would be plenty more opportunities. Sunset County had no shortage of crooks.

The only fly in the ointment was Taylor Mead. And Sharpe had an answer for that crazy old fucker as well.

WHILE she waited for Gavin Ricks's lawyer to show up, Molly went down the short list of the school's former board members.

And it's getting shorter by the day.

Most of them from the '50s and '60s had died of natural causes. Nothing unusual there. So why had four people with connections to either the school or the board been killed in such a short period of time?

Molly bet the answer lay somewhere inside one of the boxes Les Caulfield was going through. She wondered if she should have conscripted more help to go through them. It was a huge job, and Les was not all that enthusiastic about taking time away from his primary investigation.

Molly thought about calling Les but held off. She didn't want to risk pissing him off more than he already was.

Restless, Molly wondered if she should go to Les's office and go through them herself. She was terrible at delegation. "It's a trust issue," her analyst had told her. Molly questioned that reasoning. In her mind, an investigation was about the minutiae, the tiny fragments. But tiny fragments only made sense when you knew the big picture. And Les Caulfield was the only investigator who knew what the big picture at the Pine Academy was. So for now, Molly was stuck twiddling her fingers and waiting.

She stared glumly at the whiteboard on her wall. She had written the victims' names in the middle along with their individual timelines. She added Dr. Blanic's name and timeline, even though he wasn't one of the victims. Molly instinctively knew that Blanic was somehow involved.

Molly discovered there were only three years where they converged—1964, 1966, and 1967. It was obvious Gavin Ricks did not fit this timeline. He would've been too old to be a student during that time. He might, however, be able to give her some insight into the school and what it was like while he had been there.

"MY parents died in a car crash when I was nine," Gavin Ricks said softly.

He sat next to his lawyer who was making copious notes during the interrogation. Peckinpaugh had set the ground rules: no questions about the murders, and Molly could only ask about Ricks's time at the school.

"I had no relatives who could take me in, so the state sent me to the Pine Academy."

"That was in 1958?"

"Yes."

"What was it like coming here to the school?"

Ricks's features clouded. "I don't remember much from that time. It all happened so quickly. One day I was at home with my parents and then suddenly they were gone and I was in a strange place. I remember being scared a lot."

"What can you remember about the school?"

Gavin Ricks looked at his son. Molly had allowed Colin to sit in on the interview.

"It was like jail. A lot of the kids had been sent there by the courts. There were also some children who were retarded … mentally challenged. They had special classes where the staff trained those kids to wash dishes and clear tables, plus other jobs they could handle.

"We all worked at something. I would be part of the grounds crew when it was warm, and I helped shovel snow in the winter."

"What about the staff and teachers?"

"They were more like jailers than teachers. We were locked up after lights out. It would have been a disaster if there'd ever been a fire.

"I don't know what else I can tell you. When I turned sixteen, I demanded that they let me leave. I came away from the Pine Academy feeling like an outsider. When I was legally able to, I changed my name."

"Why did you do that?"

"I thought a new name would help me to leave the past behind. Being Steven Praeger was just too painful."

"But if you wanted to put that part of your life behind you, why did you come back?"

"My life was pretty much shit at that point. I was drinking too much and couldn't hold onto a decent job. I did manual labor and construction. I drifted around for a while and somehow ended up back here. They were building a lot of vacation homes and resorts in those days."

"And that's as far as we go," Peckinpaugh said.

"Earl, I'd like to ask Mr. Ricks a few more questions about his time at the school if you don't mind."

Peckinpaugh nodded and Molly proceeded.

"Do you happen to remember the woman who was the cook? She would have had a strong accent."

"Yes, I remember her. She was nice. She made us special treats. She even liked to dress up sometimes."

"Dress up? How?"

"She'd wear a clown costume, you know, with her face painted white and a big red smile. Some of the kids were really scared, but I thought it was hilarious. She was hysterical."

Molly caught her breath as the flesh on her arms rose up.

"Can you remember when she'd do that?"

Ricks nodded. "At Christmas and on the Fourth of July. Oh, and sometimes when we were sick. She came to visit when a bunch of us had the measles. I remember that because I thought I was dreaming."

"Oh?"

"Yeah, it was kind of strange because it was late at night and everyone was sleeping. I thought I saw the clown dancing in the corridor outside the infirmary."

BEFORE she was five, Molly had been terrified of clowns. Later, her analyst told her the phobia was defined as *Coulrophobia*. The fear of clowns was quite common, especially among young children. It's easy to understand why. Clowns are both familiar and disturbing. The fear comes from not knowing who is lurking under the greasepaint.

Even though she was long over her fear, Molly avoided clowns whenever she could. This, however, was one clown Molly couldn't avoid. She looked at the whiteboard once again and tried to fit the pieces together.

First, Mark Barnard had seen a clown dancing outside the house after his father had been shot. Then there were the traces of makeup on Delores Marsh, on Frank Brighton, and on the ropes holding Vandermeer against the light. Finally, there was the stolen clown costume, which brought Molly back to Norma Cartier. When she'd asked Cartier about the missing costume, the woman had been evasive. Molly knew she wasn't telling the truth.

What else isn't she telling the truth about?

Molly wrote CLOWN in bold letters in the center of the white board. She stood back and stared at the word. The idea of a murderer dressing up as a clown was the fodder of bad fiction.

This isn't a Batman film.

Molly contemplated the word CLOWN for a few minutes.

She circled Delores Marsh and the Pine Academy and drew lines to the word. Marsh dressed as a clown at the Academy during the '50s and early '60s.

Deputy Jeff Cunningham stood in the doorway looking at the board.

"Clown? What's that about, Molly?"

Molly winced and wished she'd erased the word before anyone could see it. And then she noticed Jeff's strange expression.

"Not sure. Why?"

He cleared his throat, obviously stalling for time.

"I investigated an accident a couple of days ago … I think it was the morning Delores Marsh was killed. Clark Benjamin ran his pickup off the road and flipped into a ditch."

Molly looked at him impatiently. "So?"

Jeff coughed. "The accident was one county road over from the place in the woods where Marsh was killed. Less than half a mile away."

Molly waited for her deputy to get to the point.

"Clark was pretty banged up. He was lucky he wasn't killed. When we were putting him in the ambulance, he was out of it. He kept ranting about not letting the clown get him."

Clown?

Jeff now had Molly's full attention.

"I didn't really pay too much attention. As I said, he was banged up good. Then I got the call about Delores Marsh and headed over there. I meant to follow up with Clark on the accident. Looks like he was going too fast."

"Was he drunk or something?"

"Nope. I figure he was just speeding."

"Is he still in the hospital?"

"They held him overnight and then let him out."

Molly grabbed her jacket. "Let's go."

CLARK Benjamin lay on his living room couch watching golf and resented the interruption. His head was still pounding like a son of a bitch after it bounced off the steering wheel when his pickup flipped. When the truck rolled, he felt like he'd been tumbled inside a clothes dryer. Benjamin's body was bruised from his shoulders to his ankles. The doctors wouldn't give him anything for the pain because of the head injury, but that was okay. Benjamin self-medicated by puffing on a joint despite the two deputies in his living room.

Molly motioned at the joint. "Can you put that down, please. We need to talk."

Benjamin smiled and stubbed it out. "Can't this wait until tomorrow?"

"Sorry, Clark, it's important," Jeff said in a conciliatory tone.

Clark shrugged. "Okay, let's get it over with."

He'd turned down the sound on the television, but his eyes kept darting to the screen as they talked. Tiger Woods was making his latest comeback.

"I understand you flipped your truck on County Road 7," Molly said.

Clark was only half paying attention as Tiger nailed it straight down the fairway and onto the green.

"Yeah, the truck flipped."

"You remember what you told me when they were putting you in the ambulance?" Jeff asked.

"Nope. I got knocked out."

"But you were talking," Molly said.

He nodded, still distracted by the television.

"And you told Deputy Cunningham about the clown."

Benjamin froze like he'd been stabbed with an icicle.

"I was flipping out and seeing things."

"You're saying it was a hallucination then?"

"Yeah, most likely."

"How did you manage to crash like that? It was dry, and from what I understand, you're an experienced driver."

"It was an accident."

Molly sensed he was lying.

"You know what I think, Clark?"

He shook his head.

"I think you saw a clown before you had the accident."

"No, there was no clown!" he shouted. "It was all in my head."

"We need the truth, Clark. Lives depend on it."

"What the fuck would a clown be doing out in the woods anyway? It doesn't make sense."

You're right about that, my friend.

Molly took a breath. "We think there was someone in the woods dressed as a clown, and we believe that person murdered Delores Marsh."

Clark Benjamin considered this for a few seconds.

"I was late so I pushed up my speed. The clown stepped out of the woods and freaked me out. I jerked the wheel to the left and the next thing I knew I was upside down in a ditch."

"Is there anything else you can remember?"

"No, it's all pretty hazy after that, though I think I saw the clown in the rear-view mirror when I was in the ditch. It looked like he was dancing."

Dancing?

Molly felt a chill creep up her spine.

"Can you describe the costume he was wearing?"

Benjamin shrugged. "I only saw him for a second. I remember shiny red stripes ... and maybe white ones.

A red and white striped clown costume. The description matched the one that had been stolen from the parade warehouse.

AFTER they left Clark Benjamin, Molly asked Jeff to drive her to the scene of the accident.

The earth was scarred where the pickup had landed. Molly looked back along the road at the small crest about a hundred feet away and visualized the accident—Benjamin speeding along in his pickup was startled when he saw something entirely unexpected come out of the forest.

Molly walked along the shoulder. There were tread marks in the gravel where the truck's wheels skidded when Benjamin jammed on the brakes. Molly continued down the road to the spot where the skid marks began.

Standing at the edge of the thick woods, Molly scanned them for any sign of a disturbance and saw a place where it was obvious someone had recently passed by. She took out her cell phone, called

Kurt Harbou, and gave the crime tech the GPS coordinates. Kurt promised he would come right away.

She crossed over to the other side of the road and rejoined Jeff. They walked up the slight rise in the road.

"He came out of the woods back there and went this way according to Benjamin," she narrated, still working it out in her head.

At the top of the rise, there was a track leading off into the woods. It was wide enough for a car and Molly could see impressions in the mud. Carefully, she and Jeff followed the track. The ruts led to a small meadow where there would've been enough room to park a car.

Jeff fixed crime scene tape across trees to cordon off the area.

Kurt Harbou arrived a little while later. Molly explained what she wanted Kurt to check. When she finished, she saw a tuxedo rental catalog on the passenger seat beside Kurt.

Molly nodded toward it. "Avoid lime green or mauve. They clash with your eyes."

Kurt laughed and climbed out of his van. Molly asked Jeff to stay and show Kurt where they believed the clown had been.

Molly borrowed Jeff's cruiser and headed for Pine. When she and Jeff had been stomping around in the woods, she'd had a thought.

MOLLY sat across from editor Randy Darmor in his office at the Pine Whisperer newspaper. Molly knew Darmor had been a student activist before coming to work at the paper in the '70s. In the late '60s, he'd been a member of the Port Huron circle who founded the SDS, Students for a Democratic Society. But like most of the radicals from that era, Darmor had been turned off by increasing violence in the movement and had quietly walked away to start a new life.

Molly met him for the first time when he interviewed her about her campaign. She'd tried hard to charm the old radical. Darmor had been noncommittal, though Molly felt she'd made a good impression. Her positive feeling had been confirmed when she leafed through the latest issue of the paper and saw he'd endorsed her in an editorial.

"Alfie Iannarelli said you might be able to help me out."

"Oh, yeah? How?"

His tone made it obvious he had a newsman's skeptical view of law enforcement.

"I was hoping I could look at photos from the last Thanksgiving Day Parade."

Iannarelli had told her the Pine Whisperer ran a two-page center spread on the parade. He'd also asked her if she'd like to have dinner sometime. Although Molly had declined his offer—"because I'm too busy"—she;d left the door open for the future.

"Well, you've aroused my reporter's curiosity. I'm obliged to ask why."

Molly sighed and wondered if she could trust Darmor.

"I'm interested in any pictures you have of the clowns, especially if you have one of William Vandermeer."

"Vandermeer?"

He fixed her with a steady gaze. The truth, she decided was the best approach.

"I need your promise not to publish what I'm about to discuss with you until my investigation is finished. I'll let you know when you can. You'll have a head start on the other papers. I guarantee it."

Darmor looked skeptical but agreed, and Molly spent a few minutes taking him through the case.

"But, how does it all tie together?"

"I don't know."

Darmor had the same instincts she did and recognized Molly wasn't telling the whole truth. Darmor let it go, however, because what she had revealed was electrifying enough. He smelled a Pulitzer in his future. If he played his cards right, this might be the cap on an otherwise mediocre newspaper career.

Darmor went to the file room and returned a few minutes later with a thick folder of photographs marked THANKSGIVING DAY PARADE.

He and Molly sorted through the shots and put the clown pictures in a separate pile.

"I took these myself," he bragged, holding up a nicely composed shot of a group of clowns standing in front of a flatbed trailer.

Darmor was right. The photographs were very well done. And to top it off, the editor had noted names of the clowns on the back of the photo. Molly picked out Vandermeer standing dead center in the shot. She put it aside and selected another one with Vandermeer in full profile.

Luckily, Darmor had shot in color. She could see Vandermeer's clown costume had alternating red and white stripes with yellow fringe around the neck, wrists, and ankles. Vandermeer's face had been painted white with red tears and a ghoulish red grin outlined in black.

"Can I borrow this?"

"Sure, it's only a copy. I have the negatives in storage. You can take the whole file if you'd like."

THE file boxes were in the corner of the conference room still untouched. Molly struggled to keep her annoyance in check.

Les Caulfield smiled apologetically. "Sorry, Molly, I haven't had time to crack them yet."

"That's okay, Les. Get to them when you can."

She showed him the picture of Vandermeer dressed in the missing costume.

"If you don't mind me saying so, Molly, all this sounds a little crazy."

"Arnie called this morning and asked if I thought these murders connect to our investigation at the school."

"What did you tell him?"

"I said there are some interesting coincidences and we need to take a closer look."

"Thanks, Les."

Molly was relieved Arnie had supported her. She was concerned that a serious rift may have opened up between them because she wasn't taking the election seriously, and he resented her interference in the Gavin Ricks case.

"WHEN are you going to tell her?" Betty Voxx demanded that morning.

Arnie poured himself a cup of coffee and saw Betty hadn't made breakfast for him. Each morning for the past fifty years, Betty had faithfully cooked his bacon and eggs. The only time she hadn't was when she was angry with him.

"It doesn't matter. It's none of her business."

Betty looked across at him, and Arnie knew she was angry.

"You're just a stubborn old man."

"Stay out of this, Betty."

Arnie got up from the table and took his coffee into the living room. Copies of *The Sunsetter* and the *Detroit Free Press* were on the table next to his armchair.

The Pine murders were the front page headline of *The Sunsetter*. Arnie flipped to the editorial page. The paper had endorsed Kenton Sharpe for sheriff.

Shit!

Cummings, the paper's editor, was an idiot anyway. He crumpled the paper and tossed it on the floor.

Betty followed him into the living room. Arnie knew she wasn't going to let up.

"Why do *you* get to make that kind of decision?"

"Betty, you sound just like her."

"Well, I can relate to Molly. You're letting your pride overrule your common sense."

"Gavin Ricks is guilty as hell. You didn't see that baby he killed. I did. I'm not going to let Molly muddy the case."

"What are you afraid of? That maybe he isn't as guilty as you believe? Maybe you need to read *Les Miserables* again."

"You think I'm obsessed?"

"Well, I certainly don't think you're acting objectively."

He set the coffee down so hard it sloshed over the edge of the cup. His wife fixed Arnie with a reproachful glare.

"You don't want to give it up, do you? You can't stand that the job is coming to an end. This is closure for you."

During all their years together Betty had mastered the art of cutting to the bone when it came to dealing with her husband. She alone knew how to get past the bullshit and into his heart. The only other person who came close in this respect was Molly Parsons.

"You tell her today, or I will," she threatened as he put on his coat and headed for the door.

"She's a good investigator. I'll let her find out for herself."

"And what will she think of you when she does?"

ARNIE thought about what Betty said as he drove to the office. He couldn't remember a time when he'd seen her so angry. It made him pause and consider what she'd threatened. Finally, he decided on a solution.

THIRTY-ONE

MOLLY found a thick file sitting on her desk.

The file was ancient. Once blood red, the folder had faded to a soft rose and smelled musty like it had been hidden away for a long time.

What the hell?

Molly was astonished to discover this file was the complete account of the double homicide that Gavin Ricks was accused of. It was much thicker than the file Arnie kept in his desk drawer.

Curious, Molly opened the file and began to read, becoming increasingly engrossed. When she finally closed it, she was furious.

Molly rushed into Arnie's office and slammed the door shut. She threw the file onto his desk.

"All this time you kept me in the dark."

"Have a seat," he sighed.

She continued to stand.

Arnie motioned at the chair facing his desk. "Sit down, Molly."

She paced restlessly for a few minutes, unsure of what to do. Finally, she sat down.

"I let you go off half-blind because I let my biases get in the way."

She exhaled in exasperation.

"Damn right you did. I thought we trusted each other."

"It had no bearing on the case. After all, it happened in 1967."

"This whole fucking case seems to be leading me backward."

"I still don't think there's any connection to what's happening now and what happened back then."

"Maybe not, but at least now I have a chance to consider it."

Molly jumped up and stomped from his office.

Arnie looked down at the file and felt ashamed. Molly was right. As his wife had reminded him that morning, he'd let his prejudices affect his better judgment. He had a feeling he'd be making amends for a long time.

Arnie picked up the phone and called Peckinpaugh. He informed him that he intended to question Gavin Ricks again. Before the attorney could object, Arnie hung up. His phone rang immediately, but the sheriff just stared at it.

MOLLY was still angry when she entered the school's main lobby. Students jostled her as they hurried to their next class. Molly stepped out of the way and let them pass. She glanced at the empty display case and was touched for some unfathomable reason by the faded condolence messages that had been written by grief-stricken students so long ago.

Once the hall had cleared of students, Molly entered the main office where the receptionist coldly informed her that Rita was in a meeting.

Molly was tempted make a snarky remark to the aloof woman, but instead asked if Sara Lapeen was available. A few minutes later, the harried-looking school's archivist appeared in the office doorway. Molly estimated Lapeen had to be at least seventy.

Once a teacher at the Academy and then the librarian, Lapeen had returned as a volunteer a few years after retiring to maintain the school's archives. She was a formidable presence, and in the wake of the scandal had appointed herself to safeguard whatever legacy was left.

Molly had run into Lapeen a few times during the Akron investigation and found her helpful but cool. As an archivist, Lapeen was obligated to provide any materials requested, but she didn't have to like it, or Molly, for that matter.

After Molly told her what she was looking for, the archivist fixed her with a skeptical stare. "I should call the director and get her permission. Elsie Maranello was a long time ago, and I'm not sure your warrant covers that far back."

Damn!

Molly had hoped Lapeen wouldn't question the validity of her request, but the woman was no fool.

"Were you here when she was?"

Lapeen nodded. "Elsie Maranello was a friend. It was so sad about what happened to her and her little girl. I hear they finally caught the bastard who killed them."

"Maybe …"

Lapeen cocked an eyebrow. "But you don't think so, do you?"

Molly nodded thoughtfully.

Sara Lapeen considered Molly's request for a few seconds then flipped through a thick three-ring binder on her desk and ran a finger down the left column.

"Box 1504, shelf A4."

Sara Lapeen wrote the information on a yellow sticky note in neat, flowing letters.

"Now, let's see what we can find."

GAVIN Ricks sat between his son and his lawyer.

Instead of using one of the interview rooms, Arnie suggested they use his office. He set a digital recorder on the edge of the desk facing Gavin Ricks.

"I am Sunset County Sheriff Arnold Voxx. Also in attendance are Gavin Ricks; Colin Ricks; and Mr. Ricks's attorney Earl Peckinpaugh. Mr. Ricks has previously been advised of his rights."

Arnie paused.

"This interview concerns the deaths of Elsie Maranello and her daughter June Maranello on the evening of March 14th, 1967. Mr. Ricks, could you please explain to me the nature of your relationship with the victim?"

Ricks slumped forward.

"I lived with her."

"Were you lovers?"

"I loved her if that's what you mean."

Gavin Ricks began to sob and his son put an arm around his father's shoulders.

"Would you describe the events of that evening please."

"I worked late and got home around 7:30. Junie was already asleep. I went in and kissed her good night."

"Was June Maranello your child?"

"No. Junie was Elsie's from her marriage to Sam Maranello. He was killed at Suoi Bong Trang the year before."

"He was in the army?"

"Yes, 1st Infantry. There was a battle during the night and he was wounded. He died a couple of days later. Elsie never got over it."

"Had she been drinking on the evening of her death?"

"Yes, she was pretty upset."

"Why was she upset?"

"I don't know. Elsie wouldn't tell me."

"And you had no idea what might have upset her?"

Gavin Ricks looked up and wiped the tears from his eyes.

"I think it was something at the school. She'd come home late a couple of nights in a row and she wouldn't say why. Of course, I was a mess myself … drunk and stoned most of the time."

"Were you drunk and stoned that evening?"

Earl Peckinpaugh stopped Ricks from replying. He leaned over and had a whispered conversation with his client. Peckinpaugh frowned and sat up straight.

"This is Earl Peckinpaugh, Mr. Ricks's attorney. I have advised my client not to answer the sheriff's previous question. Mr. Ricks has declined my advice."

Gavin Ricks looked straight at Arnie.

"I was out drinking for most of the afternoon. I had also smoked marijuana."

"And you arrived home in an impaired condition?"

"Yes."

"Did you continue to drink with Mrs. Maranello?"

"Yes."

"The neighbors reported hearing shouting during the evening. Did you and Mrs. Maranello argue?"

"Yes."

"What was the nature of your argument?"

"I tried to get her to tell me what was wrong. She refused."

"What happened then?"

"Elsie went to the bedroom to go to sleep. I stayed in the living room and watched television. Dean Martin was on."

"Did you continue to drink?"

"Yes," he replied meekly.

Gavin Ricks averted his head to avoid looking at his son. Colin Ricks squeezed his father's shoulder in support.

"What were you drinking?"

"I'd been drinking beer, but we ran out. Elsie had finished the wine. The only thing left was a bottle of brandy that Elsie had won in a school raffle. I cracked it open and had a couple of shots. It was pretty potent and I passed out."

Arnie remembered the bottle of brandy, it had been knocked off the table and had spilled all over the floor next to the victim.

"What happened when you came to?"

Ricks's eyes filled with tears again.

"Please ..." Arnie said softly.

Gavin Ricks wiped at the tears with the back of his hand.

"I found Elsie ... She was on the floor. She'd been beaten with a baseball bat."

"Do you know where the bat came from?"

"Yes, it was mine. I played softball in the summer."

"Where was the bat?"

"It was sitting next to me on the couch. It was covered in blood."

"Did you touch it?"

"Yes, I picked it up and then threw it into the corner of the room."

"What did you do next?"

"I tried to clear my head. I felt sick."

"Did you kill Elsie Maranello?"

"I don't know. I can't remember a thing."

"And there was no one else there?"

There was a long pause. Ricks struggled with the memory of that night of horror.

"I kept blacking out. One time when I came to, I thought I saw the silhouette of someone in the hall, but I passed out again. When I woke up, I was alone."

"Do you have any idea what time you woke up?"

He shook his head. "Johnny Carson was on TV, so it had to be after 11:30, but I can't be sure of the exact time."

"When you were finally able to get up, what did you do?"

"I went down the hall to check on Junie." Gavin Ricks broke down in racking sobs. "But she was dead too. She'd been stabbed."

Arnie shuddered at his own memory of this.

"Did you recognize the knife?"

"It was one of our kitchen knives."

Arnie tried to keep himself under control and just listen to the man's story, but his simmering anger over the child's murder finally boiled over.

"And you don't remember using the knife to kill June Maranello?"

Gavin Ricks, sensing the interview had turned hostile, leaned back in his chair and crossed his arms.

Earl Peckinpaugh stepped in. "Sherriff, I think this interview is at an end."

Arnie fought hard against his rage. Molly was right, it was blinding him. He needed to hear the rest of the story.

"Mr. Ricks, I apologize for my last remark. I appreciate that you volunteered to tell your side of the events. I would like to continue it if you're willing."

Gavin Ricks was an emotional wreck, devastated by finally verbalizing his recollection of the night of the murders.

Arnie looked at him carefully, and for the first time wondered if Gavin Ricks could have been capable of killing Elsie Maranello and her daughter.

"There's not much more that I can tell you, Sheriff," Ricks said quietly. "I snuck away. Believe me, in the last fifty years a day hasn't gone by that I haven't thought about how much of a coward I was."

He looked at his son in anguish.

"No matter what successes I had, it will never make up for what I did. I built a new life for myself, had a family and the respect of my community, and all the time I had to live with the awful truth of that night. Finally, I couldn't stand it anymore."

"And you started drinking again, knowing that you were likely to get caught when you got behind the wheel."

"I needed to be caught."

Gavin lifted his head and stared directly at Arnie.

Doubt tickled the back of Arnie's neck, yet he flushed with rage.

He's guilty as hell!

All the physical evidence pointed to Gavin Ricks. The scenario hadn't changed. Gavin Ricks had killed Elsie Maranello and her daughter in a fit of drunken rage.

Those were the facts.

Arnie thought about the silhouette Ricks claimed to have seen in the hallway. It was nothing, a figment, part of a hallucination. There was no reason to reopen the investigation.

What could he find now? The evidence was a sad catalog of a sordid crime—baseball bat, butcher knife, victim's clothes, broken glasses, bits and pieces, and not much else. It was still locked away, waiting for the day when the murderer was finally apprehended.

Elsie Maranello's trailer had been hauled away years ago and sold for scrap. The entire trailer park no longer existed. It had gone bankrupt and closed in the 1990s. All that remained of the park now was a few rotting hulks overgrown with weeds.

There were no new facts to lead Arnie away from the conclusion that Gavin Ricks was the murderer. But a sliver of doubt about Ricks's guilt had taken hold of the him. It throbbed in the back of Arnie's mind like an abscessed tooth.

What if Gavin Ricks is innocent?

The feeling stayed with Arnie long after Gavin Ricks, his son, and his attorney had left his office.

The case file was still on his desk where Molly had tossed it. Arnie opened it and began to carefully read the report he'd written all those years ago.

THIRTY-TWO

THE secret meeting was held at Jack Smythe's old cottage on Shadow Lake.

The gathering was deliberately kept low-key, attended by only the most trusted members of the Boyle Citizens Committee. Their leader, Boyle mayor Adam Gmerek, had organized the group to counteract the influence of Taylor Mead and his henchmen.

Before Mead came along, Boyle had been a decent place to live. No one paid much attention to how the town was being run as long as taxes stayed low. Mead kept things status quo and, if anything, business got better. Local merchants were excited at first by all the new customers who seemed to be flush with cash.

Many were willing to turn a blind eye to the insidious business being conducted under their noses. So slowly the town's moral core was eroded by the promise of a roaring economy. Legitimate merchants soon found themselves sleeping with the devil, but by then it was too late. They'd already sold their souls.

Adam had been born and raised in Boyle. When he was growing up, Boyle was peaceful and thriving. He left for Iraq with his National Guard unit in 2005 and, when he returned, he was shocked by what he saw—a town overwhelmed by corruption. He pleaded with state and federal government officials to do something about the meth trade, but no one listened, or cared. Finally, he had enough and stood for election as mayor. Despite the best efforts of Taylor Mead and the

Atkinson brothers, Adam was elected by a substantial majority. It was obvious other citizens of Boyle were tired of the disgrace their town had become.

After Adam's victory, Taylor Mead made it known this unfortunate lapse in immorality would not be repeated. He still pulled most of the strings in town, and quite a few in the county as well. Taylor Mead had managed to get one of his toadies appointed clerk to oversee the forthcoming election.

To counter this attempt at election fraud, Adam had assembled a group of trustworthy people who would watch the polling stations and document any attempts to subvert the democratic process.

The citizen's group spent a good part of the evening reviewing their strategy for the next day's election. They'd taken on a big task, but weren't naïve when it came to understanding the risk they faced. And they were united in their mission to seize back their town.

The meeting broke up a little after 10:00 and everyone headed back to town. They spaced their departures out so there wouldn't be a stream of cars heading into Boyle at the same time. And they split up taking different routes, again in an effort not to tip their hand.

WES Chandler worked as a mechanic at the Atkinson brothers' dealership. Chandler had also ridden with the Atkinsons in the Devil Stompers. Chandler, a loser in his mid-thirties with tiny insect eyes and a permanent smirk branded on his face, fit right in with the motorcycle gang.

That afternoon Sammy Atkinson had assigned him to watch Old Whatley Road, which ran north out of town. Chandler hid in the woods next to the bridge over Sawyer Creek. The span was narrow and everyone crossing it had to slow down. Sammy Atkinson had given him a pair of night-vision glasses, so Chandler could note license plate numbers on any cars crossing the bridge. It had been quiet most of the evening, but now traffic had picked up which was definitely unusual for this time of night.

Chandler jotted down the plate number from a gray minivan and cross-checked it against his list. He confirmed it was Gmerek's van.

Buddy, your luck just ran out.

Wes Chandler used speed dial on his cell phone to call Sammy.

MOLLY helped Sara Lapeen wrestle a box down from one of the higher shelves in the back of the storage room. They'd been at it for several hours with no luck so far.

The normally unflappable Lapeen was mystified.

"I don't understand it. Elsie's day books and teacher's notes should be in here. That's what the records show."

"Maybe they were misfiled."

From the severe look shot her way, Molly knew that wasn't likely. Sara Lapeen was meticulous, a real anal-retentive type who would never allow such an error to happen.

"They were definitely in that box five years ago," Lapeen muttered. "We did a full inventory when we moved to the computerized system."

Molly looked at the thirty pound box they'd just manhandled off the shelf. From the thickness of the dust, it hadn't been opened in a long time.

"Who did the inventory?"

"I supervised some students and they did it."

"Must have been fun for them," Molly said lightly.

"It was punishment. They never broke curfew again."

The woman had no sense of humor. Sara Lapeen was devoid in the personality department. She alternated between fussy and autocratic. Molly wondered if this was the result of working long hours in a gloomy room with dusty documents.

In their short time together, Sara Lapeen had also expressed some shocking views on minorities and what she saw as "lower classes." Molly thought about challenging the woman's bigotry but held her tongue. She needed Lapeen's help so, instead, Molly changed the subject.

"You taught with Elsie? What was she like?"

"She was an excellent teacher. All the students liked her. They were devastated when she was murdered."

"Yes, that must have been shocking."

"Not to me. I was expecting something like that."

"Why?"

"Because she was a wanton woman."

Lapeen's mouth twisted into an unpleasant smile. "Some of the other teachers complained to the director at the time, but he wouldn't do anything about it."

"Complained? About what?"

Lapeen sniffed. "Why her drinking, of course, and that awful man she lived with. He was a disgrace."

Molly thought back to when they first discussed Elsie Maranello, Lapeen had described her as *a friend*. Lapeen's lofty and snide remarks certainly didn't sound that friendly. In fact, they sounded downright hostile.

Lapeen interrupted Molly's recollection. "I understand that you arrested the man responsible for her death."

"We have a suspect in custody."

Molly changed the subject abruptly hoping to catch Sara Lapeen off guard.

"Can you tell me what the school was like back then?"

"Well, it's much different today. In those days, most of our students were sent by the courts."

"I understand some of them were mentally ill, or had intellectual disabilities."

"Intellectual disabilities? You mean were they *retarded*?" Sara said with a grin. "Yes, we had all kinds of subhuman types in those days."

Subhuman types?

Molly thought back to Delores Marsh's diaries.

"I understand there was an infirmary."

"The state required it."

"And you even had a doctor on staff."

Lapeen's eyes narrowed with suspicion. "Yes, Dr. Blanic. He was a saint.

Molly struggled to remain nonchalant.

"But there isn't an infirmary here anymore?"

"No, just a nurse. Anything serious goes to the county hospital in Sunset."

"So, what happened to the infirmary?"

Sara waved an arm around the room.

"This was originally the surgery. The classroom next door was the ward."

"How many patients could be treated at one time?"

"I can't recall. I think there was space for six beds."

Molly tried to think of a reason to ask Lapeen to show her Blanic's personnel file. But she had no logical reason for the request, and Lapeen would probably demand a court order. Instead, Molly asked the archivist for directions to the washroom.

THE late afternoon sunshine was intense and suffused the hallway outside the school's records office with an orange glow. As Molly walked down the hall to the washroom, she dialed Les Caulfield. When he finally answered, Les sounded flustered.

"Les, you have a copy of the file inventory from the school, right?"

"Yes, of course."

"Can you look up the personnel file for a Dr. Blanic? I need to know which box it's in."

Molly expected him to object, but Les only sighed. Then she heard the distinctive clicking of key strokes, a sound that grated on her nerves.

"Yes, there's one on the inventory list. It's in Box 68 B. That's 1968, Molly. What the hell is going on?"

Les sounded tired. Molly wondered if he wasn't feeling well, or if his patience with her had worn thin. Before she could ask Les what was wrong, he began speaking.

"The special prosecutor called me again this morning. She's getting concerned about the speed of the investigation. This is an important case for her, and she doesn't want hiccups."

"Sorry, Les. I'm going to wrap it up as quickly as I can."

There was silence for a few moments.

"Fine. See that you do," he replied curtly and hung up.

When she turned, Molly was startled to see Sara Lapeen standing behind her. The grim expression on the woman's face made it obvious she had overheard Molly's conversation with Les.

"I've locked up. We're finished for the day. If I locate Elsie Maranello's file, I'll call you."

From the frosty tone of her voice, Molly knew that it was unlikely she would ever hear from Sara Lapeen again.

LAPEEN was still fuming an hour later as she sat at her desk with a smug smile and tapped her keyboard.

That goddamn Parsons woman!

Well, Molly Parsons didn't know where Elsie Maranello's day books and records were. Lapeen's smile broadened. They'd been deliberately misfiled. Lapeen knew because she was the person who had hidden them.

Why can't they leave us alone!

The school was silent. It was after 6:00 and classes had ended for the day. Any students still in the school at this hour would be eating dinner in the dining hall in the residence building next door.

Sara Lapeen thought about her own dinner, a square of spinach lasagna wrapped in foil thawing in her refrigerator. She wasn't hungry right now. She didn't have much of an appetite at all these days.

Lapeen speculated about what Molly Parsons had been looking for, and why had she been asking about dear old Dr. Blanic.

Luckily, the archivist had the foresight to misfile Blanic's records as well. It would take at least a year of searching to find. Lapeen had memorized a simple key so she could quickly locate them on the system. Her password key was elements of her late husband's dog tag number. He'd given her his dog tags when he returned from Korea, and Lapeen had worn them around her neck ever since.

Molly Parsons's visit had piqued Lapeen's curiosity. Why was that bitch interested in Elsie's files and day books, and how did Dr. Blanic fit in? Maybe she needed to look. Lapeen slipped the tag from around her neck and stared at the number stamped on the aluminum surface. She'd made a series of tiny knicks above the numbers that corresponded to the number of the box where she'd hidden Elsie's and Dr. Blanic's files, along with other sensitive files.

A long time ago, when she first took over as an archivist, Lapeen had considered destroying these records but she couldn't. She had a duty as conservator to preserve and protect the school's history, no matter how awful it had been.

Lapeen locked the heavy door to the records room. She didn't want anyone disturbing her while she examined the files. She made her way carefully down the aisle to the back of the room where the oldest records were stored.

Lapeen heard something and froze.

The sound of soft wheezing was coming from nearby.

"Who's there?" Sara Lapeen's voice with cracked fear.

She listened, heart racing, as the wheezing rose in volume. Lapeen wished she had the pistol concealed in her purse, but her handbag was locked in her desk drawer.

She desperately needed to escape. She sensed whatever was in here was close, and the room closed in around her. Her aged body refused to budge. Lapeen twisted her head around and gasped as a figure stepped from the shadows between the shelves. When she saw what it was, Lapeen went numb with terror. She stumbled back toward the door which was impossibly far away.

The voice was soft and mocking. "Hello, Sara."

The clown's painted smile widened as he towered over her.

Sara Lapeen whimpered.

The clown reached for her with an egg-white hand.

Paralyzed, Lapeen was unable to scream or resist as he gripped her shoulders and pulled her close.

THIRTY-THREE

MOLLY couldn't decide what she was more tired of—murder or campaigning.

Well, at least one will be over tomorrow.

Molly decided to treat herself to dinner at The Villager. She'd never been much of a cook, and the prospect of frozen pizza didn't appeal to her.

Hank Summerville greeted her at the door and showed her to a table. He was treating her extra sweetly, and Molly figured he must have seen the last polls, which showed that Kenton Sharpe had a slight lead.

"Hank, I'll have a double-shot of Absolut, neat, please."

He looked at her in surprise. Molly generally drank beer.

"What's the special tonight? Not pizza, I hope."

While she liked most of the items on The Villager's menu, Molly loathed their pizza, which she found greasy. Her opinion, though, was not shared by most of The Villager's customers and pizza night was always the restaurant's busiest.

"Double patty melt with American cheese, fresh cut fries, coleslaw, and a pickle." Hank was a little too enthusiastic.

"Sounds good."

Hank went off to get her drink and Molly looked around. The restaurant was unusually quiet.

Must be the calm before the storm.

Deep in thought, Molly was startled when Balthazar Piotrowski sat down across from her. His face was creased with deep worry lines. The contractor, normally jovial and outgoing, had become gloomy since he'd translated Delores Marsh's diaries. He seemed to have internalized the horrors they contained.

"I talk to my uncle again in Poland."

Molly noticed his accent had thickened.

"He suggest you talk to Simon Wiesenthal."

The name was familiar to her, but she couldn't quite place it.

"He keep lists of Nazis and their crimes. They should have records because Wiesenthal was prisoner at Gross-Rosen. It will have particular significance for them."

She remembered now—the Simon Wiesenthal Center for Holocaust Studies. They helped track down war criminals after World War II. She would give them a call in the morning.

Molly had been trying to find out what had happened to Dr. Blanic after he'd left the Pine Academy in the 1960s, but he'd disappeared without a trace. Maybe the Wiesenthal people might be able to give her a lead.

Hank's daughter Jennie brought Molly's dinner. Balthazar stood up and pointed at Jennie's nearly full-term belly.

Balthazar's gloom lifted. "Soon I have little nephew," he told Molly with pride.

"Or little niece," Jennie corrected.

He smiled broadly. "Or little niece."

They left Molly to eat her dinner in peace, and she decided not to think about the case for a while.

Tonight is for me.

No matter which way the election went tomorrow, this was her last night as a deputy. Molly decided to relax and enjoy it.

> *"What's in a name? That which we call a rose*
> *By any other word would smell as sweet.*
> *So Romeo would, were he not Romeo call'd,*

Retain that dear perfection which he owes
Without that title. Romeo, doff thy name,
And for that name, which is no part of thee
Take all myself."

Daphne Grange tried to focus on her lines and not on Bradley Thorn, her Romeo standing below the balcony.

God, he's hot!

Bradley's tight T-shirt and jeans accentuated his buff body, especially in the blue spotlight which simulated the moon for the play's most famous scene.

Daphne and Bradley were in the auditorium. Daphne knew they weren't supposed to be there but jumped at the chance to be alone with Bradley to "rehearse" for the school's production of *Romeo and Juliet*.

The set wasn't finished and the balcony where Daphne stood was a scaffold fifteen feet above the stage floor. The bars of the structure creaked and groaned ominously. The whole thing felt unstable, and Daphne hoped the set design crew would make it a lot steadier before opening night. She didn't relish hanging on for dear life while trying to deliver her lines.

"I take thee at thy word. Call me but love, and I'll be
new baptis'd; Henceforth I never will be Romeo."

Her heart beating wildly as Bradley stared longingly into her eyes, Daphne momentarily lost her place. She reached for her copy of the play which she had set on the railing and felt the scaffold shift. Her script hit the stage at Bradley's feet and he looked up at her in alarm as the scaffold began to rock back and forth. Daphne instinctively grabbed at a rope tied to the railing to steady herself, but it came loose in her hand and whipped up into the shadows above. She followed its movement and blinked in surprise as something hurtled down toward her.

A sickening snap echoed through the auditorium.

Daphne gasped in horror and almost tumbled off the scaffold. A body swung in wide arcs over the stage. She recognized the person hanging from the fly loft—Sara Lapeen. The librarian hung from a crudely fashioned noose, neck broken, her head lolling to one side.

Daphne was momentarily stunned but came out of it at the sound of a high-pitched shriek from Bradley. He looked up at the body in terror and ran from the auditorium.

AT the other end of the county, Adam Gmerek checked on his children.

Both were sound asleep and Adam closed the door quietly so he wouldn't disturb them. Adam went back to the living room where his wife Allison sat watching television.

Allison wasn't happy about his involvement in the citizen's committee and his tenure as mayor. She'd grown up in Boyle and was as disgusted as Adam was at what her town had become. She constantly reminded him, however, they had two children and Taylor Mead was ruthless when it came to protecting his interests. Allison Gmerek was terrified that Mead saw her husband as a threat.

Adam walked to the living room window and closed the curtains. Earlier he had done a perimeter sweep around the house, checking that all doors and windows were securely locked. This precaution made his wife even more apprehensive.

"You know they're going to come."

Adam shook his head. "They're not *that* stupid."

"Don't bet on it," Allison snapped a little sharper than she intended. "And don't bet *our* lives on it."

His stoicism, while appealing, was also damned annoying. Adam hid his feelings under a thick layer and rarely let them show. But when he did, as he had when he swooped their children into his arms on his return from Iraq, her heart melted.

Allison thought of Gary Cooper in *High Noon* and his sense of duty to a town that wouldn't stand with him. That film was a lot like their current situation. When push came to shove, as she was sure it would, Allison was terrified they would be left standing alone to face Taylor Mead and his thugs.

"I'm going to bed."

"I'll be up in a few minutes."

Adam felt restless, and didn't know why. His fingers and toes tingled uncomfortably, a feeling he'd had a few times in Iraq. It was a kind of sixth sense warning him danger was close.

"DON'T kill him," Sammy Atkinson ordered, his voice thin in the Bluetooth headset. "Just scare the shit out of him."

Wes Chandler sneered and muttered into the mouthpiece, "Yeah, a little fear goes a long way."

Atkinson hung up and Chandler went back to watching the house, which he'd been doing since Gmerek had returned from the meeting.

Strong floodlights were mounted along the back wall of the Gmerek home to illuminate the entire backyard. The lights forced Wes Chandler to hide in a stand of birch trees in the woods at the back of the property. It was freezing back there, and a dead animal smell filled the air. Chandler stamped his feet and wished he'd worn warmer boots.

The first week of November and it already feels like fucking winter!

Chandler hated snow and cold. And winter meant he would have to put his Harley away. He tried not to think about the changing season and focused on the house. The living room blinds were closed, but he could see a silhouette move back and forth as someone paced in front of the window.

Hurry up and go to bed, asshole.

Once the lights in the house went out and Gmerek was in bed with that hottie of a wife of his, Chandler would make his move.

Wes Chandler was built like a professional wrestler and would scare the shit out them when he burst into their bedroom wearing the Halloween mask he had crumpled inside his jacket.

He imagined Gmerek and his wife, sheets pulled up their chins, begging him not to hurt them or the kiddies.

Yeah, you're gonna streak your undies tonight.

The living room lights went out.

At last!

Chandler was careful not to step into whatever rotting critter was making the stench. He took out his pistol, a .44 magnum just like Dirty Harry's, and held it at his side. The house was far enough away from the neighbors that he could use the gun. He'd put a slug into the bedroom ceiling just over their heads and let plaster rain down on them. His thumb massaged the hammer of the large handgun like it was a talisman and he started to move toward the house.

Chandler froze as the ice-cold barrel of a gun pressed against the underside of his ear.

Without being told, he set the .44 on the ground in front of him.

"Kneel down."

Now it was Chandler's turn to shit his pants. He looked around helplessly, hoping the cavalry would arrive. But no such luck, Wes Chandler was on his own.

"Lace your fingers behind your neck."

Chandler shifted his weight, and rifle caressed his left cheek.

"Now!" spat a second voice.

"Please. I was just going to scare him, honest."

There was no reply. Instead, he felt fingers explore the inside of his jacket and extract the cell phone from his pocket.

Who cares? It's a burner.

He had half a dozen more.

Oh shit!

It dawned on him that this phone's call record was intact. He felt sick to his stomach. His most recent call to Sammy Atkinson was still there.

Fuck, how could I have been so stupid!

Someone spun Chandler around and pulled a hood over his head. The world went black and, before he could object, a pair of handcuffs were snapped onto his wrists.

"Hey, don't you gotta read me my rights?" Chandler's voice was muffled by the hood.

Chandler was jerked to his feet and frog marched through the woods.

"I got rights!"

Strong hands lifted Chandler and tossed him onto a hard, carpeted surface.

I'm inside the trunk of a car?

"Where the fuck are you takin' me!"

"For a long ride, Wes."

The lid slammed and a few minutes later he felt the car move.

THIRTY-FOUR

MOLLY had just come through the front door when her cell phone rang.

"There's been another one at the Pine Academy. I'll pick you up in five minutes." The grim tone in Arnie's voice told her all she needed to know.

WITH the siren wailing and lights flashing, Arnie got them there in record time to Molly's relief. She found the uncomfortable silence between them unbearable.

An ambulance screamed to a stop in front of the school just behind Molly and Arnie.

Molly noticed two teens huddled on a bench next to the front entrance. The boy was practically catatonic, although the girl seemed oddly composed. Next to them, Les Caulfield had a comforting arm around Rita John who was in shock.

"What happened?" Molly asked Les.

"Apparently these two students were rehearsing for *Romeo and Juliet*. When the girl tugged on a rope, it released the body hidden on a catwalk above the stage. The victim had a rope tied around her neck. The fall snapped it like a twig."

Another execution.

"Do we know who the victim was?" Molly feared hearing the answer.

"Sara Lapeen," Rita blurted. "The school's archivist."

Molly went pale.

"What is it?" Arnie asked, seeing her expression.

"I was with her this afternoon."

Rita turned and fixed her with an accusing glare. "What? You didn't clear it with me."

Molly shook her head. "I tried to, but you were in a meeting."

"I thought we had an understanding, Molly, that any requests for information would go through me."

Molly nodded.

"I'm surprised that Sara would even talk to you."

"Well, I think she had the idea that I'd spoken to you first."

Rita shook her head. "And you let her believe that?"

"I needed some quick answers."

"And did you get them?" Les asked.

"No, we couldn't find any of the files on Elsie Maranello."

Rita looked amazed. "Elsie Maranello? What's she got to do with any of this?"

"She came up in a related investigation."

Molly looked at Arnie, hoping he would step in.

Pissed off, Les turned to the sheriff.

"Arnie, what the hell is going on here? You told me she was good, the best you had, but instead of helping me with my investigation she keeps running off in all different directions. The special prosecutor is all over my ass about this."

Arnie sighed, looked at Molly, and then back at Les.

"Sorry, Les, I understand how you must feel, but I trust Molly's instincts on this and I'm standing behind her investigation. We've got five murders that all seem to lead back to this school. If Molly says she thinks they're related, then that's all I need. Until we catch whoever's doing this, it's her case to run any way she feels will get results."

"Well from what I hear, she won't be running anything after tomorrow. I'm going to speak to the special prosecutor about the lack of cooperation on the part of the county sheriff's department. Hopefully, the new sheriff will be more supportive."

It was never Molly's intention to give Les's investigation short shrift. He looked so weary and defeated. Molly wanted to apologize. Instead, she let Les Caulfield walk off in disgust.

SARA Lapeen's body was hanging from the lighting grid above the stage. Ronnie Kolmenn stared at it and shook his head. The coroner smiled weakly when Molly stepped up beside him and looked at the corpse.

"It's about time you got here."

"I know, you're tired of *hanging* around," Molly said with a chuckle.

"No. Actually, I was waiting so you could view the body in situ before we took it down."

Molly climbed the stairs to the stage and shone her flashlight on the body.

"Careful, there's urine."

Molly stopped and looked down at a yellow pool on the stage below the body.

On the catwalk above, Kurt snapped a picture. He looked down at Molly grimly.

"The dust has been disturbed. It looks as if the body was draped over the railing. When the girl pulled the rope ... " Kurt made a tumbling motion with his hands.

"From the angle of the neck, it was a clean break," Kolmenn observed.

Molly avoided looking at Sara Lapeen's horribly distorted face. Even though she hadn't liked Lapeen, or her haughty attitude, the fact that she'd been with the woman just hours before she was killed creeped Molly out.

Molly was convinced Lapeen had been covering up the location of the missing files and now she was afraid she'd never find them.

"Okay if we bring her down now?" Kolmenn asked as he rubbed his chin. "I'd like to get back to my warm bed. It looks like I'm going to have another busy day tomorrow."

To Molly, the coroner looked lost. Usually, Ronnie wouldn't even perform an autopsy a month, and now he'd done four in less than a week, with another to come tomorrow.

"You can take her down now."

The coroner nodded and waved to Kurt on the catwalk. He untied the rope holding Sara Lapeen and lowered her body to the stage.

Arnie pulled Molly aside, out of earshot of the others.

"This is a mess."

Molly's head throbbed just thinking about the case.

"I'll keep Les off your back for a day or two, but the school administrator is going to make a lot of noise. She's desperate to save this place, and if she can deflect some of this shit onto you, I think she will."

"I'll talk to her, Arnie. It's in the best interest of the school for all this stuff to come out."

Arnie looked around at the auditorium. His eyes stopped on the body now lying on the stage under a sheet.

"I think she's fighting a lost cause. This place is doomed."

ANOTHER *sleepless night.*

A carousel of clowns and victims swirled past Molly as she tried to put the pieces of the murders together. She rolled the elements of the crime over and over, but nothing fit.

The glowing numbers on the bedside clock flipped to 3:06 am.

It was officially Election Day. Molly couldn't shake the feeling that she'd blown it. Maybe it was for the best. The case would then become Kenton Sharpe's mess, and he had neither the skill or resolve to crack it.

Finally giving up on sleep, Molly went to the kitchen and put on a pot of coffee. She stared out the window while she waited for it to brew.

Her thoughts shifted from the case back to the election. On their way back to town from the school, Arnie had laid out the strategy for getting voters out. He assured her his campaign workers would do an excellent job on election day.

Molly hoped so because it was now out of her hands.

But in spite of his assurances that she would win, Arnie was angry with her. Molly kicked herself for barging into the Gavin Ricks case. At the same time, she cursed Arnie's stubbornness and his inability to look beyond his own obsession. She recognized that fifty years was a long time to carry the burden of the horror he'd witnessed that night, but that was no excuse for his tenacious behavior.

Molly regretted the rift the Ricks case had caused between them. She was going to have to apologize for not taking Arnie into her confidence in a situation he was deeply involved in. She didn't want their final days together in the department to be tense and formal. A lump was forming in her throat, and Molly was overcome with emotion. Today was truly the final day, no matter which way the election went.

Molly thought back to what Arnie had said about the school the previous evening.

Is it doomed?

The sexual molestation lawsuits would bankrupt the school, and rightly so. Those young men deserved amends for what their coach had done to them.

Molly agreed with Arnie. The Pine Academy was fated to die a humiliating death.

But none of the murder victims could be tied to the Akron lawsuits and the investigation into involvement by the school's board of directors. Delores Marsh and Sara Lapeen were at the school when Akron was there, but the other victims hadn't been involved with the school or its board for at least a generation. That meant there had to be something else that tied the victims together.

Molly sipped her coffee as she contemplated the possibilities. The brew was bitter, so she added more milk.

How do Elsie and June Maranello fit into this?

Their murders could be a coincidence, but Molly didn't believe in coincidences. They were like ghosts—they didn't exist.

There was, however, an intersection: Brighton, Barnard, and Vandermeer were on the board; Delores Marsh was the school's cook; and Sara Lapeen was a teacher.

All at the same time.

This juncture was hard for Molly to ignore.

What happened at the school during that period of time?

And what about the mysterious Dr. Blanic?

His tenure at the school, in addition to his previous relationship with Delores Marsh when they worked together at the same concentration camp, meant he was somehow tangled up in whatever had happened at the Pine Academy during the '50s and '60s.

Marsh's diaries had raved about 'subhumans' and the need to eradicate them. Maybe she and Blanic had participated in mass exterminations at Gross-Rosen and, by the time they arrived at the Pine Academy, they'd refined their racial theories and practices.

Jesus, that's a stretch!

But not out of the realm of possibility. Molly had read that forced sterilization was part of public health policy in the state of Michigan until the 1970s. She wondered how many of the school's students had been victims of this cruelty through the years. Molly felt sick just thinking about it.

Sara Lapeen had been somewhat cooperative the previous afternoon, until she'd overheard Molly asking Les about Dr. Blanic. After that, Lapeen's attitude changed.

Dr. Blanic?

Blanic certainly seemed to be at the center of the vortex, but was he the key?

Molly decided that finding out as much as she could about Blanic would be the first order of business in the morning.

THIRTY-FIVE

WHAT the fuck was going on?

Wes Chandler was still shaking with fear. The previous night he'd bounced around in the car's trunk for what seemed like hours before he felt the vehicle jerk to a stop. They dropped him on the ground like a sack of potatoes. Someone took off the handcuffs, and his hands burned as the circulation returned.

"Leave the hood on for ten minutes after we go."

The threatening voice scared the piss out of Chandler. He nodded frantically in agreement even though he was sure they couldn't see his head under the cowl. Then he lay on the ground as instructed until the roar of the car's engine had long faded. By then he guessed at least ten minutes had passed and he tugged off the hood with shaking fingers.

Skeletal hands reached out of the darkness. In a panic, Chandler slithered away from them until he realized they were just broken corn stalks. The air was thick with a loamy smell that reminded him of his uncle's pig farm. He got to his feet and looked around, trying to figure out where the hell he was.

The middle of fucking nowhere!

His feet were blocks of ice because whoever had jumped him had taken his shoes and socks. They'd also stolen his jacket and the frigid night air cut into him like a razor blade.

I'm gonna fucking freeze to death.

Chandler had no idea how late, or early, it was. He never wore a watch. He normally used his cell phone to tell him the time, but they had taken that too.

A voice inside his head told him it was time to move. As if to emphasize his thought, the moon slid from behind scuttling clouds to light his way. Chandler started to walk, careful not to step on the sharp edges of the corn stalks.

"Son of a fucking bitch," he muttered over and over as he trudged out of the field.

CHANDLER was exhausted when he finally reached a BP station. It was closed for the night, but miraculously a working pay phone was next to the front door.

He got Sammy Atkinson out of bed, which didn't make Atkinson happy at all. Atkinson swore and ordered Chandler to wait where he was. The frigid tone of Atkinson's voice made Chandler consider making a run for it, but he wouldn't get very far, and it would only piss off Atkinson even more.

"WHAT the fuck's going on?" Atkinson demanded as Chandler gratefully absorbed as much warm air as the pickup's heater could pump out.

Chandler stumbled through an explanation of what had happened and how he ended up in the middle of a corn field.

"That was pretty fucking stupid!" Atkinson growled.

"They got the jump on me," Chandler whined, "like they knew I was coming."

Atkinson gripped the steering wheel in an attempt to suppress his rising dread. A voice in his head told him to run while he still had the chance.

AFTER he dropped Chandler off at his house, Sammy Atkinson drove around for a little while trying to figure out what was going on. Wes Chandler may be stupid, but he was loyal and Atkinson didn't doubt that his story was true. That meant Boyle's mayor had friends watching out for him, maybe even some buddies from the service.

No, that sounds too much like a bad Bruce Willis movie.

Atkinson had another thought. Maybe the person behind this fuck up was Mead.

The old bastard's trying to prove he's still got it.

Atkinson thought back to their conversation on Mead's front porch. That son of a bitch had brought in some weight from outside to mess up Atkinson's plans. The old man was shrewd, you had to give him that.

Maybe Mead already had Gmerek in his back pocket, a thought that left Sammy Atkinson cold. If it were true, that would mean Mead might be tying up loose ends, and Sammy Atkinson was the loosest end of all—Atkinson knew way too much about Mead's business.

THE follower was five-hundred feet behind Sammy Atkinson's pickup truck.

He was an expert at not being seen, even on lonely country roads on a dark night like this. He'd mastered the art of invisibility, driving dark, his headlights and running lights turned off.

The only sound in the interior of the Chevy was the soft hum of the night-vision goggles he was wearing. The glasses gave him an uncanny look, like a praying mantis. The follower would like that analogy because he felt like a predator. Sammy Atkinson would never even know he was there. A second man in the car, also wearing night-vision glasses, remained silent. Between them on the bench seat were Wes Chandler's cell phone and his .44 magnum pistol.

KENTON Sharpe woke up on the morning of the election humming *It's a Beautiful Day in this Neighborhood*.

Sharpe was confident he was going to win. No question about it. He didn't need the polls to tell him this. He only needed Taylor Mead and his thugs.

Sharpe imagined they were already fanning out across the county ready to strategically harass and intimidate voters. Around breakfast time, thousands of citizens would receive robocalls informing them their polling stations had changed and directing them to voting booths miles away from where they lived. Sharpe smiled at the thought of all these voters saying "Fuck it" and not voting.

The previous day, many less-educated voters received an official-looking notice in the mail advising them the date of the election had been changed from Tuesday to Wednesday. And then there would be the concerned citizens acting as self-appointed poll watchers who would challenge certain voters to produce government-issued picture IDs.

I certainly do love the democratic process!

Sharpe lived alone in a small cabin on the east end of Granite Pond. His home, like his life, reflected his utter lack of passion for anything. The living room was decorated in a style that could only be described as early *Field and Stream*. Most of his furniture had been in the place when he bought it. Recently, he'd replaced a worn-out armchair with a new leather recliner. This was Sharpe's favorite throne. He spent most of his free time there with his feet up and a fresh tumbler of bourbon in hand.

Sharpe had consumed a dozen shots of the golden liquid the night before and felt somewhat fuzzy.

Hair of the dog.

As Sharpe headed to the kitchen to put the coffee on, he froze, realizing he wasn't alone.

Taylor Mead sat on a chair in the far corner of the room. Through the window behind him, Sharpe saw a couple of large goons he didn't recognize standing on the porch.

"Taylor. How are you? I was just about to make some coffee. Would you like some?" Kenton Sharpe's tone was a little too cheerful.

"I think it would be a clever idea to be there when the polls open this morning," Mead began. "It makes a good show for the press."

"Yeah, sure. I'll get dressed and go over there now."

Mead had the eyes of a cottonmouth, tiny black orbs sunk into deeply recessed sockets. Mead fixed them on Sharpe and flicked the tip of his tongue along his upper lip.

Sharpe found the old man's silence unnerving and rushed to fill the gap.

"Where's Sammy today? He and I usually talk first thing."

Mead regarded him like a side of beef being sized-up by a master butcher.

"He's out and about, I guess. Election Day you know."

Sharpe nodded nervously.

"After the debate the other night, I just want to be sure of our position with respect to each other. You may have an understanding with Sammy Atkinson and his brother, but I know that you realize your deal is with me."

Kenton Sharpe's head bobbed up and down. Taylor Mead's smile sent a chill down Sharpe's spine.

"It makes me nervous when I hear you've been making secret recordings."

Sharpe's right eyebrow twitched, but he managed to smile reassuringly.

"Well, as I explained to Sammy, that recording was only to derail Parsons's campaign. That bitch is a mess of trouble."

Sharpe waited anxiously for Taylor Mead's reaction, but Mead stayed silent. Finally, he fixed Kenton Sharpe with a frosty stare.

"I've gone a long way out on a limb for you, Kenton. I've made a sizable investment in your candidacy, and I expect that my faith in you will pay real dividends."

"You can certainly count on that, sir."

Mead's arthritic joints cracked as he stood up. Mead hid his pain well, but the sound of those creaking bones told Sharpe he most likely wouldn't be dealing with him much longer. Old age was going to do in Taylor Mead, if he lived long enough. Kenton Sharpe took comfort in this notion. Mead gave him the creeps.

"Thanks for your time, Kenton. Good luck at the polls today."

Taylor Mead opened the door and went onto the porch. The two goons fell into step on either side of Mead.

Sharpe, watching Mead walk stiffly to the car looking frail enough to blow away in a gentle breeze, smiled as he thought about the strong wind that was coming.

THIRTY-SIX

SIMON Wiesenthal Center information officer Avi Marcovitch sounded skeptical.

"We get a couple of calls a month like yours, Deputy," Marcovitch said. "If you give me a few minutes, I'll check the names against our database."

She gave Marcovitch both names—Martin Broder and Michael Blanic.

"I'm surprised that you still get calls about war criminals. Most of them would be dead now, right?"

"That's true," Avi Marcovitch grunted. Biology is taking its toll, but there are still a few around, and as long as there are ... Yes, we do have a case file on Martin Broder."

Molly detected awe in his voice.

"What year was he last seen in your town?"

"Around '69 or '70. He worked as a doctor in a state school here."

"Thank you. That information fills in a gap for us. There was no sighting of him since 1946 in Austria. We think he escaped Europe in a rat-line set up by the Spanish."

"A rat-line?"

"An escape network for fleeing Nazi war criminals. They were set up by sympathizers who provided escapees with false identities and passage to a safe destination."

"Like South America?"

"Yes, and other places. The Third Reich didn't die with Hitler."

"Can you track Blanic down?"

"I wouldn't hold out much hope of that, not after all this time. But having a name helps. It gives us somewhere to follow from. Who knows though, sometimes we get lucky."

"And if you were to locate him, what would happen then?"

"If he was still alive and living in the United States, we'd turn the information over to the Office of Special Investigations at the Justice Department. They'd handle the prosecution."

"And if he was found guilty?"

"His naturalization would be revoked and he'd be deported. Though by the time that process is finished, the bastards are usually dead of old age."

"What happens when they're all gone? Do you shut down your organization?"

"Not at all. We mostly focus on education these days. There's still plenty of anti-Semitism in the world to keep us busy. Unfortunately, hate never dies.

"If you give me a few hours, I'll run Blanic's name through our system and call you back. We might be able to find out what rock he crawled under."

Molly thanked Marcovitch for his help and wished him good luck, even though she thought the chance of finding anything was slim. Blanic was good at covering his tracks.

KURT Harbou came in early to run the evidence from the Sara Lapeen crime scene. He sipped green tea from a ceramic mug as he worked.

"Anything?"

Kurt looked up and nodded as Molly entered the crime lab.

"Looks like our clown again." Kurt pointed out a tiny white stain on the shoulder of the sweater Lapeen had been wearing.

"Damn," Molly sighed.

"There was nothing else on her clothes or shoes."

Molly picked up dog tags dangling from a chain.

"I ran it through the DoD database. It belonged to her husband. He was killed in Viet Nam in the '60s."

Molly examined the dog tags carefully. The aluminum had blackened with age, but as she turned it over, a glint caught her eye. Molly moved the dog tag under a stronger light and it sparkled again. A tiny line was scratched above the second digit of the serial number. She saw an identical scratch a few numbers over and then another.

Molly's heart began to race. This was no accident. Someone had deliberately marked the dog tag.

6—7—5?

What the hell did 675 signify? Molly turned the tag over again and saw smaller scratches below some of the other numbers as well.

0—9?

675 and 09?

What the hell is this?

Some sort of code? A combination?

"Can you look at these scratches under the glass for me?"

Molly handed the dog tag to Kurt. He slid it onto the platform of his scanning microscope and adjusted it until one of the scratches appeared on the screen. Then he dialed up higher resolutions until details of the mark appeared.

"It's deliberately made."

"How can you tell?"

"From the depth. Most scratches are from surface wear. Lapeen had this around her neck, so the chances of it getting scratched are slim. If I had to guess, I'd say the mark was engraved with a pin."

675 and 09?

Molly looked up at the sound of footsteps to see Arnie enter the room. She looked at him in surprise.

What the hell is Arnie doing in the crime lab!

Being an old-fashioned lawman who didn't subscribe to the cult of forensics, the sheriff had never set foot in here. In Arnie's opinion, too many crime shows had made people believe there was some magical technology that would solve every crime. Real life wasn't like that. There was no disputing that forensics played an important part in modern law enforcement, but most crime solving came down to diligent and determined investigation. Most criminals were just plain stupid and left a trail of evidence that even the Hardy Boys could follow.

"Did you get it?" Arnie asked Kurt brusquely.

Kurt walked to his desk and handed a report to Arnie. The sheriff scanned it carefully and his shrewd eyes narrowed.

"Thanks," he said to Kurt and left with out even acknowledging Molly.

Arnie was obviously still angry with her.

This must end now.

Molly followed Arnie down the hall and into his office.

"Arnie, I'm sorry. I never should've interfered with your case like that. I was way out of line and I apologize."

Arnie sat down and motioned for her to do the same. He pointed to the picture of Ray Allen, sheriff of Sunset County in the late 1950s. Allen was a fat man with small, squinty eyes who reminded Molly of an overweight version of George W. Bush.

"Ray Allen was the most corrupt man this county ever elected for sheriff. He shook down the helpless and took tons of graft from developers to look the other way."

Molly nodded. She'd heard the stories.

"He was involved with Linda Schiller, one of the dispatchers. A real looker. She was also married to one of the deputies, Justin Schiller. Can you believe that? A fat pig like Ray Allen messing with a man's wife right under his nose.

"Well, one day Justin cracked. He walked into Allen's office and shot him dead. Then Justin killed Linda and finally blew his own brains out. That was probably the worst day this department has ever seen."

Molly waited patiently for Arnie to make his point. Instead, he pushed a crime scene photo of Elsie Maranello in front of her. Maranello lay on her side, her head resting against the fridge.

"What do you see?"

She stared at the picture intensely. Elsie Maranello's head was turned away from the camera, so Molly couldn't see all her injuries clearly. The room was a mess with papers and furniture strewn around. Pieces of a shattered bottle were scattered around her legs.

"What's she wearing?" Arnie asked wearily. He was sick of looking at the picture.

"Slacks and a white blouse. Two-tone shoes."

"Ricks told me he'd passed out from drinking the night of the murders. That's a broken bottle of brandy by her legs. See the stain on the slacks?"

Molly saw a darkish blotch on the pant leg.

"She won the bottle in a raffle at the school. Elsie didn't drink brandy, but Ricks did and it knocked him out.

"I had Kurt run a test on the slacks. They've been sitting in an evidence box for fifty years, but he was still able to detect chloral hydrate in the fibers."

"A Mickey Finn?"

"Yup."

"I believe someone deliberately knocked Ricks out with it and then murdered Elsie and June. Being dosed with chloral hydrate leaves the victim disoriented. Ricks likely came to and discovered Elsie and the baby were dead and figured he'd done it in a drunken rage. He's believed it all these years. And so have I."

Molly worked at processing this new information. If Gavin Ricks hadn't done it, then who had? Who would be that heartless? Who would kill an innocent woman and child in such a horrible way?

Blanic!

The doctor's name came to Molly in a flash. She thought of the death camps and then later the Pine Academy.

All those dead children.

Molly filled Arnie in on what she'd learned about the doctor. When she finished, he shook his head, perplexed.

"It doesn't make any sense. Blanic flees Europe after the war and ends up here working in a school. Even if he was performing forced sterilizations on the children there, it was most likely state-sanctioned.

"I know," she agreed. "It's something darker than that. I can feel it. Sara Lapeen was deliberately hiding Elsie Maranello's files."

"You think there was something in there?"

"Yes, and I think it got Elsie and June killed. I also believe it's the key to the other murders as well. Arnie, I need your help to get a look at the files at the school."

"I'm not sure I can get the school to cooperate. The administrator is really pissed with you."

"She's only trying to shield the school from more scandal. I'll talk to her."

"Okay. I'll speak to Les Caulfield and the special prosecutor. And I'll talk to the DA about Ricks as well and let him know new evidence has surfaced."

Molly knew it had taken a lot for Arnie to admit he'd been wrong about Gavin Ricks.

"Molly, you were right. I did let my feelings get in the way of my better judgment. I was so poisoned by hatred that I almost railroaded an innocent man to jail for the rest of his life. I owe you a debt of gratitude." Arnie's eyes teared up. "No matter what happens at the polls today, I can't think of a better person to sit in this chair."

He looked over at Ray Allen's picture on the wall again and shook his head in disgust.

"Kenton Sharpe makes Ray Allen look like Wyatt Earp."

Molly didn't have time to think about that. She needed to drive to the Pine Academy and persuade Rita to let her into the file room.

MOLLY drove past the polling station on the way out of town. She was tempted to stop and cast her ballot. Kenton Sharpe had been on the morning news—first in line at the polling station, waving his ballot high in the air like it was a victory laurel.

There would be plenty of time to vote later, right now she had to see those files.

THIRTY-SEVEN

THE clown woke in a fever, the remnants of a bad dream rattling around inside his skull.

In his nightmare, the clown's baby sister Darcie was smiling sweetly, her eyes filled with innocent wonder. The clown squeezed back tears at the memory and tried to drive it away.

But he couldn't, and it overwhelmed him.

Darcie crying in terror during a violent electrical storm …

Darcie tearfully holding a piece of shattered robin's egg …

Darcie filled with delight at what Santa had brought her …

Darcie tenderly cradling the newborn she'd been allowed to hold, cooing out a tuneless lullaby to "baby Junetie" …

Darcie who would never get any older than this precious little girl in his dream …

Darcie who needed to be protected from the awful things …

Darcie who had been taken away by an evil Harlequin …

Sweet Darcie who he never saw again.

In the early morning light, the clown choked back tears and swore on her soul that it would soon be over.

He would wash all the crimes away.

RITA John was surprised to see Molly Parsons standing in the hallway outside her office when she arrived for work.

"Molly, whatever it is you want, you can speak to our lawyers. I'll give you their number."

Molly admired Rita's steely resolve.

"Rita, could we talk? Please." Molly didn't have to work at sounding contrite.

Rita ignored Molly and walked into her office, slamming the door behind her. Molly stood in the hallway for a few minutes before she knocked softly on Rita's office door.

The school's administrator didn't answer.

Molly rapped again.

"Please, Rita."

"Go away," Rita replied bitterly.

"I need to look inside one box in the archives. It's important."

"Like I said, talk to our lawyers about it."

Rita was immovable. Desperately Molly tried a different tack.

"Okay, why don't you look inside the box yourself and decide. It's number 675 on shelf 9."

There was silence from the other side of the door.

"Please leave immediately," Rita's muffled voice responded.

"Box 675, shelf 9 ... box 675, shelf 9. Go look for yourself."

Silence.

Molly curbed the impulse to smash the door in and drag Rita down the hall to the storeroom. Then Rita would see for herself and hopefully believe.

Molly stood with her hands clenched at her side waiting, but there was no sound from the office. Finally, frustrated and afraid of what she might do, Molly stalked to the front entrance of the school. She paused, gazing at the long line of people waiting to vote. Molly considered going back to Rita's office to make one final try. Instead, she walked out to her cruiser and headed back to Sunset.

Fuck it. It's time to vote.

RITA John sat gripping a pencil. She tapped the eraser on the leather desk pad.

Box 675, shelf 9.

Rita continued to stare at the door wondering if Molly was still in the hallway. The desperation in Molly's voice had disturbed her.

Rita considered Molly's situation.

Is she using her investigation as a ploy to get elected?

Rita wouldn't put it past her. The woman had no shame. Molly was only looking for another way to discredit the school, to bring more disgrace to them.

For the thousandth time, Rita cursed Gregory Akron and her predecessors who had looked the other way while the coach had committed terrible crimes.

Saving the school was hopeless. She wasn't going to save this place. There were too many secrets still buried here.

Box 675, shelf 9.

Rita John threw her pencil across the office and grabbed the phone.

MOLLY dropped by to see Les Caulfield on her way out of town. She realized she needed to do some repair work if she had any hope of salvaging their relationship.

Les didn't look up from his laptop when she entered the conference room. Molly noticed the boxes she'd brought from the school were still neatly stacked along one wall. It was apparent they had not been opened.

Molly awkwardly faced Les.

"Les, I just wanted to apologize."

He nodded, his gaze fixed on the computer screen.

"Arnie called me first thing and already did that for you."

"That was good of him, but I need to make my own apologies. I abandoned you. I know this investigation is necessary, and if there's anything I can do to make amends, please let me."

"Molly, I got out of bed this morning and could hardly move from the pain."

She started to respond, but he held up his hand.

"I don't want sympathy. Ever since that drunken bastard ran into me, my career's been on borrowed time. I should've been pensioned off already, but I wanted to finish on a high note. This investigation might bring closure to a bunch of innocent kids who Gregory Akron was allowed to soil. He was protected, Molly, by the bastards who should have been protecting those students. And for what? So that the school could win some basketball games. That seems like a good reason to let a monster to prey on children, doesn't it?"

Les was hurting, both physically and emotionally. Molly felt bad she hadn't been able to help him more.

"Because of your actions, I now have to apply for a new subpoena for every piece of evidence. It's going to set me back by months."

"Les, I ... I don't know what to say."

He shook his head. "It's going to give them more time to anticipate the charges and for the bastards to prepare their defense. And I guarantee that when we do get into court, it won't be pleasant. Those boys are going to be raped all over again on the stand in the name of justice.

"That school's been an evil place for a long time, and I suspect it's going to continue to be."

Molly didn't know how to respond. Instead, she walked to the wall and began to stack the boxes one on top of the other.

"I'll take these back to the school."

"Do whatever you like," Les replied without emotion.

LES Caulfield was right, Molly reflected as she drove back to Sunset. Pine Academy *had* been an evil place for a long time. For almost a century, the school had humiliated and brutalized the children who had passed through its doors. The people who were supposed to protect the children had ignored them and instead had protected the monsters who abused them.

Rita should be commended for her efforts to turn the place into what it should have been in the first place—a safe haven for children.

But it was too late for that. There had been too much evil, too many victims.

Molly thought about Dr. Blanic. The Academy had allowed him to continue his twisted, racist eugenic experiments.

What else were you up to, Doctor?

Molly was confident there was something in Elsie Maranello's notes that would give her a clue.

She was still considering what Elsie's notes might reveal when her cell phone rang. It was Avi Marcovitch from the Wiesenthal Center.

"Deputy Parsons?"

"Please call me Molly."

"Okay, Molly. Our researchers were able to run down some more information on Dr. Blanic."

"You work fast."

"We have to. Anyway, after Blanic was dismissed from Pine Academy, he found work as a doctor in a prison in Oregon. He retired from there in 2004."

"Where is he now?"

"Dead. From natural causes in 2009. We're waiting to hear back from our contacts in Eugene to confirm this, but the information is reliable."

The biological clock really was working against them.

"Thanks very much for your help, Mr. Marcovitch."

"Not at all. I should thank you, Molly. We can cross another one of these bastards off our list."

Molly smiled weakly, taking little consolation from his words.

"Can I ask you something else?"

"Sure."

"When I first mentioned Dr. Blanic ... Broder, you sounded a bit in awe. Was I wrong about that?"

"No, not at all. Dr. Broder worked at the Gross-Rosen camp. We have a particular interest in that camp because it was one of the ones that Simon Wiesenthal was interred in."

"I see."

"Thanks again, Molly."

"Could I ask another question? I want to know if you've ever heard anything about a clown leading children to the gas chambers?"

She thought of Delores Marsh.

"It's a myth. There was a Jerry Lewis movie about a clown who did that."

"God, it sounds really horrible."

"Apparently it was so awful the film company never released it. Anyway, the Nazis didn't need clowns to lead the way to the gas chambers, they had guns."

"Sorry."

"No, it's an important part of what we do here. We separate out myths from reality and educate about the consequences of lies."

THIRTY-EIGHT

MOLLY'S polling station was at the main branch of the Sunset library.

The line stretched out the front door, and Molly admired all the people waiting patiently in the cold drizzle. As cynical as she was about most things political, the sight of voters standing in line to exercise their democratic right never failed to inspire her.

Molly went to the back of the line.

"Hi, Molly."

She felt a clap on her back and turned to greet Hank Summerville. He moved his umbrella to cover her head. Jennie and Andrzej stood with him. Andrzej held an umbrella protectively over Jennie.

"Andy, are you looking forward to being able vote?" Molly asked Andrzej.

He smiled proudly and nodded. "Maybe by next election, Molly, I am American citizen."

Molly hoped so. It was a long, arduous grind for an immigrant to gain citizenship. But Andrzej desperately wanted to greet his newborn as an American. From the size of Jennie's belly, however, Molly thought he was going to run out of time.

They chatted while the line crawled along. Finally, they were inside the building, now uncomfortably humid from the damp bodies passing through. Molly's thoughts morbidly turned to concentration camp prisoners lined up waiting patiently for their turn to be gassed. It was a vision that made what they were doing here today all the more meaningful.

When her turn came, Molly looked down at the ballot in the voting booth. She flipped the switches next to candidates' names for various offices. Molly knew many of them personally. When she got to **Sheriff** on the ballot and saw her name, she paused before flipping the switch next to it.

Done!

Molly took her ballot to the registrar. She'd known Brenda Kramer since elementary school.

"Just put it in the box, Molly," Brenda said with a smile

Molly returned Brenda's smile and pushed the folded ballot into the slot on top of the box.

At the sound of loud voices coming from across the room, Molly turned to see a burly man being escorted from the library by a security guard. An angry man holding a clipboard was speaking to a woman in her late seventies.

"It's been like that all morning," Brenda said.

"What's going on?"

"They won't say, but that fellow with the clipboard is from the state elections commission. The other man is some thug they sent up here to try to challenge people's right to vote. They aren't very subtle about it, though."

Molly had an excellent idea who "they" were.

So, it's a knife fight then.

Molly watched the door close behind the burly man.

RITA John sat through the lunch hour absorbed in her thoughts. Gregory Akron had been allowed to perpetrate his crimes because the school had looked the other way. She imagined the board of directors and the administrator had justified their actions as "for the sake of the school." The board members of the and the administration had deluded themselves into thinking they were protecting this institution.

Am I doing the same thing?

A distant throbbing in her temples warned Rita a migraine was on its way.

Jesus, not now!

Rita inhaled and slowly released her breath. The spring inside her released some of its tension as she continued to breathe methodically until the pain receded.

Box 675, shelf 9.

Rita had written the information on a slip of paper. Her hand shook as she picked it up.

THE heavy box left a thin line of dust on Rita's blouse. She barely noticed it as she peeled away the dried-out packing tape sealing the carton. When she was done, Rita studied the box. To all appearances, it was just another banker's box. The number 675 had been printed on one end. From the amount of dust on the lid, the carton hadn't been touched in a long, long, time. It reminded Rita of a coffin inside a mausoleum.

Just leave it alone. Put it back.

Finally, like Pandora, Rita lifted the lid expecting something evil to fly out and consume her. She sighed in relief when she saw the box was only filled with discolored file folders.

Rita riffled the folders like a blackjack dealer. The papers inside— ledger sheets and budget reports from the 1930s—were yellow and fragile, the edges flaking away. She dug deeper into the carton and discovered newer folders near the bottom. And teachers' day books.

Rita stiffened as she stared at the writing on the cover of one of the books—Elsie Maranello.

Under the day book was Elsie Maranello's personnel file. Rita gripped the documents like they were religious icons. She set them reverently aside and continued to root through the box, adding more documents to the neat pile next to the carton. When she finished, Rita began to read.

The documents were mostly routine, the mundane detritus of any teacher's career. She recognized the same terminology she had used over the years when evaluating teachers. Rita suppressed a smile as she read some of the comments.

No, nothing's changed all.

As she worked her way through the material, Rita's dread rose. The comments had stopped being tedious and ordinary. Toward the bottom of the pile was a series of pointed memos from Elsie Maranello to the head administrator of the school. They'd been written in an ordered script, the kind of neat handwriting developed over many years of teaching cursive. The neatness of the writing contrasted with the horror of the words.

Rita sat back in her chair. Stunned and sickened, she was on the verge of tears. She stifled a sob and immediately transformed her grief into fury.

Rita yanked open her desk drawer and searched for Molly Parsons's business card.

AFTER voting, Hank had urged Molly to come back to The Villager for lunch. He poured them both a glass of wine and toasted her 'victory.'

"It was going to be a surprise, Molly, but what the heck … We're planning a victory party for you here tonight. I'm going to close early and we've invited a bunch of friends and supporters."

Molly smiled, touched by Hank's gesture.

"I hope we have something to celebrate."

"You think a few goons are gonna make a difference? Sharpe is a lying weasel. Everyone knows that. You may not believe it, but people really appreciate what you've done for this town. Arnie made an excellent choice when he nominated you."

Did he?

She flashed back to Les Caulfield. His bitter rebuke that morning had gotten under her skin. Molly detested the hurt she saw in Les's eyes.

"Molly!"

She looked up to see Colin Ricks walking toward her. He offered his hand and she shook it.

"Thank you so much."

Arnie had spoken to the DA about the new evidence they'd discovered. He'd asked that they move for bail for Gavin Ricks, with a possibility the charges would be dismissed.

"When's your dad getting out?"

"This afternoon. The DA asked for a special hearing."

"I'm happy for him. How's he doing?"

"He's relieved."

"I can't imagine what it must've been like dragging that kind of guilt around for fifty years."

Colin Ricks declined Molly's invitation to join her for lunch. He wanted to pick up some fresh clothes for his father.

"Another happy ending," Hank observed.

"Maybe."

Molly thought about the Pine Academy's dark history. There would be no happy ending there.

She nibbled at her sandwich pensively and finally pushed it away. Hank looked sternly at the half-eaten sandwich and Molly shot him a meek smile.

"Sorry, Hank. Nerves about the election."

Molly had the uncomfortable foreboding that once this cycle of murders was finished, the killer would be impossible to catch. This clown would likely disappear back into the woodwork.

I'll be damned if I'm going to let that happen.

GAVIN Ricks was released on bail. As soon as the hearing was over, his son hustled him from the building into a waiting Lincoln Navigator and drove off.

Arnie stood in the doorway of his office. Molly had a tough time reading the expression on his face.

"So?"

"Redemption," he replied softly.

231

This must be terrible for him.

Arnie had been tormented by the murders of Elsie and June Maranello for all this time and just when he thought there was going to be closure, it was torn away. She felt a small stab of guilt over the part she had played, but there was no justice in convicting an innocent man. And Molly was convinced that Gavin Ricks was blameless in the double murder.

"So, what now?"

Arnie turned to Molly with a forlorn smile. "We find the real killer."

MOLLY rarely closed her office door. But when she did, the closed door sent a clear message to everyone that she wasn't to be disturbed. Even Arnie kept away when her door was shut. She also forwarded her phone to the switchboard so she could focus on the murders.

Molly crossed her hands on the top of her desk and lay her head down on them while the case bounced around in her brain like a pinball. She inhaled slowly, focusing on the simple act of breathing. Finally she exhaled in a long rush of breath that cleared her mind. The frantic jumble in her head began to recede and was replaced with a serene clarity.

Molly felt like she'd left her body and was free-floating among the facts she'd collected. Each was in its own little compartment and she was among them, turning them over slowly and re-examining each one from a different angle.

Three members of the board ...

A cook ...

A teacher ...

A teacher and her child ...

The doctor ...

Forced sterilization ...

Students ...

1967 ...

"I could never figure it out ... "

Jesus!

A cold steel core had formed in her stomach and a sickening realization flooded through her.

Don't jump to conclusions.

A knock on her office door startled Molly.

"Sorry to bother you, Molly," said Blyth Simmons, the department's head dispatcher, "but there's a Rita John on the phone. She sounds really upset."

Molly looked at the blinking light on her desk phone for a moment before she picked up the receiver.

"Molly, I found the file. You need to see it."

The flat tone of Rita's voice chilled Molly to the bone.

"I'll be there as quick as I can."

THIRTY-NINE

KENTON Sharpe knocked back his fourth shot of bourbon.

The drinks were doing nothing to calm him down after Taylor Mead's unexpected visit. Sharpe considered calling Sammy Atkinson and pleading to get out of their arrangement, but it was too late for that. He'd sold his soul to the wrong devil. This one would definitely have his due.

Sharpe considered what options he had, but there were no really viable ones. There wasn't enough cash in his offshore account to provide a decent standard of living for very long if he ran now. But did he have a choice? Whoever had made that recording knew all about his agreement with Atkinson and Mead. If he tried to run, those two would track him down and feed him into a wood chipper just to keep him quiet.

Sharpe knew the best scenario was to lose the election and then just disappear. But that wasn't going to happen either with Mead and Atkinson bringing all their muscle to the polls. His campaign had the benefit of the best machine that corrupt money could buy.

Kenton Sharpe poured himself another drink and contemplated just how fucked he was.

THE rats were abandoning the ship, or at least one rat was.

After Sammy Atkinson had dropped him off near the center of town, Wes Chandler decided it was time to run as fast and as far as he could. But it turned out flight wasn't going to be quite that easy. When Chandler returned to the spot where he'd parked his car the night before, it was gone. That scared him into action, and he used most of his cash to buy a one-way ticket to Motor City.

The bus left at noon and so far the journey was maddeningly slow, stopping at every crossroad in the county. By 1:30 the Greyhound had only reached Sunset. The driver announced they would be stopping for fifteen minutes. Wes Chandler tapped his fingers tensely on the armrest. Finally, to settle his nerves, he went across the street to the diner and ordered a coffee to go. He asked to use the washroom.

"Restroom back there," the old man behind the counter said in broken English.

Greek. All the diners are owned by Greeks these days.

A few minutes later he came out of the bathroom and found a large man blocking his way.

"Hello, Wes."

Chandler recognized the voice from the night before and turned quickly to make a run for it. His escape route was blocked by another large man, both stamped from the same mold.

"What's your hurry, Wes?"

The first man twisted him around and pinned his arms behind his back. Chandler felt cold steel against his skin as a pair of handcuffs were snapped on his wrists. Before he could even open his mouth to protest, he was hustled through the kitchen and out the back door into the alley behind the diner.

JEFF Cunningham was just coming on-shift. Molly caught up with him in the squad room.

"I need you to do me a favor."

"Sure," he replied, happy to delay his patrol by a few minutes.

"Can you go down to records and pull the jacket on Davy Snider?"

She told him what she was looking for and Jeff nodded. He headed for the file room with determined urgency.

Then Molly called Kurt Harbou in the forensics lab.

"Hey, did you manage to get a cast of those tread marks the other day?" Molly asked, thinking of the accident scene on the county road.

"Yeah, the ground was wet and the vehicle must have been sitting there for a while."

"Anything distinguishing?"

"Yes, ma'am. The left front tire. There was a notch in the outer tread like a piece of it had been gouged. Probably hit a piece of metal on the road. Why?"

"Because I think I know where we can find a match."

"Really?"

When she told him where to look, he couldn't believe it.

"Be careful and take Jeff with you for backup. If there's any chance you might be discovered, don't take the risk." Molly added with a smile, "After all, I don't want to screw up your wedding plans."

THE rain turned into plump snowflakes as Molly drove north toward Pine. The temperature had dropped steadily during the afternoon and now hovered around zero making the roads slick. She had to cut her speed or risk skidding off the road.

It was nearly dark by the time Molly reached the Pine Academy. Rita John stood by the front door haloed in light. Her sunken eyes were red-rimmed. Without saying a word, Rita led Molly to her office. Classes had ended for the day, and the hallways were dimly lit and foreboding.

"Why did you change your mind?"

"You were right. The school did try to get Elsie to stay quiet about it, but she was determined to go to the authorities." Rita's voice was emotionless. "I think that's what led to her death."

"How many?"

Rita looked at Molly in surprise. "At least twenty, maybe more."

"I need a list of the names."

Rita opened her desk, took out a piece of personalized stationery, and handed it to Molly.

236

Molly scanned the list to see if any names were familiar. They weren't.

"Do you believe in evil, Molly?"

Most cops believed in evil after they'd been on the job for a while and it was a question Molly had considered from time to time, especially since she'd had a strict religious upbringing. Her father had been an itinerant preacher who only saw the world in absolutes of sin and salvation. So to Molly, evil was a biblical concept and implied some sort of underlying mystical influence.

But we humans can't get off that easy.

You don't get to pass the buck to some supernatural force that makes people do evil. Molly believed people *chose* to do horrific things and justified it by refusing to think of their actions as bad.

She thought of Dr. Blanic and Delores Marsh. They had deluded themselves into thinking they were doing something good by helping to cleanse the Aryan race of impurity when they worked at the Nazi death camp.

"What does it matter anyway? We don't have any proof," Rita said sadly. "There's no one left to testify about what happened. They're all dead now."

Rita was right. The clown had seen to that.

"I need to get a look at the student files from that time period," Molly said.

"Sure, but you already have them. You took them with the fingerprint cards."

The boxes—they're still in the trunk!

"I'll get them. Would you help me look through them?"

Rita agreed and said, "But they were children. They wouldn't have known what was going on here."

"One of them did," Molly said quietly.

Damn that woman!

The clown watched as Molly walked briskly out of the school. She opened the trunk of her cruiser and started lifting out file boxes.

This wasn't part of the plan. The plan was to bring all this to an end, to cleanse this place once and for all. The clown considered what to do next. It had taken a long time to get to this point. A little more patience would be required.

The clown retreated into the darkness still clutching his instruments of purification—a road flare and a red plastic container of gasoline.

FORTY

TAYLOR Mead liked using brothers as bodyguards.

The Cotter twins, his most recent bodyguards, stoically bracketed his front door. Harlan and Don Cotter were as dumb as maple trees but they knew how to obey orders.

Not like the Atkinsons.

Mead was convinced Sammy and Tommy had turned against him, a feeling reinforced after his visit to Kenton Sharpe. Once upon a time, the Atkinsons had been like the Cotters—a pair of biker thugs you could point at problems. But a touch of the high life and a little bit of respectability had turned the brothers into a big problem.

Sharpe was lying, and Mead wondered what kind of a deal he'd made with the Atkinsons.

A problem the Cotter twins will have to handle.

It was a familiar story. Mead had seen it all before. Give the hired help a tiny taste and the next thing you know they want it all.

Mead understood. He'd felt the same way himself when he worked for an old-time mob boss in Cleveland a long time ago. He thought about killing that angry old fuck but knew if he did, the entire organization would've come after his ass. So instead, Taylor Mead started his own thing hundreds of miles away from his boss in a region the bastard wouldn't consider a threat.

The tiny town of Boyle, Michigan, had been good to him. By the time Taylor Mead arrived, Boyle was already known as the place to score high-quality meth and was ripe for the picking. The drug trade was chaotic and disorganized. But the product was superb, which was a miracle considering it was cooked up by a disparate group of hillbillies spread throughout the woods surrounding the town.

Taking his leave with the blessing of the Cleveland mob, Mead arrived in Boyle promising prosperity and order. Mead saw that his best opportunity was to lock up the town as a distribution center because the cookers were struggling to get their product to markets around the country.

Mead had a plan. He bought an old warehouse on the edge of town and created Valu-Rama, a gigantic liquidation business. Mead bought up excess stock from bankrupt companies for pennies on the dollar and sold them for a fraction of their original cost. The store was an immediate hit and soon became a 'destination' for bargain-hungry shoppers from all over the Midwest.

This meant trucks, lots and lots of them—big and small—all coming and going from his warehouse. He rented most of the trucks from a company that was a front for the Satan Stompers biker gang in Traverse City.

Mead particularly kept an out eye out for drugstore bankruptcies and snapped up a lot of bargain Sudafed, which contained the key ingredient amateur chemists used to make crystal meth.

Taylor Mead bought cheap and sold high. And got rich.

It wasn't a surprise the Atkinsons were making a play. They saw Mead as a weak old man who was past his best before date. Mead needed to show them his claws.

Mead had only one nagging concern today. There wasn't much information coming back from his 'campaign workers' who had spread out across the county that morning. He could keep Kenton Sharpe happy and content as long as he could get him elected.

It had been a lucky break for him that the current sheriff didn't appear interested in what was going on in Boyle. Mead figured Voxx stayed out of their business so he could protect the aunt who lived just outside of town.

What will happen if that Parsons woman gets elected?

From everything Taylor Mead understood about her, Molly Parsons would be a formidable enemy. He had no illusions that she wouldn't unleash the dogs on him and his empire. It would leave him with few options. The most pragmatic one would be to take his money and run.

Mead knew he could live comfortably for the rest of his life somewhere where he couldn't be extradited, but the prospect of leaving was unpalatable for him. That left him with one alternative—something bad would have to happen to Molly Parsons.

KURT came back to the cruiser where Deputy Jeff Cunningham was waiting. "It wasn't there."

Jeff put the car in gear and they drove off.

"I'm almost glad it wasn't," Kurt said. "I'm having a tough time wrapping my head around this."

Jeff tapped a folder on the seat beside him. "Take a look in here."

Kurt picked the thin file labeled **Davy Snider**. He opened it and started to read. A few minutes later he put it down in awe.

"Jesus!" he gasped. "What the hell is Molly doing?"

"More importantly," Jeff added, "what are we going to do about it?"

IT was after 9:00 and the night air was biting into the clown as he continued to watch the dark and quiet school. The simmering resentment about Molly's interference grew into full-blown rage.

A voice in the clown's head screamed, "It's time! It's time! It's time!"

Unable to contain his fury any longer, the clown rose on stiff legs and picked up the can of gasoline.

If she gets in the way, it will just be too fucking bad.

The clown headed toward the school.

It ends now.

THEY'D spread the files out on the desk and couch in Rita's office to cross-reference the list of students who died and had come up short.

"We need more," Molly told Rita.

"I don't know if there is anymore." Rita got up from her chair and rubbed her eyes. "Let's go take another look."

Rita led the way down the corridor and unlocked the storeroom. Molly was surprised that it was already dark outside. It had to be after 7:00. She reached for her phone to check the time and realized she'd left it in her purse which was in Rita's office.

The polls would probably be closing soon and her fate would be decided in the next three hours or so. Molly followed Rita into the darkened storeroom.

THE hallway was dim and empty. The clown carefully pushed down on the bar to open one of the side doors. It wasn't locked.

Great security considering what happened here last night.

The clown moved silently down the corridor imagining Darcie was watching. Maybe she was wearing that adorable grin that made everyone love her.

The heavy can of gas gave off a faintly sweet odor.

Fire will be the final act of purification and will wipe away the evil of this place forever.

He prayed his sister would understand what he was doing, that this cleansing act was for her and all the other children who had suffered here.

Although Dr. Blanic was now out of reach, robbed of his rightful punishment by a peaceful death, the others had been eradicated like the disease they were.

Well, nearly all …

Now, finally, this place would be reduced to ash and buried.

The clown's shoulder erupted in pain and he set the gas can down.

Maybe I should drag it along the corridor. No, that would make too much noise.

He muttered a curse softly and picked up the can again, wincing at the ache in his shoulder. He regretted filling such a large container, but wanted to make certain he had enough fuel to finish the job, to purge the evil and sanctify the innocent.

Rita and Molly were in the school and that was good—Molly had been digging around, and would have learned the school's darkest secrets. If only Molly hadn't been so curious. And now, she'd involved Rita. He felt sorry for both of them, but there was no other way, they would burn along with the rest of this evil place.

The clown kept struggling down the corridor hauling the heavy can until he heard faint voices. He continued toward the sound, listening carefully as it grew louder. He paused outside the file room door. Now he knew where Molly and Rita were.

The hallway swirled in front of him as other, higher, voices floated around him. He recognized his sister's voice among them. The clown squeezed back tears.

"Soon …," he whispered, "soon."

IN the storeroom, Molly and Rita leaned over the desk and sorted through file folders.

Rita looked like she was going to be sick to her stomach. Molly tried to keep her usual clinical cop's demeanor but couldn't. The enormity of what these benign looking tan folders contained overwhelmed her.

The horror of what had happened here washed over Molly and unleashed repressed feelings of grief and anger at the senselessness of what she'd experienced in her years of law enforcement—a tragic litany of drunken car crashes, brutal beatings, random destruction, and the theft of everything precious to the innocent.

She was always led to a single question: How could anyone do something like this?

Because we're so good at justifying our own dark impulses.

Molly and Rita turned as the stockroom door opened with an ominous creak. Molly moved toward the open door but fell back as the clown stepped into the light. Behind her, Rita gasped in horror.

With a contemptuous red smile on his painted white face, the clown's visage was something out of a nightmare.

The clown advanced slowly into the room and Molly desperately looked for something to use as a weapon.

Why did I leave my phone and gun in Rita's office!

The clown's massive hand shot out and grabbed Molly by the throat. He dragged her closer until his terrifying face was only inches from hers. The strong odor of greasepaint—along with something more primordial, like air escaping from an ancient swamp—filled her nostrils as she desperately strained to get a glimpse of the person beneath the makeup.

The clown's jaundiced eyes glittered in the feeble light and his crimson smile widened. Madness radiated from the clown as he lifted Molly and threw her backward. She banged into a shelf and went down hard, blacking out for a few seconds.

When Molly came to, Rita was screaming and the clown had disappeared. She tried to make sense of what was happening, but the blow to the back of her head scrambled her thoughts.

The door slammed shut with a crash that reverberated through the room. Rita ran to the door and tried the knob. There was a loud click from the other side as the deadbolt slid home. She pulled at the door frantically but it wouldn't budge.

Molly staggered to her feet, the room whirling around her. Rita jumped back from the door as a liquid seeped under it. The dry mustiness of the stockroom was cut with the smell of gas as it flowed in a widening pool under the door.

"We have to get to the back," Molly said weakly.

A faint whoosh came from the corridor then blue flames crawled under the door and exploded in a brilliant flash that knocked them off their feet.

"Is there a back door?" Molly yelled over the roar of the fire.

Panic overwhelmed Rita and she screamed, "No!"

The room, illuminated by the growing blaze, was not that large. Molly and Rita were trapped in a tinder-dry forest of boxes. Flames were already consuming the file boxes near the front. Thick smoke crept along the ceiling and reached downward to devour them.

"Is there a phone?"

Rita pointed to the table by the door. It was burning intensely and the old-fashioned dial phone had melted into a pool of black plastic.

They huddled against the back wall of the room, watching in terror as box after box burst into flames.

The room was quickly filling with noxious fumes.

"Breathe shallowly," Molly said as she pulled Rita down to the floor where there was still a little precious oxygen.

HEAT and smoke set off the school's sprinkler system and water cascaded down from the ceiling. The clown hesitated at the entrance to the school as drops of white makeup rain down his face, staining his colorful costume. Silhouetted against the raging inferno, he danced in glee.

As the clown ran out the side door, the hallway exploded into flames behind him. He fell to his knees on the lawn and sucked in the cool night air. Turning his grotesquely streaked face to the heavens, the clown let out a bellow that was half laughter and half pain.

The deed has been done!

FORTY-ONE

"JESUS Christ!" Kurt Harbou screamed.

He sat beside Deputy Jeff Cunningham as Jeff raced his cruiser up the driveway to the Pine Academy.

Jeff wasn't sure what Kurt was reacting to—the sight of a clown running from the building, or the conflagration that had engulfed the front of the school.

Through the glass entrance doors, they could see fire rolling down the corridor and shooting across the ceiling. Parts of the building were wood-frame, and Jeff figured the entire structure would be gone in a matter of minutes.

With shrieking alarms audible all over the school's campus, Jeff was certain the fire department was already on the way but called it in anyway.

Jeff considered pursuing the fleeing clown who'd disappeared into the trees near the road.

"Molly!" Kurt shouted as he pointed to her car parked next to the school's entrance.

Jeff slammed the cruiser into the curb in front of the building.

A crowd of students had been evacuated to a safe distance on the lawn. Jeff frantically searched the crowd for Molly.

"Where the hell is she, Kurt?"

Kurt shook his head. They shared a look and without another word ran to the front door. A wave of heat enveloped them as Jeff kicked open the door and he and Kurt dashed inside. Kurt looked into the wall of flame.

We're too late!

MOLLY felt surreal, floating discorporate above the scene.

So this is what it's like to die.

On the floor next to her, Rita was gasping for breath. Molly reached through the smoke and pushed the administrator's head down.

"Keep your nose to the floor," Molly said, her voice strangled by phlegm.

Molly didn't know whether or not Rita had heard her. It really didn't matter at this point. The smoke was already killing them. Her head throbbed painfully, and she lost focus. She was staring across a vast expanse of space, barely conscious, trying to hold onto life. Molly's mind swam with images from the past.

Her father holding his worn bible aloft.

Steve, her late husband, smiling lovingly.

Her mother crying in the dark.

Friends mourning her loss.

Arnie Voxx standing over her grave.

Molly knew her life was now down to the last few seconds. Once the air in her lungs ran out, she would have to breathe in the toxic smoke and surrender to death.

That damned clown!

The killer stepped from the shadows and, with makeup running off his face, had revealed himself. But the clown's identity no longer mattered. He would never be caught.

Now it's time to die ...

A loud boom made the walls shake.

Something exploded.

But Molly was beyond caring. The fire flared brighter around her, causing shadows to do a death dance inside the smoke. Beside her, Rita moaned softly.

Molly reached out and gripped Rita's hand.

Let's go together ...

The pain in Molly's chest was unbearable. The air in her lungs was used up and she had to breathe again. Molly exhaled slowly, letting the carbon dioxide dissipate before she took a final breath.

KURT and Jeff searched the offices for Molly and Rita but found no trace of them.

A stack of old file folders on Rita's desk made him pause.

"Where the hell is the file room?" he asked Jeff.

Jeff shook his head and ran to a framed map of the school on the office wall.

He ran his finger along it and stopped.

"This way." Jeff shouted and ran into the hall.

THE hallway outside the file room was completely engulfed in flame and Jeff feared that they were too late.

Despite the raging fire, Kurt ran through the flames and slammed into the door to the file room. He felt a jolt of pain in his shoulder, but the solid oak door wouldn't budge. Jeff joined him and they smashed against the door in unison. The deadbolt ripped free of the doorframe and the door swung inward. A wall of smoke and flames punched out into the hallway bowling them over.

The fire had already breached the ceiling and the room was blazing. Smoke burned their eyes and flames wavered before them like a desert mirage. Most of the smoke was still rolling along the ceiling and hadn't started to sink yet. But it was only a matter of time before it did. If they were caught in the hallway, they wouldn't stand a chance.

Kurt stumbled in the darkness and reached out to steady himself. His hand touched a smooth glass surface. He wiped at the tears stinging his eyes and saw what he was touching—the glass door of a fire hose cabinet. Kurt got Jeff's attention and wordlessly indicated what they needed to do. Kurt hoped the water supply hadn't been affected by the fire.

Together they dragged the fire hose out of the case. Jeff aimed it at the center of the inferno and Kurt turned the handle. The flat canvas tube came to life as water roared along its length and sprayed out the nozzle, hissing like a striking cobra as it doused the flames. Jeff worked the stream of water back and forth across the ceiling to cool the air as they advanced into the room, driving the fire back.

Outside, the wail of a siren rose in the night air. Although the fire department had responded quickly, Kurt and Jeff knew they needed to focus on getting to Molly and Rita and searched frantically. Kurt felt a sickening lump form in his gut, fearing they were too late.

COLD water slapped Molly's face, knocking the remaining air from her lungs. She sucked in a shallow breath and an intense burning ripped down her throat causing her to gag uncontrollably.

Molly was still disoriented from the blow to her head, but she could tell the room was a little cooler. Knowing the smoke would kill her instantly, Molly resisted the urge to raise her head.

She heard someone calling her name from inside the swirling, dense smoke.

Molly ... !

The dead were calling to her. She would be with them soon. Then there would be no more pain.

Molly ... !

She raised her head and smoke wrapped around her mouth and nose like cellophane. She couldn't breathe.

This will all be over ...

Strong hands gripped Molly's shoulders and she was yanked forward toward the most intense part of the fire.

No!

Molly fought back.

They're not going to take me like this!

Then she tumbled headlong into darkness.

Molly inhaled and felt cool air soothe her smoke ravaged throat. She pitched forward and vomited, choking as the bile burned her raw esophagus. Molly wanted to see, but her eyes were glued shut by dried mucus.

A familiar voice reached out to her through the darkness.

Kurt!

"Just lie still, Molly. The ambulance is on its way."

"Rita?" she gasped and was seized by a coughing fit. When it stopped, Molly still had a difficult time breathing.

Her fingers worked at her eyelids, trying to pry them back so she could see.

"Molly, don't … there might be damage," Kurt cried.

Determined, Molly sat up. Through blurred vision, she saw they were on the lawn. On the grass beside her, Jeff Cunningham was pressing desperately on Rita's chest. Molly tried to crawl toward them but the scene tilted wildly.

The last thing Molly heard before she passed out was Jeff calling Rita's name.

FORTY-TWO

TAYLOR Mead dreamed of an all-consuming fire.

Mead had fallen asleep in his easy chair in the living room. He awoke feeling disoriented and disturbed by the vividness of his dream. He glanced at the clock on the mantle above the fireplace. It was after 10:00 in the evening.

Something's wrong.

Although not a superstitious man, Taylor Mead had long ago come to heed his visions. While maybe not supernatural, he believed his dreams were a mirror of his inner turmoil, and he could sense impending danger like an animal before an earthquake.

Taylor Mead had lived a long time by trusting his instincts, and right now those instincts were screaming at him to run. Things must have gotten out of control. He hadn't received the calls he'd been expecting from his people around the county.

Had the Atkinsons stepped up their game?

He'd always anticipated their potential for treachery. The Atkinsons had attitude, but he knew they would reveal their hand sooner or later because they were stupid and blatantly transparent. Mead recalled Sammy's smugness the other day when they'd met on his porch.

But this feeling was something stronger, less defined—and felt much more dangerous.

Mead got up from his chair and crossed to the small bedroom. Earlier in the evening he'd packed a small overnight bag. It was one that had come in with a shipment from a bankrupt luggage supplier. Sturdy and well made—waxed canvas joined together with brass and leather—Mead had liked it instantly. And even though it was brand new, the bag had an aged patina.

The overnighter was small and couldn't hold much, just a few toiletries, some essential medications, one change of clothes, $10,000 in hundreds, and a pistol.

Taylor Mead picked up his bag, took a final look around, and turned out the cabin's lights. He opened the door and hesitated, his eyes and ears attuned for anything out of place. The night was still.

Satisfied that he was safe, Mead closed the door quietly behind him and moved across the porch to the steps. Yet he just couldn't shake the feeling of impending doom.

The shadows wrapped around him like a straightjacket and Mead shivered, feeling the bite of real fear.

Mead's car was a deep matt black that absorbed light and was practically invisible in the dark. The car also had a switch under the steering wheel that killed the brake and running lights, so he could roll in stealth mode. Mead always kept his gas tank filled in case he had to make a quick escape. He wouldn't need to refuel for at least three hundred miles.

Taylor Mead had an new identity in the glove compartment and, if he needed them, several sets of false IDs stashed in bank safety deposit boxes scattered around the country.

Like a snake shedding its skin, Mead had left his wallet containing his Taylor Mead ID on the dresser in his bedroom. All would disappear in seven hours when the bomb under the propane tank behind the cabin exploded.

The bulk of his fortune was spread out among various banks around the world in numbered accounts. He'd draw on them slowly so as not to attract attention. Mead was used to a modest lifestyle and with the money he had squirreled away he could live a hundred lifetimes. All he had to do was disappear.

Without looking back, Taylor Mead guided the darkened automobile down the driveway and turned left. Mead had practiced many times and his route was imprinted in his brain. Five miles from the cabin he felt confident enough to finally turn on his headlights.

Mead looked at the empty road behind him and smiled. Now, it was time to sew up some loose ends. He pushed the Bluetooth control on his steering wheel and patiently voice dialed a number from memory.

"Yeah?" The voice was nasty.

Taylor Mead spent the next few minutes giving the man specific details of what he needed done. When finished, Mead disconnected the call with a satisfied grin. By that evening, the Atkinson brothers and Kenton Sharpe would no longer be a problem for him.

Only for the undertaker.

Mead took a final look in the rearview mirror and saw the road was still empty. He turned onto the main highway and after a few minutes passed a sign announcing the interstate was only three miles away. When he reached I-75, there would be a myriad of possibilities to choose from. The only sure thing was that Taylor Mead would disappear forever.

MOLLY woke up in the hospital. Her head throbbed and her eyes and throat felt like they'd been sandpapered. The clock on the far wall told her it was after 3:00.

Arnie was snoring softly in a chair next to her bed and she felt a slight déjà vu at the sight. The sight of Arnie asleep in a hospital room was a familiar one. It had happened before, once after her husband Steve died and she miscarried their child and, more recently, when she'd been wounded by a murder suspect.

Molly had an IV inserted into the back of her hand and the powerful painkillers in the drip made her feel warm and secure. While she was aware of her surroundings, nothing mattered. She lifted her hand and wiggled her fingers. The burns on her arm glowed an angry red, but she didn't feel any discomfort. She smiled placidly. The drugs they'd given her were doing their job, but they were making her thirsty.

She turned her head to see if there was any water nearby and saw Kurt and Jeff standing on the other side of the room watching her, concern etched on their faces.

Molly felt like Dorothy when she woke up back in Kansas at the end of the *Wizard of Oz*.

There's no place like home.

"Can I have a drink of water?" she rasped.

Kurt poured water mixed with ice into a cup and adjusted the straw. He held it for her while she drank.

"Rita?" Molly asked after a few sips.

Jeff smiled.

"She inhaled a lot of smoke, but she's going to be okay. They have her in ICU."

Molly plucked a piece of ice from the plastic cup and put it in her mouth. The chilled water soothed the burning in her throat.

"Any permanent damage?"

Jeff smiled reassuringly.

"You both were lucky. A pile of burning boxes fell right where you had been lying just after we pulled you out."

"Thanks." The water in the cup quivered as her hand shook.

If Jeff and Kurt hadn't arrived when they did ...

Arnie woke up with a snort. He looked around and saw that Molly was awake. He got up from the chair with a groan and walked to the bed.

"We have to stop meeting like this."

Arnie put a hand on her shoulder, his eyes glistening. Molly put her hand over his.

"The school?"

"The main building was partially destroyed. The fire department worked hard to keep it from spreading to the rest of the buildings."

"Everyone okay?"

"Yes, all the students and teachers got out. You and Rita were the only ones left in the school."

She squeezed his fingers hard. "Arnie, I thought I was going to die in there. I was certain I was."

Molly lay back on the pillow.

"I was so scared," she whispered.

Deep feelings were welling up in Molly, something that made her very uncomfortable.

Arnie squeezed her hand. "It's okay now. You made it."

"I was afraid that I'd lost the chance to say something to you, something I've needed to say for a long time."

"You don't need to say anything, Molly."

"Yes, I have to." Molly hesitated, searching for the right words through her drug-induced haze. "I need to thank you for believing in me and supporting me through everything. It kept me going."

The exertion had increased the drip, and she felt a soft wave wash over her. She closed her eyes and surrendered to it.

Arnie set her hand down on the bed and patted it.

"Have a good sleep. You'll need it," he said as Molly dozed off. Then added, "Sheriff Parsons."

FUCK!

The pain made Kenton Sharpe think there was someone inside his skull trying to break out with a sledgehammer. At some point during the night, he'd ended up on his living room floor. He felt like throwing up. Instead, he burped and tasted stale whiskey.

Fuck! Fuck!

A hole was punched in the drywall where he'd thrown the telephone after ripping it from the wall. His cell phone lay in pieces next to the coffee table. Those damn reporters and their insistent calls looking for a statement, trying to get his concession.

Fuck! Fuck! Fuck!

Sharpe's vision throbbed along with the pounding in his head.

It hadn't even been close. Sammy Atkinson and Taylor Mead had assured him the election was in the bag—bought and paid for. Instead, Molly Parsons had thumped him by twenty percent.

Bitch!

She would probably come after him with both barrels, thanks to that damn recording.

Well, let her try.

Molly Parsons was going to have something bad happen to her, something that couldn't be tied to him. Sharpe would make sure of it. He'd have the Atkinsons take care of her. Then there'd be a special election and he'd be back in charge.

He forced a smile, but it came off as a grimace.

Kenton Sharpe knew if Mead and the Atkinsons were tired of backing the wrong horse, they'd find another candidate.

Then where would that leave me?

Sharpe also knew those thugs would never tolerate a loose end.

I'll be a loose end—fuck!

He imagined himself inside a sealed oil drum at the bottom of Lake Michigan trying to guess which breath would be his last.

Fuck! Fuck! Fuck! Fuck!

Sharpe staggered to his feet and cursed the bottle of bourbon that was slowing him down this morning. He wondered what sort of victory speech the bitch gave last night. It was almost noon. He'd check the news.

Except I can't.

His 60-inch Samsung lay askew on its mounts, six bullet holes in the screen.

Sharpe had been so despondent over the election results that he'd contemplated putting the gun into his mouth and pulling the trigger. The Channel Six in-depth election coverage team seemed like a better substitute, so he shot up the TV instead.

Well, fuck that!

Right now Sharpe needed to do something about the raging storm in his head. He started in the direction of the liquor cabinet, every step setting off new waves of pain. A fresh bottle of Jack Daniels inside the cabinet was tantalizingly just out of reach, the hangover elongating time and making his surroundings appear stretched out.

The pounding in Sharpe's head morphed into a loud crash as his front door was torn off its hinges and landed at his feet. In stunned silence, Sharpe turned to face three goons filling the doorway.

'And they aren't out collecting for the Red Cross ...'

The recollection of a favorite line from *Blazing Saddles* almost made him laugh. But instead, Kenton Sharpe began to sob as the men advanced on him.

FORTY-THREE

DARCIE?

She was out there in the shadows, strapped to a gurney but still smiling sweetly at him.

Was she singing?

He loved her songs and the way in which she mangled the words taking the familiar and merging it with the unknown.

Spaggettisburg.

That's where the great battle of the Civil War was fought and Lincoln made his famous address.

Stovenator.

Her interpretation of where their meals came from.

Clocksee.

Tears filled his eyes as he remembered.

Laughter.

The mocking laughter of the other kids made him furious. He stood up to them, protecting his little sister.

Sweet innocent Darcie.

But he was not able to protect her that night. The clown had taken her to see the doctor. Then she was taken out of his life forever.

The clown.

Well, he'd finally laid her to rest. The fire had sanctified that awful place. An evil had been erased forever, an evil that would no longer torture him.

He took off his real face with cold cream. His true self was on the bureau in his bedroom smeared into little clumps of cotton. Now it was time to step back into the shadows and be anonymous again.

He felt a momentary pang of regret that those two innocent women had to die and sad this final act had been tainted by tragedy.

But so be it.

The cleansing had been done for the sake of erasing a bigger sin, and he would have to live with the consequences. At least now there would be no more deaths. All the players, the enablers, had been punished. The clown had finished with them forever.

He gathered up the used cotton balls and put them into a garbage bag. The costume was carefully hung up in its secret place in the back of the closet. Someday soon he would cast it into the flames.

SAMMY Atkinson was pissed off. He hadn't been able to reach Taylor Mead since 9:00 that morning, and it was now 11:00. That cheap old fuck didn't even have voice mail, so he couldn't leave a message—not that he would.

The election had gone badly, and he didn't know what to do. In one evening, their entire hand-picked slate of candidates had gone down in defeat, wiping away their power structure and the protection it represented. Sammy Atkinson was left feeling frustrated and scared, very scared.

Had his men skulked away into the shadows along with Kenton Sharpe and Taylor Mead, leaving him and his brother Tommy to face the aftermath?

Atkinson hit speed dial again and waited with growing anxiety as his call went unanswered.

To cap things off, two of his best salesmen hadn't shown up this morning, but that was a minor irritation. The dealership was always quiet in the morning. No customers ever showed up until at least noon.

Atkinson was surprised then when the ringer attached to the front door dinged to announce someone had entered the showroom.

Typically this would have provoked a stampede of salesmen to the showroom floor. This morning, he was the only one around.

Well, at least I can get something out of this.

Sammy Atkinson stood up and plastered a false grin on his face before he strode out into the showroom with phony confidence.

A large man stood looking at a list of options taped to the front window of a pickup. This man reminded Atkinson of Dwayne 'The Rock' Johnson—six feet of solid muscle topped off with a shaved head. The brilliant halogen lighting reflected off his bald head giving him an artificial halo.

"I'm interested in the black quad cab out there," the bald man said in a soft, friendly tone.

Atkinson relaxed a little. His greed gene kicked in and he started to calculate just how much over list he could squeeze out of this rube.

"You've got good taste. She's fully-loaded and has been well maintained."

"Any chance I could take her for a test drive?"

Sammy's smile widened. "Sure, I'll get the keys."

Maybe the morning isn't going to be a total loss after all.

When Sammy Atkinson turned away to go back to his office for the keys, he missed the large man's hard, mean smile.

KENTON Sharpe could smell his own urine from under the hood that had been placed over his head. He'd pissed himself when he was locked in the trunk.

They had driven for a while before he'd been lifted out and dragged into a building.

This is how Taylor Mead deals with loose ends.

The expected bullet and shallow grave didn't come. Instead, Sharpe was secured to a metal chair with nylon ties and left alone to contemplate all sorts of horrors yet to come.

Even though he was blindfolded, Sharpe could sense he was in a room. The air here was warm and had an institutional odor. Most of all it was unnaturally quiet.

Sharpe knew what Taylor Mead and his men were capable of. They would torture him to learn what they needed to know.

This is about the recording.

Mead would want to know who had been behind the recording. Kenton Sharpe whimpered in desperation because he had no idea who had recorded his conversation with Sammy Atkinson. It was likely Atkinson himself made the tape, maybe as leverage in case Sharpe ever got out of line.

Sharpe's heightened senses amplified the click of a lock from behind him, and he twisted around in that direction. Soft footsteps approached and stopped. He could feel the presence of someone standing directly behind him.

The hood was pulled off his head, and he squeezed his eyes shut defensively trying to block out whatever new terror was about to reveal itself.

"Did you piss yourself, Kenton?"

The voice was familiar. Sharpe opened his eyes and blinked hard against the harsh light in the small room.

A smiling Arnie Voxx walked into view.

"Voxx? What the fuck is going on?"

Arnie held up his index finger.

"One chance, Kenton. That's all you're getting."

"Untie me right now you bastard," Sharpe said defiantly.

"Kenton Sharpe, you have the right to remain silent. Anything you say can and will be used against you in a court of law. You have the right to speak to an attorney, and to have an attorney present during any questioning. If you cannot afford a lawyer, one will be provided for you at government expense."

"Fucking right I want an attorney present I'm going to sue your ass."

Arnie looked at him in disgust.

"Do you understand your rights as I have read them to you?"

Sharpe continued to struggle against his bonds.

261

"We picked up six of Taylor Mead's gang last night. They're in interview rooms down the hall. The first one who talks gets a special prize."

Sharpe stopped struggling.

"Oh yeah, what's that?"

"A reduced sentence."

"Well that's very sweet of you, but it doesn't get me out of this chair."

"That offer doesn't apply to you."

"This is pure harassment, Voxx. You've had it in for me for years."

"Maybe, but your current predicament doesn't have anything to do with my personal feelings toward you, Kenton. This is a DEA case, and they have hours of recordings of you and the Atkinson brothers conspiring in a criminal enterprise. You'd have sold the whole county to Taylor Mead if you'd been elected."

"Yeah, well prove it."

"It's not really my case. The Feds have a special prosecutor in place and a Grand Jury to deal with all the rotten shit in Boyle. You're just one of the little fish in the net."

Sharpe looked across the room at the mirror on the wall. He imagined the prosecutor was looking back at him right now. His bravado deflated like he'd been stuck with a pin.

"So what can I do?"

"They really don't need anything from you, Kenton. They've had eyes on you for almost a year. You can't give them anything they don't already have. You shit in your nest, and now you're going to have to sleep in it."

"This is about Molly Parsons, isn't it? This is your revenge for the way I treated her."

"You disgust me, Sharpe. You brought this on yourself. You betrayed the trust people put in you. For what? A pickup truck and some cash?"

"What do you want from me?"

Arnie Voxx walked to the door.

"Enjoy your stay in prison."

Arnie let the door slam after him.

Kenton Sharpe stared at the mirror in growing horror as reality dawned on him.

MOLLY was discharged from the hospital before lunch. The doctor had ordered her to go home and get some rest. Kurt came to pick her up in the Austin Healey, her pride and joy. She smiled at the sight of the big man crammed behind the wheel of the small sports car.

Kurt helped her into the passenger seat. Even with his assistance, she still felt winded from the exertion.

Kurt clumsily ground through the gears.

"Careful with my clutch," she groaned.

"This vehicle is totally unsuited to this climate you know."

"I love it anyway," she said with a painful smile as he mashed the gears again. "Thanks for getting me out."

"No problem. I've been hoping for a chance to drive your car."

"I meant out of the fire."

"I know," Kurt said as he focused on trying not to tear the Healey's transmission to pieces.

"What about the fingerprint cards?"

"Yeah, I got a match."

"It's bad, Kurt, really bad ..."

"I know. I was coming to warn you. But we were too late."

"Not too late. Rita and I owe our lives to you and Jeff."

"What are you going to do now?"

Sleep ...

"I don't know. Any evidence was probably burned up in the fire."

"But we still have the fingerprint cards."

"It's not enough, Kurt."

The car's heating system wasn't working. It rarely did. Molly felt chilled to the bone.

"Congratulations, by the way," Kurt said trying to lighten her mood, "on becoming sheriff. You'll be great."

She hadn't thought about her new job until then. There would be plenty of time to think about it later. She wouldn't take office until February. Right now she didn't even have her deputy's badge. It had been burned up in her handbag along with her Beretta and phone. Without them, she felt naked and vulnerable.

With the school gone, Molly wondered if the clown would finally find peace.

"Can I borrow your phone?"

Kurt passed her his cell and she dialed Jeff Cunningham's number from memory. He answered right away.

"Jeff, I want you to arrange for around the clock protection for Rita."

"Not necessary. I'm sitting right next to her bed and I'm not going anywhere."

"Thanks," Molly said gratefully and hung up.

"Jeff hasn't slept since it happened. It's kind of cute actually, like he's her guardian angel or something."

Molly smiled at the thought. Jeff was a veteran who'd been haunted by his experience during his tour of duty in Afghanistan. Horrible things had happened to him over there, and he'd carried the weight of them back with him.

By saving Rita, maybe Jeff had found a little peace.

She gave Kurt his cell phone back.

"Can we go to the office?"

"No. I promised Arnie I'd take you straight home."

"I need to sign out a gun and a new cell phone."

Kurt turned the Austin Healey around. Molly tried to remember what else she'd in her handbag and groaned. It would take weeks to get her driver's license, credit cards, and other essential ID replaced.

GAYLE Tippett peered at Molly over the top of her reading glasses.

"You're supposed to be at home in bed," she told Molly sternly. "Sheriff," Gayle added with a smile.

Molly propped herself on the edge of Gayle's desk.

"My Berretta burned up. I need a replacement."

Gayle pulled a worn three ring binder from her desk drawer and leafed through it. In addition to making sure every officer in the department qualified on the range twice a year, as the department's firearms officer, Gayle was also in charge of issuing weapons.

"I don't have any M9s in inventory. I can give you a Glock 19."

"Sure, that's fine."

Gayle handed Molly a Requisition for Firearm form. Molly appreciated that Gayle was strictly by-the-book when it came to her responsibilities. She completed the form and handed it back to Gayle.

Gayle opened the safe built in to her office wall. She took out a box and gave it to Molly along with a carton of ammunition and two extra magazines. It was light compared to her Beretta.

Usually, at this time of day, the office was busy with deputies coming on and going.

"Where is everyone?" Molly asked.

"Arnie called them in last night. There've been raids all over the county this morning. Some big deal with the DEA."

Molly knew Arnie would fill her in later. Right now, she felt her energy flagging. She sagged against the desk and Kurt guided her back to the car.

Sitting in the passenger seat, Molly took the Glock out its box and began to feed bullets into one of the clips.

"Feel a little more secure now?" he asked.

In response, Molly slapped a clip into the butt of the pistol.

FORTY-FOUR

WHY isn't Darcie at rest?

He rose on one elbow and looked around the bedroom. It was late morning, but the blinds were sealed tight letting in no light. He thought once his tasks were complete the dreams would stop and he'd never see his baby sister again.

But he'd been wrong. He was still dreaming of her dancing in the corridors of the school singing her silly little songs. In the darkness, behind her, he could just make out the faint visage of someone standing.

The doctor? The clown?

The furnace hadn't kicked in yet and his bedroom was cold. He got up and pulled on his robe.

Coffee.

In the kitchen, he put the kettle on and turned on the small TV. The local news was detailing the results of the election. The anchor segued from the outcome of the sheriff's race to the story of the school and Molly Parsons's close call in the fire. The reporter went on to describe the scene of the blaze—the fire department had arrived in time to save most of the building. In the early morning light, he could see the Pine Academy, while having suffered significant damage, still stood.

Rage welled up within him. He gripped the coffee cup in his painfully clenched fingers. The reporter speculated that the school would be rebuilt to its former glory.

He heard a mocking tone in the reporter's voice, as if the man were speaking directly to him, taunting him for screwing up his task.

Madness overwhelmed him. He threw the coffee mug across the kitchen and it shattered near the fridge. He sank to his knees and began to cry.

Will this ever end?

MARK Barnard stood mutely as the pastor finished the benediction at the committal service for his father. The coffin was covered by a flag, as befitting a war hero and senator.

The last few days had been a nightmare for Mark. They'd finally released him from jail, but there'd been no apology. Not that he'd expected one. Mark knew he was the most obvious suspect, plus the killer had used his gun to commit the crime. Although infuriated knowing the murderer was still out there, Mark stoically masked his rage.

Mark looked at the group gathered by the graveside. All the bereaved were friends of his father—political cronies and war vets. Mark wondered if one of them was might be his father's killer.

Rifle shots startled Mark as the honor guard fired a volley before the coffin was lowered into its crypt. The sound of the guns took him back to the evening of his father's death—those two terrible bangs from the house and the clown doing its bizarre dance along the driveway.

Was the clown real, or a stress-induced hallucination?

The police seemed to take the clown seriously when Mark finally told them what he'd seen.

Two of the soldiers ceremonially folded the flag. The officer in charge presented it to Mark, stepped back, and saluted him.

For the next few minutes, his father's friends greeted him with words of encouragement and sympathy, but it was awkward and forced. They knew Mark had been suspected of murdering his father and released for "lack of evidence."

Mark knew he'd be gossiped about for years to come, however, he wasn't planning to stay in Pine. He'd never felt connected here and had spent most of his life elsewhere, either at boarding school or in the army.

He was certain the life insurance companies would try to delay payment, but eventually they would settle. In the meantime, he could sell the farm and the dairy. The sale would give him a sizeable fortune which he planned to use to start a new life somewhere else.

Mark turned from the grave and walked back to the funeral home limousine. Mark Barnard would no longer be just his father's son, he would now be his own man.

MOLLY slept until after 6:00 that evening. She staggered to the bathroom still short of breath, but felt more human after a long, hot, shower.

There wasn't anything to eat in the fridge, so she put bread in the toaster and brewed a cup of coffee. After four slices of toast slathered with peanut butter, her energy started to return.

She tried calling Arnie at home, but there was no answer.

Maybe he's still out on the raids.

She wondered what that was all about, but had a strong suspicion it involved Boyle and Taylor Mead.

Had they finally nailed that old prick?

Molly dug around in her closet and found an old handbag from her bounty hunting days. She groaned at the thought of having to replace all her identification and credit cards.

At least she had a gun, though she missed her Beretta. The gun had been a gift a long time ago and it was a totem to her.

Some folks carry a rabbit's foot, I had a lucky pistol.

It was stupid to mourn a gun but Molly felt like another piece of her past had been stripped away.

Molly had baited the trap that morning and made the call. It would be interesting to see what happened next. She knew she should've waited to speak to Arnie before putting their plan into play, but Molly had the feeling that time was not on her side. Any chance she'd have depended on quick action.

A knock at the door interrupted her thoughts.

Molly flicked on the outside light and held the Glock behind her back as she opened the door. Colin Ricks stood on her porch holding up a bottle of wine.

His smile faded when he saw her.

"Jesus, what happened to you?"

She stepped aside and let him in, keeping the gun out of sight.

TAYLOR Mead kept to the back roads until he was close to I-75. The Vanderbilt entrance to the interstate was just ahead. He'd programmed the Lincoln's GPS with his destination. It would take him three and a half hours to reach the airport in Detroit. After that, Taylor Mead would disappear forever.

Mead didn't give a second thought to what he'd put in motion back in Boyle. By now the Atkinson brothers and Kenton Sharpe would no longer be an issue. They would all be safely planted deep in a landfill outside Mackinaw City.

Mead smiled as he waited for the light to change, tapping the top of the steering wheel in time with the Eagles' *Hotel California*. A movement on the right side of the car caught his eye. Mead saw a dark blue Ford pull into the intersection against the red light and block his lane.

Son of a bitch!

A second Ford boxed him in from behind. Then all hell broke loose—blue and red flashing lights, whooping sirens, and men leaping from cars pointing guns at him.

Mead glanced at the armrest where he'd concealed a pistol and then back at the badges and guns. It would be suicide to try to shoot his way out, and he wasn't ready to die yet. Instead, Taylor Mead turned off the ignition, put his hands on the wheel where they were clearly visible, and waited.

With practiced precision, they pulled Mead from his car, handcuffed him, and read him his rights. When asked if he understood, Mead shrugged and nodded. He would keep his mouth shut. What could they prove? The Atkinson brothers and Kenton Sharpe were already dead. Now it was time for his $10,000 a month legal eagle to start earning his retainer. This was merely a momentary setback on his road to retirement.

Mead was shoved into the back of the blue Ford. With lights flashing and sirens wailing, the procession made its way back to Sunset.

WHILE Colin Rick opened the bottle of wine, Molly slid her Glock under a magazine on the coffee table.

"How's your father doing?"

"He's relieved."

"I can't imagine what he went through all those years believing he was guilty of such a horrible crime."

Colin contemplated this as he slowly sipped the wine.

"Thanks again for taking a closer look. That sheriff of yours would have railroaded my father into prison for the rest of his life. And Dad would have gone to his grave believing he'd killed Elsie and her child." Colin made no attempt to conceal his bitterness.

"Arnie's a fair man. He's been carrying the weight of that night with him for as long as your father has. Once he saw the evidence, he came around."

Colin smiled weakly. "Yeah, I guess he did."

They drank some more of the wine in silence.

"So if my father didn't do it, who do you think did?"

Molly stared off into space for a few moments before answering.

"My guess would be Dr. Blanic. Elsie Maranello discovered what he was doing at the school, and he killed her and her daughter."

Colin shuddered.

"What was he up to at the school?"

"I'm not sure, and any hope of finding out burned up in the fire."

"Sorry."

"Not as much as I am," Molly replied regretfully.

Now there would never be closure for the victims at the school. Not that Molly believed in closure. In her experience, closure was just a cliché trotted out by some investigators to bring nobility to their quest for justice. If there was anything like closure in this case, it came at the hands of a psychopath who dressed up as a clown to extract revenge against those who covered up the school's monstrous past.

Too bad Blanic's dead. He's the one who really deserves the clown's wrath.

Molly wondered how accurate the Wiesenthal information on Blanic was. The doctor had been excellent at covering his tracks for the last sixty years.

Maybe he'd done it again.

Molly refused to let this slim possibility get her too excited. She would make another call to Avi Marcovitch in the morning to see how solid their information was.

And then another possibility began to grow in her mind.

FORTY-FIVE

BIRDLAND is where all the canaries come to sing.

Nicknamed by a cynical field agent, Birdland was a black site jointly operated by the FBI and the DEA. The secluded facility was located off a country road south of the Gaylord State Forest and was designed to intimidate.

To a casual observer, from the outside Birdland appeared to be just a small industrial building surrounded by a high, electrified fence. On the inside, however, were six cinderblock cells, three on each side of a single corridor running the length of the facility. Every cell was painted light gray and had no windows or decoration of any kind.

Each cell, or room as the agents preferred to call them, contained a high-profile detainee. The most high-profile was Taylor Mead. Sitting alone, chained to a metal table, Mead was not the least bit intimidated by his surroundings.

In separate cells across the hall were the Atkinson brothers. Because the cells were soundproof, Mead was completely oblivious of his proximity to the brothers.

Mead assumed they were making audio and video recordings of him and, with a bored glance around, tried to spot the hidden cameras. Unable to locate them, he leaned back casually in the chair confident they couldn't touch him. He was satisfied that by now the Atkinson brothers and Kenton Sharpe were cooling in the morgue.

Without their testimonies, there would be nothing to link him to whatever crimes the government suspected him of.

ACROSS the hall, Tommy Atkinson drummed his fingers nervously on the metal arms of the chair and waited. He'd been waiting a long time in an empty room and the isolation was getting to him.

Tommy jumped at the squeal made by the door as an interrogator entered and sat down across from him. Atkinson grinned as if he didn't have a care in the world. He thought about whistling a tune to piss off this inquisitor but resisted. Atkinson wasn't that brave, at least not without his brother Sammy around.

Where the fuck is Sammy?

The man didn't say a word for five minutes, he just silently stared at Atkinson with piercingly dark eyes. Finally, he slapped a thick file folder on the table. Atkinson didn't bother to look at it.

"We have Taylor Mead, seven of his men, and Kenton Sharpe in custody. They're all competing to see who can give the other up first. It's kind of like musical chairs," his interrogator said with a smile.

Tommy's shit-eating grin faded.

"And my brother Sammy?"

The investigator shook his head. He opened the file, took out a photograph, and slid it across the table. Atkinson blanched at the sight of his brother with a large wound on the side of his head.

"Sorry for your loss."

The investigator's tone told Tommy the investigator was delighted to be breaking the news.

"We couldn't get to him in time. Mead had him hit early this morning."

Atkinson continued to stare down at the photograph. His fingers gripped the edge of the table.

Fuck, it could be a cop trick.

But his eyes riveted to the picture told him it wasn't.

"What the fuck do you want me to do about it?"

"That's kind of a stupid question, Tommy, but then Sammy was always the brains of the family, wasn't he?"

Tommy thought about kicking the agent's face in, but it would be useless—he was securely manacled to the table.

The agent, sensing Tommy Atkinson's rage, dropped his smile.

"Don't be mad at me. I'm only the messenger here."

He paused to let his words sink in, and Atkinson slumped back in his chair. The interrogator tapped the picture of Atkinson's dead brother.

"You don't want to be the last one standing when the music stops do you?"

Tommy Atkinson considered this. He glanced at the picture again and finally shook his head. The investigator pulled out a sheet of questions he was confident Tommy would be willing and able to answer.

DOWN the hall, Sammy Atkinson was going through the same ordeal. He looked down at the doctored picture of his brother Tommy with a good part of his head blown off, churning with fury toward that bastard Taylor Mead.

Like a good bird, Sammy Atkinson also began to sing. And when he did, he was a regular *Rockin' Robin*—tweet, tweet, tweet.

WHEN Molly got off the phone with Avi Marcovitch from the Wiesenthal Center she marched down the hall and knocked on Arnie's door. He looked up from the mound of paperwork on his desk.

"You're supposed to be at home," Arnie said gruffly.

Without being invited, she sat down.

"I'm recuperated."

He shook his head and tried to continue to work his way through the case files on his desk.

"I won't miss any of this paperwork," he muttered tapping the pile.

"I think I caught a break in the murders of Elsie Maranello and her daughter."

Arnie put his pen down and looked at her.

"Remember how we believed that Dr. Blanic had died out west?"

He nodded, waiting.

"Well, the death certificate was false. The investigators at the Wiesenthal Center figure there's a possibility he might have filled it out himself."

"So, is he dead or isn't he?"

Molly shrugged. "No one knows for sure, but we might be able to use that to our advantage."

Molly filled Arnie in on the rest of what she'd learned. When she finished, Arnie shook his head in disbelief.

"And you think we can take him?"

"I think it's your call. You deserve to make the arrest."

Arnie considered this.

"You'd better call Les Caulfield. He'll want to be in on it too."

Molly wasn't looking forward to talking to Les. He was already furious with her about derailing his investigation.

Arnie noticed her discomfort.

"You might as well start honing your diplomatic skills."

Once Molly left his office, Arnie took the old file folder from his desk and flipped it open to look at the crime scene photos once again.

TAYLOR Mead looked around the room and wondered what was keeping his lawyer. He was starting to get really pissed off. He'd been in custody for hours and that thieving prick of an attorney hadn't shown up yet.

He'd better be standing before a fucking judge getting my bail set!"

Meanwhile, Mead was just keeping his mouth shut. He was sure his silence would drive the cops crazy. They'd seized his new ID along with the money when they'd searched his Lincoln. It was no big deal, he had another set of ID papers stashed away in a safety deposit box in a Cleveland bank along with plenty of traveling cash.

He felt their eyes on him.

"I'm not going to say anything without my attorney present," Mead said to whoever was listening.

A loud click came from a hidden speaker in the ceiling and Sammy Atkinson's shrill voice filled the room. Atkinson had rolled over and was spilling the beans. Mead's ears began to pound painfully in sync with every damning word.

Cold sweat began to roll down the back of Taylor Mead's neck.

"It's just his word against mine," Mead said defiantly toward the ceiling.

Tommy Atkinson's voice joined his brother's and he detailed what he knew.

Jesus! They're both supposed to be dead.

He cursed his ineffective hitman as Kenton Sharpe's terrified voice joined the chorus.

The drone of voices went on and Mead's head continued to pound as his blood pressure climbed into the danger zone. Lightning bolts flashed in the corner of his eyes and the pain was so severe he felt as if his head was being split in half with a meat cleaver.

DR. Ronnie Kolmenn was at home. He met Molly at the door with a glass of Scotch in his hand. From the look of him, it wasn't his first drink of the day.

"Ronnie, I need a favor," she asked after declining his offer of a drink.

Kolmenn looked terrible. Molly recognized the signs of too many nights with too little sleep. She'd suffered through a period of insomnia herself not that long ago and it had really messed her up.

Kolmenn had been like this for weeks. At first, she'd thought it was the pressure of the election—technically Kolmenn was up for reelection, but he'd been unchallenged.

Over the years, Molly had grown to like the cynical coroner even though his acerbic wit made it difficult at times. It bothered her that Kolmenn did not always acknowledge the gravity of the deaths he was investigating and made jokes at the expense of the deceased. But Molly knew this was his way of coping with the senseless carnage that came with his job.

"Ronnie, I have to ask … Is something wrong?"

He didn't respond. Instead, he walked over to the sidebar and poured more whiskey into his glass.

Molly looked at him with concern.

"I mean it's been noticeable the last couple of weeks. You haven't been … well … yourself."

"Define 'myself,'" Kolmenn challenged.

"In the past, you've always been quick with a sarcastic quip or bad pun at a crime scene. Recently you've been serious, more like a regular coroner would act. Plus, you look horrible, like you haven't been sleeping."

"I'm an old man. I don't sleep as much," he snapped. "And don't the dead deserve some respect?"

"Not from you. You like to liven things up, make things less grim for the rest of us."

"Maybe I'm tired of being the clown then."

Kolmenn hesitated.

"Sorry, wrong choice of words," he muttered.

"I just want you to know that you can talk to me about whatever is bothering you."

"Right now, the only thing that's bothering me is you."

Molly held her tongue. She deserved his anger. She had no right to be poking her nose into his affairs. Molly was never good at this touchy-feely kind of stuff. She would feel the same kind of resentment if someone tried to butt in on her privacy. Molly let it drop.

"Sorry, that was harsh of me," Kolmenn apologized.

This took Molly by surprise. In the entire time she'd known him, she'd never seen him say he was sorry about anything.

"Let's call it *man-o-pause*. I go through it every election. It reminds me of the passage of time."

She'd learned to expect a lot of things from Ronnie Kolmenn, but maudlin wasn't one of them. And yet here it was—the despair of old age.

"It comes so soon, the moment when there's nothing left to wait for."

"That's very eloquent."

"Happiness is beneficial for the body, but it's grief that develops the powers of the mind." He smiled sadly. "Marcel Proust. I reread *In Search of Lost Time* during each election year, and then I drink too much. It helps me wash away the clutter, so I can reemerge as a beautiful, sarcastic butterfly once again."

"And that's the Ronnie Kolmenn we all know and love," Molly said emphatically.

Kolmenn held his glass high and then drained it.

"So, you need a favor?"

Molly spent the next few minutes explaining just what she wanted from him. As she neared the end, his mouth turned up into a wicked smile.

"Will you do it?"

His smile broadened. "It has a particular appeal."

She was about to thank him when his phone rang. He answered and listened for a few minutes. After he hung up, he went to the sink on the wet bar and poured the whiskey out of his glass.

"It appears I am needed at the jail. There has been an incident."

"An incident?"

"It seems Mr. Taylor Mead has blown a head gasket."

"He's dead?"

"Yes, of a massive stroke."

"What caused it?"

Dr. Ronnie Kolmenn smiled. "Apparently he was listening to bird songs."

FORTY-SIX

MOLLY walked tentatively into the conference room.

Les Caulfield was pulling pictures off the wall and dropping them into an open file box.

"What are you doing?"

He continued pulling the pictures down.

"Putting all this away," he said coldly, struggling to contain his rage.

"Why?"

He sighed and turned around. His anger faded, replaced with fatigue.

"Most of my evidence burned up in the fire."

"Not everything."

He shook his head. "It's over, Molly. The special prosecutor is shutting me down. No one has the heart to pursue it any longer."

"What about all those kids?"

"Akron's dead, the school's gone ..."

"I'm so sorry, Les."

"It's not your fault, Molly. I appreciate your help, I really do. It was a fool's errand anyway. A make-work project for a broken old man."

"But what about the children, how do they get justice?"

He shrugged. "They're going to tear down the school and bury it. It's for the better."

"Well, if it's any consolation, I think we're going to be able to bring at least one of them to justice."

"Oh yeah? Which one?"

"Blanic."

Les hesitated, a frown crossing his face. "I thought he died out west."

"Apparently not. That was a false trail. He's been living nearby for the past fifteen years."

"That's all well and good, but we don't have any evidence left."

"Not at the school, but I had a bunch of file boxes in my car, and Arnie thinks we might be able to pull DNA off Elsie's clothing. If we can tie the old fucker into her murder, we can put him away for the rest of his life."

"Sounds thin to me."

"Maybe, but I have an idea to lure him out."

Molly explained to Les what she was planning. When she finished, he shook his head.

"I can think of a dozen reasons why that will never work."

"Want in on it?"

Les Caulfield shook his head again. "No, it's your thing. I'm just going to put this stuff away and quietly shuffle off into retirement. Tell Arnie that we should play golf sometime."

"Again, Les, I'm sorry for the way it turned out."

He offered her his hand.

"Molly, I think it turned out just about the way you thought it would. You knew this was a lost cause right from the beginning."

She started to protest and then held her tongue. He was right. She had.

Molly smiled. "Sometimes lost causes are the only ones worth fighting for, Les."

He nodded gravely.

WHEN Adam Gmerek woke up that morning, he had no idea Boyle had changed. He didn't hear the sound of the sucking void left by Taylor Mead and his buddies. Adam had gone to bed early on election night without bothering to listen to the final returns. He assumed his bid for another term was a waste of time.

Adam's first inkling that something unexpected had happened was when his wife, Allison, woke him with an excited scream. She was in the kitchen near the front of the house, and the sound was still making the walls of their bedroom vibrate. A second later she threw open the door.

"You'd better get up, Adam!"

Adam groaned.

Allison grabbed him and pulled him from the bed.

"Come on, you're not going to believe this."

She dragged him through the house to the kitchen. When he saw the headline in the morning paper, Adam understood.

"Jesus!" he said in awe.

"The radio says there were raids all over the county last night. Apparently, Taylor Mead died of a stroke after he was arrested."

The doorbell chimed, interrupting further discussion.

Skip Harmer, his campaign manager and best friend, was practically dancing a jig on the front porch. Skip gave him a big hug.

"The Federal Election Commission seized all the ballot boxes before Mead's men could take them away to do the count. They also locked down the counting room and found an enormous amount of fake ballots. The Feds took the boxes up to Sunset and did the count there. Congratulations, buddy, you won by a landslide."

"You're kidding!"

"Nope, and I hear that Mead's head exploded when they arrested him. The rest of them are clamoring to rat each other out. They even arrested Kenton Sharpe on corruption charges."

Adam sat down, the enormity of what happened sinking in. They'd been given their town back. It was more than he ever expected. The challenge now would be to rebuild. Their economy had been based on drug profits for so long that it was hard to imagine where they would even begin.

Adam had no illusions that the town's criminal element was gone forever. The woods were still full of meth cookers and, sooner or later, some other operator would arrive, like Mead had, with grandiose plans to make Boyle bigger and better, and it would start all over again.

But at least now they would have law enforcement as an ally. If Kenton Sharpe had been picked up, that meant Molly Parsons was the new sheriff, and that was a great thing. Although Adam didn't know her well, he had the impression she followed Arnie Voxx's philosophy of strict but fair.

Adam thought about the days to come. He hoped he had the strength and courage needed for the task ahead.

MOLLY Parsons was wondering the same thing as she huddled in the darkened upper hallway of the Pine Academy.

The school was silent, all the students having been relocated to temporary quarters after the fire. An overpowering smell of charred wood and plastic filled the corridor, and smoke had stained the walls a sooty gray.

The plan was a desperate one driven by a case they had no chance of proving, but Molly was out of options. She shuddered at the acrid smell, flashing back to the horror of the fire that had almost killed her. The memory fueled her anger.

This fucker's not gonna get away with it.

Still, Molly was taking a big chance. If her plan went south, there would probably be more bloodshed and destruction.

Not the best way to start off as sheriff.

Since winning the election, Molly had not taken any time to think about her new role. This case had absorbed her, and she'd been focused only on bringing the perpetrator to justice.

Sheriff Parsons.

Just hearing it in her mind made Molly feel strange. Up until now, the notion of being in charge of the department had been an abstract concept. Now that the job was hers, Molly wasn't sure she wanted it.

She thought about Arnie and his struggles with the county commission, of how he had to fight for and justify every penny in the budget. As a criminal investigator, she only had to focus on her cases.

As sheriff, she would now be front and center as the public face of law enforcement in the county. Instead of solving crimes, her job would be hours of grindingly dull administrative work—performance reviews, reports, business cases, budget variables, and fucking routine paperwork.

On the other hand, she could make an impact. Arnie was a fine lawman, but an old-fashioned one. He mistrusted technology and emerging communication trends such as social media. Their forensics were excellent but also dated. Too much evidence had to be sent to more modern facilities for processing.

Her first hurdle would be to gain the department's respect and support. Over the years, Molly had rubbed some of the deputies the wrong way, and there were others who were not pulling their weight.

Oh, Lord, save me.

FROM her hiding place beside a bank of lockers, Molly heard footsteps approaching.

The footsteps stopped, and she held her breath.

He took the bait!

A momentary silence was followed by the unmistakable sound of liquid splashing onto the floor, immediately accompanied by an overpowering smell.

Gasoline!

Molly tapped the radio button once and pulled her gun out of its holster.

Time for the show to begin.

"Who's there?" The harsh German accent was apparent even though the voice was barely above a whisper.

The owner of the voice limped toward where the gas was pooled on the floor.

Molly looked down the corridor to her left and then to her right. The two men stood twenty feet apart.

The shriveled man with the German accent continued to approach. The other, holding a large container, was frozen in place.

Molly stepped out of her hiding place and stood between them. She pointed her flashlight at the silhouette holding the gas can and flicked it on.

Trapped in a halo of light, the clown turned toward her. Molly gasped in horror. An impossibly wide, blood-red grin was grotesque against the stark white face. Her thoughts reeled back to the scene in the file room and the flashlight beam wavered in her shaking hand.

As the clown turned away from Molly to face the man with the German accent, he dropped the gasoline container. It hit the floor at his feet and rolled away, the rest of the fuel spilling out.

"Are you ready to lead the children's parade?" the German asked.

The clown began to shake his head. "You can't make me, I won't let you!"

The one thing Molly hadn't anticipated was a gun. But there it was, in the clown's right hand. He raised the pistol and sighted it on the approaching specter.

Molly brought her gun up and centered it on the clown. The Glock felt unfamiliar and strangely weightless in her hand.

"Doctor, get down!"

The smaller man jerked to one side as the clown fired and the bullet zinged harmlessly off the wall. He rolled behind a row of lockers, and the clown turned toward Molly with his gun raised.

The clown's hideous grin slowly widened. Molly remembered this same ghoulish visage mocking her through the flames in the file room.

She fired a shot instinctively, but it tore wide. The clown returned fire, and Molly spun to the left. Her elbow banged painfully against the cement wall and the gun flew out of her hand.

A bullet smacked into the wall where Molly had been standing only a moment before.

The clown took a step toward her, his pistol pointed at her chest. Molly's blood turned to ice. She was cornered, helpless.

Molly frantically raced through her options and then said, "Don't do it, Les. You're surrounded."

Confused at hearing his name, Les Caulfield staggered backward, dropping his gun hand to his side.

"But they took Darcie …" His voice was flat, devoid of emotion.

"I know they did, Les, and they took the others too." Molly held out her hand to him. "They killed all those children. But you've already punished them, Les. You've made them pay for their crimes."

"Not all of them!" Les screamed hysterically.

Molly's stomach lurched in fear at the sheer violence in his voice.

The spilled gasoline was slowly spreading across the floor and Molly inched away. The overpowering gas fumes rose around Les Caulfield, and his painted face wavered in front of her.

"Les, please, we know what they did was evil. They used their power to exterminate children who were not their twisted idea of perfection."

"Darcie … She was beautiful … "

"And you couldn't protect her, Les. I know. You were only a child yourself."

"I was her older brother. It was my job to protect her!"

From the shrillness of his voice, Molly knew she couldn't reason with Les Caulfield. There was no escape from this madman. Les raised his pistol again and aimed it squarely at her, a frenzied gleam in his eyes.

At that moment, Arnie Voxx charged out of the shadows straight at Les Caulfield. With unbelievable speed, Les spun around and fired twice. Arnie grunted and crashed to the floor.

While Les was distracted, Molly scooped her Glock up from the floor. Without taking time to sight on her target, she squeezed the trigger and prayed.

The bullet caught Les Caulfield in the shoulder. He jerked his trigger reactively as he staggered backward, but his gun wasn't aimed at Molly—it was pointed downward. With a massive roar, the muzzle flash ignited the puddle of gasoline at his feet. Flames immediately engulfed Les, fusing the polyester costume to his skin.

It was a scene out of hell—the clown frantically batting at the fire as he ran down the corridor in a blind panic trying to escape the flames consuming him. Les Caulfield's final piercing scream reverberated off the walls and into Molly's nightmares.

But Molly didn't have time to consider Les's fate right now. In the dancing firelight, she saw her mentor and friend sprawled on his back, blood flowing from under his body—and the quickly spreading flames threatening to engulf him.

Molly jumped to her feet and raced over to Arnie Voxx. She was struggling to drag him away from the fire when a pair of hands grabbed Arnie's left arm.

"We've got to get out of here right now!" Ronnie Kolmenn yelled above the din of the inferno.

Relieved that Ronnie hadn't been hurt when Les shot at him, Molly tightened her hold on Arnie's right arm. Together they pulled him toward the staircase at the end of the hallway, away from the quickly spreading fire.

Molly's eyes were burning from the acrid smoke quickly filling the hallway. Choking and wheezing, Kolmenn was ready to collapse. The dead weight of Arnie's unconscious body was getting harder and harder to drag and the stairwell at the end of the corridor seemed impossibly far away.

Arnie's face swam in her vision, a thousand happy memories flashing through her mind. A supernatural strength flooded through her, allowing Molly to yank Arnie and Kolmenn into the stairwell and slam the door behind them.

With her final reserve of strength, Molly turned and shouted down the stairway.

"Jeff ... help!"

Jeff Cunningham pounded up the stairs holding a cloth over his mouth. The heat from the fire was eating at the stairwell door as Jeff lifted Arnie.

With Arnie over his shoulder, Jeff took the stairs two at a time. Molly and Kolmenn, leaning on each other for support, staggered down the steps behind him.

Just as they reached the bottom, a blast of heat blew the hallway door above them open and flames surged into the stairwell.

JEFF carried Arnie out to the front lawn well away from the building. Molly collapsed beside Kolmenn, Arnie, and Jeff. Behind them, the roof of the school caved in and flames shot high into the sky.

Feeling helpless in the moment, Molly moaned in despair. Arnie was dying. The right side of his chest blossomed with red where the bullet had pierced him. Her dearest friend's face was ashen and he didn't respond when she tried to rouse him.

"We don't have time for the ambulance," Kolmenn shouted as he ripped open Arnie's shirt.

Jeff sprinted to get the cruiser he'd hidden nearby while they laid their trap for the clown. Forty seconds later, he returned and gently lifted Arnie into the back seat while Kolmenn kept steady pressure on the wound.

"Move it!" Ronnie snapped.

Jeff jumped into the driver's seat and slammed the cruiser into gear. Huge chunks of grass were torn up as they bounced across the lawn and onto the road. He was going nearly a hundred when they passed the fire trucks racing toward the school.

Arnie didn't move or make a sound while Kolmenn fought desperately to control the bleeding. Molly turned away and grimly faced forward.

Laying the trap had been a bad idea, but it was their only choice. They had no other evidence. Les Caulfield had been a policeman for a long time and knew how to cover his tracks.

Ronnie Kolmenn had agreed to stand in as the late Dr. Blanic and Arnie had insisted on providing backup. Molly had balked at this, but what could she say? Arnie was about to go out to pasture and he wanted one final adrenaline rush.

PETER McGARVEY

And look where it got him.

FORTY-SEVEN

"IT'S our only chance of drawing him out."

Molly's idea had sounded thin when she'd explained it to Arnie the previous morning.

Arnie wasn't enthusiastic about her plan to trap a law enforcement officer he'd known personally for twenty years. Maybe it was because arresting Kenton Sharpe the night before had hit him hard. After putting that asshole in a cell, Arnie had expected to feel triumphant, or to at least to dredge up some righteous indignation toward Sharpe. But he could only manage pity, and that left him feeling hollow and sad.

Sharpe wouldn't get a deal. He had nothing to give the DEA they didn't already have. After Taylor Mead, Sharpe was the top of the heap, a trophy to serve as a lesson for any other lawman considering malfeasance.

"LES Caulfield? What made you come to that conclusion?" Arnie asked Molly.

"In a conversation we had a week or so ago, I wondered what was wrong with the people in Pine. He told me he'd grown up there and still couldn't figure them out."

"Yeah well, I think they're a little strange too."

"Except that when I first met him, Les told me he'd grown up in Tennessee."

"Maybe he moved down there."

Molly nodded. "He did. When he was fourteen. Up until then, he was a student at the Pine Academy. He and his younger sister Darcie had been sent there after their parents were killed in a car accident. Only his last name was Brice back then. Leslie Brice. His name was legally changed to Caulfield after he was adopted."

"How in the hell did you figure that out?"

"Every student was fingerprinted in those days. I asked Kurt to compare all the prints in the files with ones in the database. Les's were on record from when he joined the state police."

"It might be a coincidence. Maybe Les didn't want to reveal it because he thought it would hurt his credibility in the Akron investigation."

"He had a motive, Arnie. His sister Darcie was murdered."

"Murdered?"

"That's right, along with at least twenty-seven other kids during a ten-year period. Dr. Blanic and the kindly Delores Marsh were systematically cleansing the gene pool by selectively killing the undesirables, a little habit they'd picked up when they worked in a Nazi death camp during the war. Rita and I discovered they'd killed an entire group of kids who had physical deformities, mental deficits, or were not racially pure enough to meet their high standards."

"And they got away with it?" Arnie's eyes grew wide with disgust and disbelief.

"The system was on their side, Arnie. He was the school's doctor. He covered up his murders saying they were the result of illness or accidents.

"Elsie Maranello had her suspicions. She tried to protect the children by going to the board about it, but they ignored her. The publicity would have killed the school, which was a sweet little cash cow for some of them.

"When Elsie finally threatened to go to the state authorities, Blanic killed her and her little girl and took off. He knew his crimes would be covered up, but he wasn't taking any chances."

"Jesus! So why after all these years did Les go off the deep end?"

"I'm not sure, but I think it had something to do with his accident. He was severely injured and got pensioned off. It was unfair. Maybe he felt it was time to start punishing the other injustice in his life, like the death of his sister."

Arnie shook his head, trying to comprehend the enormity of this revelation. "I don't know ..."

"Want to take a guess as to the name of the drunk driver who hit Les?"

Arnie thought about it for a few minutes. "Davy Snider?"

"That's right. And Les found a way to punish him as well, by making him the weapon in two murders. Something Davy will have to live with for the rest of his life.

"It's kind of ironic. Davy told me that the night Vandermeer got fried, he walked over to the lighthouse because he'd seen a police car near the bar. I checked. None of our units were anywhere near Pine that night. So if it wasn't one of ours, that only left the state boys. And they denied having anyone patrolling that area. That's when I thought of Les. He has a cruiser."

"And Les's final act in all this was to destroy the school once and for all, to wipe it off the face of the earth. So he set the fire."

"That's right, and he's going to get away with it because any evidence that wasn't burned is circumstantial."

"He's a cop. He knows how to commit the perfect crime."

Arnie thought of Kenton Sharpe.

"Well, I've got someone in jail right now who might disagree with you."

"We've got one chance to nail him, Arnie. We need to dangle something out there so tempting that he'll make a bold move."

She explained her idea of letting Les know Dr. Blanic was still alive and that she was planning to lure the doctor to the school and confront him with his crimes.

Molly prayed Les Caulfield would take the bait.

THE rest of the night was a blur—the mad drive to the hospital, Arnie being rushed into surgery, the grim faces of the medical personnel and the state police investigators.

The main building of the Pine Academy had burned to the ground before they could get the fire under control. State fire investigators were attempting to locate Les Caulfield's remains, but Molly was sure there wouldn't much of him left to find. She took little satisfaction in knowing that the clown was dead.

Molly took Bill Murphy, the lead state detective, through the facts of her investigation. As she watched his anger mount with each revelation, Molly realized she'd made a mistake by not having included the state police earlier. This had involved one of their own. But Les was respected and well-liked—and Molly hadn't been sure who to trust.

"I'm taking over the scene," Bill Murphy said with barely contained fury.

Knowing she was in the wrong, Molly nodded in agreement.

A second detective joined Bill and took him aside.

"We sent a forensics team to Les's home. They found some stage makeup and other things. It's circumstantial, but it's definitely suspicious. When we run the bullet they took out of Sheriff Voxx, we'll know for sure."

Perplexed, Murphy closed his notebook and slid it into his jacket pocket.

"I knew Les for twenty-four years. I never would have guessed he was capable of this."

"Bill, if you don't mind, I'd like to go be with Betty now."

"I hear it's bad."

"Yes, Bill, very bad."

BETTY Voxx looked up when Molly sat down across from her in the small room provided by the hospital so she could wait in privacy. From her bloodshot eyes and damp cheeks, it was apparent she'd been crying.

"Betty, I'm so sorry. This is my fault. He should never have been there."

Anger flashed across Betty's face. "Molly, don't you dare say that! Arnie was doing his job. That's what the people elected him to do. It was his call and his duty, so don't you blame yourself."

Betty paused to dry her eyes and then smiled weakly. "You know, he's been sheriff all these years, and he never fired his gun once. There were plenty of times when he should've, but he always managed to persuade the person to give up. I guess it's different now, less civilized."

Molly was inclined to agree with Betty but held her tongue.

There had been a couple of times when Arnie had waited anxiously for her to get out of surgery. Molly wondered if he'd felt the same fear and despair she was feeling now.

FORTY-EIGHT

THE news was not good.

Arnie had come through surgery and had been taken to the ICU. Ronnie Kolmenn joined Betty and Molly just after dawn.

"The shot went through his right lung and nicked his spine, but he's a tough old bird."

Betty gasped. "Is he paralyzed?"

"We don't think so." Ronnie took Betty's hand. "However, the bigger issue is blood loss. They think they've stemmed it, but they don't know for sure if there was any permanent effect on his brain. They're going to keep him under for today and then we'll see."

Molly was amazed at this sensitive side of Ronnie Kolmenn she'd never seen before.

"Betty, they are doing everything they can for him. I can't make any promises right now, but I believe he is going to be okay."

Ronnie Kolmenn stood on his tiptoes and hugged her as she cried.

LATER in the morning, Betty was allowed to sit by Arnie's bedside.

Molly looked in, unnerved by the sight of him—the breathing tube snaking down his throat was taped to the side of his mouth, IV drips fed into the back of both hands.

He's so helpless.

Molly stood in the doorway and watched as Betty slipped her hand over her husband's. It was a small gesture, but the caring behind it touched Molly profoundly and reminded her of how alone she was. Molly thought of her late husband Steve at that moment and the warmth she'd felt when they were first married. The memory dredged up a bitter sorrow that lanced through her heart.

Have I deliberately cut myself off from my real feelings?

Molly had always believed her stoicism was her greatest strength.

Is it only a wall to protect myself from being hurt again?

These were questions Molly knew only Arnie would be able to answer. Arnie understood her better than anyone ever had. She didn't know if she could face life without him.

A tear welled up in the corner of her eye and Molly swiped at it. She took a final look at Betty and Arnie and then turned away. If this was going to be the last time she'd see Arnie alive, she wanted to hold onto the memory of this tender expression of pure love.

FORTY-NINE

Three Months Later

MOLLY Parsons was sworn in as sheriff of Sunset County on the second Tuesday in February.

As deputy, she'd assumed the duties of sheriff right after Arnie had been shot. But out of respect, Molly had delayed making any changes until she was officially sworn in.

Getting up to speed had been hectic, and she missed not having Arnie's guidance. Still, Molly felt like she'd done a decent job—the department had not collapsed and the work of law enforcement went on as always.

That afternoon Molly went back to the office after the swearing-in ceremony and decided to sit in the big chair in Arnie's office for the first time. During the transition period, she'd refused to go into Arnie's inner sanctum unless it was absolutely necessary.

Now it was official—this was her office.

Molly swung around in the chair and looked at the portraits of all her predecessors hanging on the wall. She'd made sure that a framed photograph of Arnie had been put there. It was his favorite, a shot taken for the local newspaper several years ago. Unlike the stern look worn by most of the other sheriffs, there was a twinkle in Arnie's eyes and a slight smile played on his lips.

With his personal things packed away, all that remained of Arnie was this photo on the wall.

Over the past weeks, Molly had thought a lot about Arnie. When he'd first suggested that she run for sheriff, she assumed he would be there to help her adjust to the job. She'd counted on having his wisdom and counsel to guide her.

Molly was disappointed that Arnie wouldn't be there to celebrate with her.

SINCE Hank Summerville had to cancel Molly's victory party back in November, he decided to hold it the night Molly was made sheriff.

It was three below and a snow squall was coming in across Lake Michigan, but that didn't stop Hank. He declared that the show must go on come hell or deep snow.

If Molly had had her way, there would be no party at all, but she finally realized it was unavoidable.

WHILE a howling wind painted the front windows of The Villager restaurant with frost, Molly greeted each of the guests. For such a lousy night, the turnout was remarkable.

Mayor Floren Cooper and newly elected Senator Palmer March embraced Molly with warmth. They'd been strong supporters and good friends and she appreciated their presence here this evening.

Various members of the county commission greeted her less than enthusiastically. Molly suspected some of them would stand in her way as she tried to remake the department and bring it up to date. She knew that many of them had supported Kenton Sharpe in the election and were not pleased with the way things had turned out.

Sharpe was currently in jail in Traverse City awaiting trial. Molly pitied him. His incarceration was not something she'd wanted, but he had chosen his path when he got into bed with Taylor Mead and his meth-dealing cronies.

Molly finally broke away from the political circle to greet Hank Summerville who proudly cradled his two-month-old granddaughter Louise, named for Hank's late wife.

Hank passed Louise to Molly. The baby looked at her in wide-eyed wonder and then began to wail.

"I have that effect." Molly smiled and gave the baby back to Hank.

She waved to Jeff Cunningham who stood off to one side with Rita John.

Molly had been surprised when Jeff and Rita had started dating because they were from such different worlds. But they'd both experienced severe trauma—Rita in the fire and Jeff in the war—and had discovered healing strength in each other.

On the other side of the room, Kurt Harbou introduced his intended, Lawrence, to Ronnie Kolmenn. Over the past few weeks, Kolmenn had returned to being his wickedly cynical self, and his sardonic humor once again lightened up his post-mortem exams.

Molly was overwhelmed by the generosity and goodwill of her friends. Not so long ago, she had seriously considered leaving Sunset. The town had held nothing but painful memories of her unhappy childhood and the tragedy that had befallen her when she'd returned. Now, she could think of nowhere else she'd rather be.

The tinkling of a glass being tapped by a spoon interrupted her recollections.

The party guests began to shout "speech, speech" in unison.

Molly had been dreading this moment all evening. Now she'd have to somehow articulate the love and joy she felt at being part of this community. Molly began searching for the right words as the crowd quieted in anticipation.

"I'd like to say a word if I could." The voice came from the back of the room.

Molly smiled in relief as Arnie Voxx limped forward supported by Betty. He was frail after losing nearly seventy pounds during his recovery, but his physical pain was masked by a smile illuminating his gaunt face.

Arnie moved to Molly's side and took her hand in his.

"I had the best job in the world for the past three decades." Arnie grew stronger as he spoke. "I've certainly had my share of regrets—things I should've done better, things I never got to do and, of course, things I should never have done."

A ripple of laughter went through the crowd.

"But I'll spare you my maudlin regrets. Tonight, we come together to celebrate Molly Parsons, our new sheriff. I've known Molly since she was a child. We've been together through some great times and through some rough times, and I can think of no other person better suited to faithfully serve the people of Sunset County."

Arnie held his glass high.

"Let us cherish the past, trust in the future, and rejoice in the glorious now."

A few minutes later, Molly slipped out the back door of the restaurant. Arnie's speech and the outpouring of love from her friends had overwhelmed her.

Molly faced the brisk wind off Lake Michigan and thought about the remarkable journey she'd taken, a journey that had brought her to this place with this group of people. The journey had been one of fear and courage, of despair and redemption. But, most importantly, it had been a journey of love.

THE END

ABOUT THE AUTHOR

Peter McGarvey has been a magazine columnist, radio journalist, advertising copywriter, marketing and sales executive, and filmmaker. He grew up in the small Ontario towns of Orillia and Chatham and has made Toronto his home for most of his adult life.

Peter's novels include two series set in Michigan. The **Molly Parsons Mysteries,** featuring a small town criminal investigator, includes *Dark Sunset*, *Bloody Sunset*, and *Foggy Sunset*. The **Rip & Wilma Hits**, *Hair Trigger* and *Double Tap*, follow the adventures of a pair of improbable Detroit contract killers. Peter's stand-alone mystery *Dark the Light*, which is set in South Carolina in the 1920s, will be published soon. He is currently working on a series of mysteries which will take place in a small Canadian town.

For more about Peter and his books, please visit PeterMcGarvey.com, and be sure to check out Peter's Facebook Author Page. You can also follow Peter on Twitter and Linked-In. Replying to emails is one of his favorite pastimes, so give him a shout at PGM@PeterMcGarvey.com!